Praise for

JULIA QUINN

"Julia Quinn is truly our contemporary Jane Austen."
—Jill Barnett

"Like an episode of *Downton Abbey* mixed with a great rom-com."
—iBooks Best of the Month (on *Because of Miss Bridgerton*)

"If you've never read romance novels, start here."
—*Washington Post*

"Quinn is . . . a romance master. [She] has created a family so likable and attractive, a community so vibrant and engaging, that we want to crawl into the pages and know them."
—NPR Books

"Quinn is a consummate storyteller. Her prose is spry and assured, and she excels at creating indelible characters."
—*Publishers Weekly* (★Starred Review★)

"Simply delightful, filled with charm, humor, and wit."
—*Kirkus Reviews*

D0111984

Top Ten Reasons to Read this Book

10. Because Julia Quinn has finally brought back historical romance's most beloved family.

9. Because where else are you going to get such a racy archery reference?

8. Because ROMANCE.

7. Because you totally want to see a one-armed man build a house of cards.

6. Because in the battle between hero, heroine, and cat, the cat wins.

5. Because WITTY REPARTEE.

4. Because you agree that croquet ought to be a blood sport.

3. Because George Rokesby is so hot he ought to star in his own BBC miniseries.

2. Because THAT KISS.

1. Because of Miss Bridgerton.

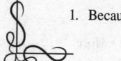

By Julia Quinn

THE BRIDGERTON PREQUELS
Because of Miss Bridgerton
The Girl with the Make-Believe Husband
The Other Miss Bridgerton • *First Comes Scandal*

THE BRIDGERTON SERIES
The Duke and I • *The Viscount Who Loved Me*
An Offer from a Gentleman • *Romancing Mister Bridgerton*
To Sir Phillip, With Love • *When He Was Wicked*
It's in His Kiss • *On the Way to the Wedding*
The Bridgertons: Happily Ever After

THE SMYTHE-SMITH QUARTET
Just Like Heaven • *A Night Like This*
The Sum of All Kisses • *The Secrets of Sir Richard Kenworthy*

THE BEVELSTOKE SERIES
The Secret Diaries of Miss Miranda Cheever
What Happens in London • *Ten Things I Love About You*

THE TWO DUKES OF WYNDHAM
The Lost Duke of Wyndham • *Mr. Cavendish, I Presume*

AGENTS OF THE CROWN
To Catch an Heiress • *How to Marry a Marquis*

THE LYNDON SISTERS
Everything and the Moon • *Brighter Than the Sun*

THE SPLENDID TRILOGY
Splendid • *Dancing at Midnight* • *Minx*

BECAUSE OF
MISS BRIDGERTON

A BRIDGERTON PREQUEL

JULIA QUINN

AVON

An Imprint of HarperCollinsPublishers

HarperCollins books may be purchased for educational, business, or sales promotional use. For information, please email the Special Markets Department at SPsales@harpercollins.com.

First Avon trade paperback printing: January 2023
First Avon Books mass market printing: April 2016
First Avon Books hardcover printing: March 2016

Originally published as *Because of Miss Bridgerton* in 2016 by Avon Books.

Library of Congress Cataloging-in-Publication Data has been applied for.

ISBN 978-0-06-327008-4 (paperback)
ISBN 978-0-06-325391-9 (hardcover library edition)

23 24 25 26 27 LBC 5 4 3 2 1

For Susan Slater.
You amaze me every day.

And also for Paul.
A well-timed phone call is
the mark of an excellent husband.
May you touch the sky this time.

Chapter 1

The roof of an abandoned farmhouse
Midway between Aubrey Hall and Crake House
Kent, England
1779

It wasn't that Billie Bridgerton was lacking in common sense. On the contrary, she was quite sure that she was one of the most sensible people of her acquaintance. But like any thoughtful individual, she occasionally chose to ignore the little voice of reason that whispered through her mind. This could not, she was certain, be considered recklessness. When she ignored this cautionary voice, it was a conscious decision, made after a (somewhat) careful analysis of her situation. And to her credit, when Billie made a decision— one that most of humanity would deem beyond foolish—she usually landed quite sprightly on her feet.

Except when she didn't.

Like right now.

She glared down at her companion. "I ought to throttle you."

Her companion let out a rather unconcerned meow.

Billie let out a rather unladylike growl.

The cat assessed the noise, judged it to be beneath its notice, and began to lick its paws.

Billie considered the twin standards of dignity and decorum, decided they were both overrated, and returned volley with an immature scowl.

It didn't make her feel any better.

With a weary groan, she looked up at the sky, trying to gauge the time. The sun was wedged quite firmly behind a layer of clouds, which complicated her task, but it had to be at least four o'clock. She reckoned she'd been stuck here for an hour, and she'd left the village at two. If she factored in the time it took to walk . . .

Oh bloody hell, what did it matter what the time was? It wasn't going to get her off this damned roof.

"This is all your fault," she said to the cat.

Predictably, the cat ignored her.

"I don't know what you think you were doing up in that tree," she continued. "Any fool would have known you couldn't have got down."

Any fool would have left it up there, but no, Billie had heard the mewling, and she'd been halfway up the tree before it occurred to her that she didn't even *like* cats.

"And I *really* don't like you," she said.

She was talking to a cat. *This* was what she'd been reduced to. She shifted her position, wincing as her stocking caught on one of the weatherworn roof shingles. The snag jerked her foot sideways, and her already throbbing ankle howled in protest.

Or rather her mouth howled. She couldn't help it. It *hurt*.

She supposed it could have been worse. She'd been well up in the tree, easily a good eight feet above the roof of the farmhouse, when the cat had hissed at her, flung out a well-clawed paw, and sent them both tumbling.

The cat, needless to say, had made its descent with acrobatic grace, landing without injury, four paws on the roof.

Billie still wasn't sure how *she'd* landed, just that her elbow hurt, her hip stung, and her jacket was torn, likely from the branch that had broken her fall two-thirds of the way down.

But the worst was her ankle and foot, which were killing her. If she were home, she'd prop it up on pillows. She'd witnessed more than her fair share of twisted ankles—some on her own body, even more on others—and she knew what to do. Cold compress, elevation, a sibling forced to wait on her hand and foot . . .

Where were her minions when she needed them?

But then, off in the distance she saw a flash of movement, and unless the local beasts had recently made the move to bipedalism, it was quite clearly human.

"Helloooooooo!" she called out, then thought the better of it and yelled, "Help!"

Unless Billie's eyesight was deceiving her—and it wasn't, it really wasn't; even her best friend Mary Rokesby admitted that Billie Bridgerton's eyes wouldn't dare to be anything but perfect—the human in the distance was male. And there wasn't a male of her acquaintance who could ignore a feminine cry for help.

"Help!" she yelled again, feeling no small bit of relief when the man paused. She couldn't quite tell if he'd turned in her direction—perfect eyesight only went so far—so she let out another holler, this one quite as loud as she could make it, and nearly sobbed in relief when the gentleman—oh, *please* let him be a gentleman, if not by birth, then at least by nature—began to move in her direction.

Except she didn't sob. Because she never sobbed. She would never have been that sort of a female.

She did, however, take an unexpected breath—a surprisingly loud and high-pitched unexpected breath.

"Over here!" she called out, shrugging off her jacket so that she could wave it in the air. There was no point in trying to appear dignified. She was, after all, stuck on a roof with a twisted ankle and a mangy cat.

"Sir!" she all but hollered. "Help! Please!"

The gentleman's gait adjusted ever so slightly at the noise, and he looked up, and even though he was still too far away for Billie's perfect eyes to see his face, she *knew*.

No. No. *No*. Anyone but him.

But of course it was him. Because who else would stroll by at her lowest moment, at her most awkward and embarrassing, at the one bloody time *she* needed rescuing?

"Good afternoon, George," she said, once he'd drawn close enough to hear.

He put his hands on his hips and squinted up at her. "Billie Bridgerton," he said.

She waited for him to add, "I might have known."

He didn't, and somehow that made her even more irritated. The world was not in balance when she couldn't predict every inflated, pompous word that rolled out of George Rokesby's mouth.

"Getting a bit of sun?" he inquired.

"Yes, I rather thought I could use a few more freckles," she snapped.

He did not immediately respond. Instead he removed his tricorn hat, revealing an unpowdered head of thick, tawny brown hair, and regarded her with a steady, assessing gaze. Finally, after carefully setting his chapeau down on what had once been a stone wall, he looked back up and said, "I cannot say that I'm not enjoying this. Just a little bit."

Any number of retorts danced on Billie's tongue, but she reminded herself that George Rokesby was the only human being in sight, and if she wished to touch her feet to the ground before May Day she was going to have to be nice to him.

Until he rescued her, at least.

"How'd you come to be up there, anyway?" he asked.

"Cat." Said in a voice that might charitably have been described as *seething*.

"Ah."

"It was in the tree," she explained, although heaven knew why. It wasn't as if he'd requested further explanation.

"I see."

Did he? She rather thought he didn't.

"It was crying," she ground out. "I couldn't very well ignore it."

"No, I'm sure you couldn't," he said, and even though his voice was perfectly cordial, she was convinced he was laughing at her.

"Some of us," she pried her teeth apart long enough to say, "are compassionate, considerate individuals."

He cocked his head. "Kind to small children and animals?"

"Quite."

His right brow arched in that monstrously aggravating Rokesby manner. "Some of us," he drawled, "are kind to *large* children and animals."

She bit her tongue. First figuratively, and then literally. *Be nice*, she reminded herself. *Even if it kills you . . .*

He smiled blandly. Well, except for that little smirk at the corner.

"Are you bloody well going to help me down?" she finally burst out.

"Such language," he scolded.

"Learned from *your* brothers."

"Oh, I know," he said. "Never could quite convince them you were actually a girl."

Billie sat on her hands. She actually *sat* on her hands, she was so sure she would not be able to resist the urge to throw herself off the roof in an attempt to strangle him.

"Never could quite convince my*self* you were actually human," George added, rather offhandedly.

Billie's fingers hardened into claws. Which was *really* uncomfortable, all things considered. "*George*," she said, and she heard a thousand different things in her tone—pleading, pain, resignation, remembrance. They had a history, they two, and no matter their differences, he was a Rokesby and she was a Bridgerton, and when push came to shove, they might as well be family.

Their homes—Crake House for the Rokesbys and Aubrey Hall

for the Bridgertons—lay a mere three miles apart in this cozy green corner of Kent. The Bridgertons had been there longer—they had arrived in the early 1500s, when James Bridgerton had been made a viscount and granted land by Henry VIII—but the Rokesbys had outranked them since 1672.

A particularly enterprising Baron Rokesby (so the story went) had performed an essential service to Charles II and been named the first Earl of Manston in gratitude. The details surrounding this elevation of rank had become murky over time, but it was generally accepted that it had involved a stagecoach, a bolt of Turkish silk, and two royal mistresses.

Billie could well believe it. Charm was inherited, was it not? George Rokesby might be precisely the sort of stick-in-the-mud one would expect of the heir to an earldom, but his younger brother Andrew possessed the sort of devilish *joie de vivre* that would have endeared him to a notorious philanderer like Charles II. The other Rokesby brothers were not quite so roguish (although she supposed that Nicholas, at only fourteen, was still honing his skills), but they easily outstripped George in all contests involving charm and amiability.

George. They'd never liked each other. But Billie supposed she could not complain. George *was* the only available Rokesby at the moment. Edward was off in the colonies, wielding a sword or a pistol, or heaven only knew what, and Nicholas was at Eton, probably also wielding a sword or a pistol (although hopefully to considerably less effect). Andrew was here in Kent for the next few weeks, but he'd fractured his arm doing some such derring-do in the navy. He could hardly have been helpful.

No, it would have to be George, and she was going to have to be civil.

She smiled down at him. Well, she stretched her lips.

He sighed. Just a little. "I'll see if there's a ladder around back."

"Thank you," she said primly, but she didn't think he heard her. He'd always had a fast, long-legged stride, and he'd disappeared around the corner before she could be properly polite.

A minute or so later he came back into view, his arm slung over a ladder that looked like it had last seen use during the Glorious Revolution. "What actually happened?" he called up, setting it into place. "It's not like you to get stuck."

It was as close to a compliment as she'd ever heard from his lips. "The cat was not as grateful for my assistance as one might have expected," she said, every consonant a haughty ice pick directed at the monstrous little feline.

The ladder *thunked* into position, and Billie heard George climbing up.

"Is that going to hold?" she asked. The wood looked somewhat splintered and was emitting ominous creaking noises with every step.

The creaks paused for a moment. "It doesn't really matter if it holds or not, does it?"

Billie swallowed. Another person might not be able to translate his words, but she'd known this man since the dawn of her memory, and if there was one fundamental truth to George Rokesby, it was that he was a gentleman. And he would never leave a lady in distress, no matter how fragile a ladder's appearance.

She was in trouble, ergo he had no choice. He had to help, no matter how aggravating he found her.

And he did. Oh, she knew he did. He had never made any effort to disguise it. Although to be fair, neither had she.

His head popped into view, and his Rokesby-blue eyes narrowed. All the Rokesbys had blue eyes. Every last one of them.

"You're wearing breeches," George said with a heavy sigh. "Of course you're wearing breeches."

"I would hardly have attempted the tree in a dress."

"No," he said dryly, "you're much too sensible for that."

Billie decided to let this one pass. "It scratched me," she said, jerking her head toward the cat.

"Did it?"

"We fell."

George looked up. "That's quite a distance."

Billie followed his gaze. The nearest branch was five feet up, and she had not been on the nearest branch. "I hurt my ankle," she admitted.

"I reckoned as much."

She looked over at him in question.

"You would have just jumped to the ground, otherwise."

Her mouth twisted as she peered past him to the packed dirt that surrounded the ruins of the farmhouse. At one point the building must have belonged to a prosperous farmer because it was two full stories high. "No," she said, assessing the distance. "It's too far for that."

"Even for you?"

"I'm not an idiot, George."

He did not agree with her nearly as fast as he should have done. Which was to say, not at all.

"Very well," was what he *did* say. "Let's get you down."

She breathed in. Then out. Then said, "Thank you."

He looked over at her with a strange expression. Disbelief, maybe, that she'd uttered the words *thank* and *you* in the same sentence?

"It's going to be dark soon," she said, her nose crinkling as she looked up at the sky. "It would have been awful to have been stuck—" She cleared her throat. "Thank you."

He acknowledged this with the briefest of nods. "Can you manage the ladder?"

"I think so." It would hurt dreadfully, but she could do it. "Yes."

"I could carry you."

"On the ladder?"

"On my back."

"I'm *not* getting on your back."

"It's not where I'd want you," he muttered.

She looked up sharply.

"Right, well," he continued, climbing another two rungs up. The edge of the roof was now even with his hips. "Can you stand?"

She stared at him dumbly.

"I would like to see how much weight you can put on that ankle," he explained.

"Oh," she mumbled. "Of course."

She probably shouldn't have attempted it. The slant of the roof was such that she'd need both her feet for balance, and her right was near to useless by this point. But she tried, because she hated showing weakness in front of this man, or maybe she tried just because it wasn't in her nature not to try—*anything*—or maybe she just didn't think the matter through in the first place, but she stood, and she stumbled, and she sat right back down.

But not before a choked cry of pain tore across her lips.

George was off the ladder and on the roof in a second. "You little fool," he muttered, but there was affection in his voice, or at least as much affection as he ever showed. "May I see it?"

Grudgingly, she poked her foot in his direction. She'd already removed her shoe.

He touched it clinically, cupping her heel in one hand as he tested her range of motion with the other. "Does it hurt here?" he asked, pressing lightly on the outside of her ankle.

Billie let out a hiss of pain before she could stop herself and nodded.

He moved to another spot. "Here?"

She nodded again. "But not quite as much."

"What about—"

A bolt of pain shot through her foot, so intense it was positively electric. Without even thinking, she yanked it back from his hands.

"I'll take that as a yes," he said with a frown. "But I don't think it's broken."

"Of course it's not broken," she practically snapped. Which was a ridiculous thing to say because there was no *of course* about it. But George Rokesby always brought out the worst in her, and it didn't help that her foot *hurt*, damn it all.

"A sprain," George said, ignoring her little outburst.

"I know." Petulantly. *Again*. She hated herself right now.

He smiled blandly. "Of course you do."

She wanted to kill him.

"I'll go first," George announced. "That way if you stumble I'll be able to stop you from falling."

Billie nodded. It was a good plan, the only plan, really, and she'd be stupid to argue just because he was the one who'd come up with it. Even if that *had* been her initial impulse.

"Ready?" he asked.

She nodded again. "You're not concerned that I'll knock you off the ladder?"

"No."

No explanations. Just no. As if it were absurd even to ponder the question.

She looked up sharply. He looked so solid. And strong. And *dependable*. He'd always been dependable, she realized. She was just usually too busy being irritated by him to notice.

He edged carefully back to the end of the roof, turning around so that he could set one foot on the top rung of the ladder.

"Don't forget the cat," Billie directed.

"The cat," he repeated, giving her a *surely you jest* look.

"I'm not going to abandon it after all this."

George gritted his teeth, said something quite unsavory under his breath, and reached out for the cat.

Which bit him.

"*Mother of—*"

Billie scooted back an inch. He looked ready to tear someone's head off, and she was closer than the cat.

"That cat," George growled, "can rot in hell."

"Agreed," she said, *very* quickly.

He blinked at her speedy acquiescence. She tried for a smile and settled for a shrug. She had two brothers by blood and three more who might as well have been brothers in the Rokesby household. Four if she included George, which she wasn't quite sure she did.

The point was, she understood men, and she knew when to keep her mouth shut.

Besides, she was *done* with that cursed animal. Never let it be said that Billie Bridgerton was in possession of a sentimental heart. She'd tried to save the mangy beast because it was the right thing to do, then she had tried to save it again, if only because it seemed like a waste of her previous efforts not to, but now . . .

She stared down at the animal. "You are on your own."

"I'll go first," George said, moving over to the ladder. "I want you right in front of me the whole way. That way if you stumble—"

"We'll both go down?"

"I'll catch you," he ground out.

She'd been joking, but it didn't seem the wisest course of action to point that out.

George turned to descend, but as he moved to set his foot on the highest rung, the cat, which had apparently not liked being ignored, let out a bloodcurdling screech and dashed through his legs. George pitched back, arms pinwheeling.

Billie didn't think. She didn't notice her foot, or her balance, or anything. She just leapt forward and grabbed him, pulling him back to safety.

"The ladder!" she shrieked.

But it was too late. Together they watched the ladder pivot, spin, then fall with a strange balletic grace to the ground.

Chapter 2

It would be fair to say that George Rokesby, eldest son of the Earl of Manston and currently known to the civilized world as Viscount Kennard, was an even-tempered gentleman. He had a calm, steady hand, a relentlessly logical mind, and a way of narrowing his eyes *just so* that ensured that his wishes were met with cool efficiency, his desires granted with breathless pleasure, and—and this was the most important part—all of this occurred according to *his* preferred schedule.

It would also be fair to say that if Miss Sybilla Bridgerton had any idea how close he was to going for her throat, she would look a lot more frightened of him than she was of the gathering darkness.

"That's *most* unfortunate," she said, peering down at the ladder.

George did not speak. He thought this best.

"I know what you're thinking," she said.

He unclenched his jaw for just long enough to say, "I am not certain that you do."

"You're trying to decide which of us you'd rather toss from the roof. Me or the cat."

She was a lot closer to the truth than one might have predicted.

"I was only trying to help," she said.

"I know." Said in a tone that was *not* meant to encourage future conversation.

But Billie just went right on talking. "If I hadn't grabbed you, you would have fallen."

"I *know*."

She caught her lower lip between her teeth, and for one blessed moment he thought she was going to let the matter drop.

Then she said, "It was your foot, you know."

He moved his head about an inch. Just enough to indicate he'd heard. "I beg your pardon?"

"Your foot." She motioned with her head toward the extremity in question. "You kicked the ladder."

George gave up all pretense of ignoring her. "You are *not* blaming this on me," he all but hissed.

"No, of course not," she said quickly, finally showing a shred of self-preservation. "I merely meant— Just that you—"

He narrowed his eyes.

"Never mind," she mumbled. She let her chin rest on her bent knees and gazed out over the field. Not that there was anything to see. The only thing moving was the wind, declaring its presence through the light ruffling of the leaves on the trees.

"I think we have another hour before the sun goes down," she murmured. "Maybe two."

"We won't be here when it gets dark," he told her.

She looked at him, then down at the ladder. Then back at him with an expression that made him want to leave her in the proverbial dark.

But he didn't. Because apparently he couldn't. Twenty-seven years was a long time to have the tenets of gentlemanly behavior schooled into one's brain, and he could never be so cruel to a lady. Even *her*.

"Andrew should be along in thirty minutes or so," he said.

"What?" She looked relieved, then annoyed. "Why didn't you say something? I can't believe you let me think we would be stranded up here all night."

He looked at her. At Billie Bridgerton, the bane of his existence since her birth twenty-three years earlier. She was glaring at him as if he'd committed some unspeakable affront, her cheeks high with color, her lips pursed like a furious rose.

With great and icy enunciation he said, "One minute has passed between the time the ladder hit the ground and this moment, right now, as these words are leaving my lips. Pray, tell me, when, during your enlightening analysis of the motion by which my foot connected with the ladder, was I meant to offer this information?"

The corners of her mouth moved, but it wasn't quite a smirk. It was nothing that indicated sarcasm. If she were anyone else, he would have thought her embarrassed, or maybe even sheepish. But this was Billie Bridgerton, and she didn't *do* embarrassment. She just did as she pleased and damn the consequences. She had done her entire life, generally dragging half the Rokesby clan down with her.

And somehow everyone *always* forgave her. She had that way about her—it wasn't charm exactly—it was that crazy, reckless confidence that made people flock to her side. Her family, his family, the entire bloody village—they all adored her. Her smile was wide, and her laugh was infectious, and God in heaven but how was it *possible* he was the only person in England who seemed to realize what a danger she was to humanity?

That twisted ankle of hers? It wasn't the first. She'd broken her arm, too, in typically spectacular fashion. She'd been eight, and she had taken a tumble from a horse. A barely trained gelding she'd had no business riding, much less trying to jump a hedge on. The bone had healed perfectly—of course it did, Billie had always had the devil's own luck—and within months she was back to her old ways, and no one thought to scold her. Not when she rode astride. In breeches. On that same damned gelding over that same damned hedge. And when one of his younger brothers followed her lead and knocked his shoulder out of joint . . .

Everyone had laughed. His parents—and hers—had shaken their heads and laughed, and not a one of them thought it prudent to take Billie off the horse, shove her into a dress, or better yet, pack her off to one of those girls' schools that taught needlework and deportment.

Edward's arm had been hanging from its socket. Its socket!! And the sound it had made when their stablemaster had shoved it back in . . .

George shuddered. It had been the sort of sound one felt rather than heard.

"Are you cold?" Billie asked.

He shook his head. Although *she* probably was. His coat was considerably thicker than hers. "Are you?"

"No."

He looked at her closely. She was just the sort to try to tough it out and refuse to allow him to behave as a gentleman ought. "You would tell me if you were?"

She held up a hand as if to make a pledge. "I promise."

That was good enough for him. Billie didn't lie, and she didn't break promises.

"Was Andrew in the village with you?" she asked, squinting off at the horizon.

George gave a nod. "We had business with the blacksmith. He stopped in to speak to the vicar afterward. I didn't feel like waiting."

"Of course not," she murmured.

His head snapped around. "What is that supposed to mean?"

Her lips parted, then hovered for a moment in a delicate oval before she said, "I don't know, actually."

He scowled at her, then turned his attention back to the roof, not that there was a damned thing he could do at the moment. But it was not in his nature to sit and wait. At the very least he could examine the dilemma, reassess, and—

"There's nothing to be done," Billie said blithely. "Not without the ladder."

"I'm aware," he bit off.

"You were looking about," she said with a shrug, "as if—"

"I *know* what I was doing," he snapped.

Her lips pressed together in perfect concert with her brows, which rose into that annoying Bridgerton arch, as if to say—*Go ahead, think what you wish. I know better.*

They were silent a moment, and then, in a smaller voice than he was used to hearing from her, she asked, "Are you quite certain that Andrew will come this way?"

He gave a nod. He and his brother had walked to the village from Crake House—not their usual mode of transport, but Andrew, who had recently been made a lieutenant in the Royal Navy, had broken his arm doing some damn fool stunt off the coast of Portugal and had been sent home to recuperate. Walking was currently easier for him than riding, and it was an uncommonly lovely day for March.

"He's on foot," George said. "How would he come if not by here?" There were many footpaths in the area, but none that wouldn't add a mile to the journey home.

Billie tipped her head to the side, gazing out over the field. "Unless someone gave him a ride."

He turned slowly toward her, dumbfounded by the utter lack of . . . *anything* in her tone. There was no one-upmanship, no argument, not even a hint of worry. Just a bizarre, matter-of-fact— *Hmmm, here's a disastrous thing that might have happened.*

"Well, he could have done," she said with a shrug. "Everyone likes Andrew."

It was true, Andrew had the sort of devil-may-care, easy charm that endeared him to everyone, from the village vicar to the barmaids at the public house. If someone was heading his way, they'd offer a ride.

"He'll walk," George said firmly. "He needs the exercise."

Billie's face took on a decidedly dubious mien. "Andrew?"

George shrugged, not wanting to concede the point, even though Andrew had always been a superb athlete. "He'll want the fresh air, at the very least. He's been climbing the walls all week. Mother has been trying to put him on broth and bedrest."

"For a broken arm?" Billie's snort gave way to a giggle.

George glanced at her sideways. "Taking joy in the misery of others?"

"Always."

He smiled despite himself. It was difficult to take offense, not when he'd spent the last week enjoying—nay, encouraging—his younger brother's frustration.

Billie gingerly shifted her position, bending her legs so that she could rest her chin on her knees.

"Watch that foot," George said, almost absently.

She nodded, and together they lapsed into silence. George stared straight ahead, but he could feel every motion Billie made at his side. She brushed an errant strand of hair from her eyes, then stretched one arm out in front of her, her elbow creaking like an old wooden chair. Then, with the tenacity she displayed in all aspects of her life, she circled back around to their previous conversation and said, "All the same, he could have got a ride."

He almost smiled. "He could."

She was quiet for a few more seconds, then said, "It doesn't look like rain."

He looked up. It was overcast, but not thickly so. The clouds were too pale to be holding much water.

"And surely we will be missed."

He allowed himself a smirk. "I will, at least."

She elbowed him. Hard. Hard enough to make him laugh.

"You're a terrible person, George Rokesby." But she was grinning when she said it.

He chuckled again, surprised by how much he enjoyed the light fizz of amusement in his chest. He wasn't sure that he and Billie qualified as friends—they'd butted heads far too many times for that—but she was familiar. That wasn't always a good thing, but right now . . .

It was.

"Well," she announced, "I suppose there's no one with whom I'd rather be stranded on a roof."

He swung his head toward her. "Why, Miss Bridgerton, was that a compliment?"

"You can't tell?"

"From you?" he parried.

She smiled in an endearingly lopsided manner. "I suppose I deserve that. But, you know, you're very dependable."

"Dependable," he repeated.

She nodded. "Very much so."

He felt himself scowl, although for all that was holy, he had no idea why.

"If I hadn't hurt my ankle," Billie continued blithely, "I'm sure I would have found a way down."

He regarded her with clear skepticism. Aside from the fact that this had nothing to do with his dependability . . . "Didn't you just say that it's too far to jump?"

"Well, yes," she said, her hand making a dismissive little wave in front of her face, "but I would have thought of something."

"Of course," he said, mostly because he lacked the energy to say anything else.

"The point is," she continued, "that as long as I'm here with *you* . . ."

Her face went suddenly pale. Even her eyes, normally a fathomless shade of brown, seemed to blanch down to something decidedly more tepid.

George's heart stopped. He had never, *ever* seen Billie Bridgerton with such an expression on her face.

She was terrified.

"What is it?" he demanded.

She turned to him. "You don't think . . ."

He waited, but she seemed beyond words. "*What?*"

Her ashen face took on a greenish hue. "You don't think that someone would think that you . . . that we . . ." She swallowed. "That we disappeared . . . *together?*"

George's entire world lurched. "*God*, no," he said. Instantly.

"I know," she agreed. With equal alacrity. "I mean, you. And me. It's laughable."

"Absurd."

"Anyone who knows us . . ."

"Will know we'd never . . ."

"And yet . . ." This time Billie's words did not merely trail off, they sank into a desperate whisper.

He gave her an impatient look. "What?"

"If Andrew doesn't come along as expected . . . and you're missed . . . and I'm missed . . ." She looked up at him, her eyes huge and horrified in her face. "Eventually someone will realize that we've both been missed."

"Your point?" he snapped.

She turned to face him directly. "Just that why wouldn't someone assume . . . ?"

"Because they have a brain in their head," he shot back. "No one would ever think I would be with you on *purpose*."

She lurched back. "Oh, well, *thank* you."

"Are you saying you wish someone *did*?" he retorted.

"No!"

He rolled his eyes. *Women*. And yet, this was Billie. The least womanly woman of his acquaintance.

She let out a long, steadying breath. "Regardless of what you think of me, *George* . . ."

How did she make his name sound like an insult?

". . . I do have my reputation to consider. And while my family knows me well enough, and"—her voice took on a reluctant edge here—"I suppose trusts *you* well enough to know that our concurrent disappearances signify nothing untoward . . ."

Her words trailed off, and she chewed on her lip, looking uncomfortable, and, if one was honest, vaguely ill.

"The rest of the world might not be as kind," he finished for her.

She looked at him for a moment, then said, "Quite."

"If we're not found until tomorrow morning . . ." George said, mostly to himself.

Billie finished the horrifying sentence. "You'd have to marry me."

Chapter 3

"What are you doing?" Billie nearly shrieked. George had sprung to his feet with speed that was *highly* reckless, and now he was peering over the edge of the building with a calculating, furrowed brow.

Honestly, it looked as if he was performing complicated mathematical equations.

"Getting off the damned roof," he grunted.

"You'll kill yourself."

"I might," he agreed grimly.

"Well, don't I feel special," Billie retorted.

He turned, staring down at her with heavy-lidded superiority. "Are you saying you *want* to marry me?"

She shuddered. "Never." But at the same time, a lady didn't want to think that a man would prefer to hurl himself from a roof just to avoid the possibility.

"In that, madam," George said, "we are agreed."

And it stung. Oh, how it stung. Ah, irony. She didn't *care* if George Rokesby didn't want to marry her. She didn't even like him most of the time. And she knew that when he did deign to choose a bride, the oh-so-grateful lady wasn't going to be anything like *her*.

But still, it stung.

The future Lady Kennard would be delicate, feminine. She would have been trained to run a grand house, not a working estate. She would dress in the latest of fashions, her hair would be powdered and intricately styled, and even if she possessed a backbone of steel, she would hide it beneath an aura of genteel helplessness.

Men like George loved to think themselves manly and strong.

She watched him as he planted his hands on his hips. Very well, he *was* manly and strong. But he was like the rest of them; he'd want a woman who flirted over a fan. God forbid he married someone *capable*.

"This is a disaster," he spat.

Billie only somewhat resisted the urge to snarl. "You're just realizing this now?"

His response was an equally immature scowl.

"Why couldn't you be *nice*?" Billie blurted out.

"Nice?" he echoed.

Oh, God, why had she said that? Now she was going to have to explain. "Like the rest of your family," she clarified.

"Nice," he said again. He shook his head, as if he couldn't believe her gall. "Nice."

"*I'm* nice," she said. Then she regretted *that*, because she wasn't nice. At least not all the time, and she had a feeling she wasn't being particularly nice right now. But surely she could be excused, because this was George Rokesby, and she couldn't help herself.

And neither, it seemed, could he.

"Has it ever occurred to you," he said, in a voice that was positively bathed with a lack of niceness, "that I am nice to everyone but you?"

It hurt. It shouldn't have, because they'd never liked each other, and damn it, it shouldn't have hurt because she didn't *want* it to.

But she would never let it show.

"I *think* you were trying to insult me," she said, picking disdainfully through her words.

He stared at her, waiting for further comment.

She shrugged.

"But . . . ?" he prodded.

She shrugged again, pretending to look at her fingernails. Which of course meant that she *did* look at her fingernails, which were revoltingly filthy.

One more thing she didn't have in common with the future Lady Kennard.

She counted silently to five, waiting for him to demand an explanation in that cutting way he'd perfected before he'd been old enough to shave. But he didn't say a word, and finally she was the one to lose whatever asinine contest was simmering between them, and she lifted her head.

He wasn't even looking at her.

Damn him.

And damn her, because she just couldn't help herself. She knew that anyone with an ounce of restraint would have known when to hold her tongue, but no, she had to open her stupid, stupid mouth and say, "If you can't muster the—"

"Don't say it," he warned.

"—generosity of spirit to—"

"I'm warning you, Billie."

"Are you?" she shot back. "I rather think you're threatening me."

"I will do," he nearly spat, "if you don't *shut*—" He cut himself off with a muffled curse, snapping his head in the other direction.

Billie picked at a loose thread on her stocking, her mouth pressed into an angry, trembling pout. She shouldn't have said anything. She'd known that even as she spoke, because as pompous and annoying as George Rokesby was, it was entirely her fault that he was stuck up on the roof, and she'd had no call to be so provoking.

But there was something about him—some special talent that only he possessed—that stripped her of years of experience and maturity and made her act like a bloody six-year-old. If he were anyone else—*anyone* else—she'd be lauded as the most reasonable and helpful female in the history of Christendom. Tales would be spread—once they'd got off the roof—of her bravery and wit. Billie Bridgerton . . . so resourceful, so reasonable . . . It's what everyone said. It's what everyone had reason to say, because she *was* resourceful, and she *was* reasonable.

Just not with George Rokesby.

"I'm sorry," she mumbled.

His head turned slowly, as if even his muscles could not believe what they'd heard.

"I said I'm sorry," she repeated, louder this time. It felt like an antidote, but it was the right thing to do. But God help him if he made her say it again, because there was only so much of her pride she could swallow before she choked on it. And he ought to know that.

Because he was just the same.

His eyes met hers, and then they both looked down, and then after a few moments George said, "We are neither of us at our best just now."

Billie swallowed. She thought maybe she ought to say something more, but her judgment had not done her any favors thus far, so instead she nodded, vowing that she was going to keep her mouth shut until—

"Andrew?" George whispered.

Billie snapped to attention.

"Andrew!" George all but bellowed.

Billie's eyes did a frantic scan of the trees at the far end of the field, and sure enough . . . "Andrew!" she screamed, reflexively starting to rise before remembering her ankle.

"Ow!" she yelped, plunking back down on her bottom.

George did not spare her so much as a glance. He was too busy over by the edge of the roof, waving his arms through the air in wide, vigorous swoops.

There was no way Andrew could miss them, hollering like a pair of deranged banshees, but if he picked up his pace, Billie couldn't see it. But that was Andrew. She should probably be glad he hadn't fallen over with laughter at their predicament.

This was not something he was going to let either of them forget.

"Ahoy there!" Andrew called out, once he'd halved the distance between them.

Billie glanced over at George. She could only see him in profile, but he looked visibly relieved at his brother's appearance. Also, oddly grim. No, not odd at all, she realized. Whatever ribbing she was going to get from Andrew, George would suffer it a hundredfold.

Andrew drew closer, a spring in his step despite the sling on his arm. "Of all the delightful surprises," he declared, his face nearly split by his grin. "If I thought and thought and thought . . ."

He stopped, holding up one elegant forefinger, the universal sign, Billie realized, to ask for a moment's pause. Then he tipped his head as if getting back into the swing of things, and said, "and *thought*—"

"Oh, for the love of Christ," George growled.

"All that thinking for *years* . . ." Andrew chortled. "I still couldn't have come up with—"

"Just get us off the bloody roof," George snapped.

Billie rather sympathized with his tone.

"I've always thought the two of you would make a splendid pair," Andrew said slyly.

"Andrew," Billie growled.

He rewarded her with a purse-lipped smile. "Truly, you needn't have gone to such extremes for a moment of privacy. The rest of us would have been more than happy to oblige."

"Stop it," Billie ordered.

Andrew looked up, laughing even as he affected a frown. "Do

you really want to take that tone, Billie-goat? I *am* the one on *terra firma*."

"Please, Andrew," she said, trying her very best to be civil and reasonable. "We would very much appreciate your help."

"Well, since you asked so nicely," Andrew murmured.

"I'm going to kill him," she said under her breath.

"*I'm* going to break his other arm," George muttered.

Billie choked down a laugh. There was no way that Andrew could have heard them, but she looked down at him, anyway, and that was when she realized he was frowning, his good hand on his hip.

"What is it now?" George demanded.

Andrew stared down at the ladder, his mouth twisting into a curious frown. "I'm not sure if it has occurred to either of you, but this isn't the sort of thing that's easy to do one-handed."

"Take it out of the sling," George said, but his last words were drowned out by Billie's shriek of "Don't take it out of the sling!"

"Do you really want to stay on the roof?" George hissed.

"And have him reinjure his arm?" she returned. They might have joked about breaking Andrew's good arm, but *really*. The man was a sailor in the navy. It was essential that his bone healed properly.

"You'd marry me for the sake of his arm?"

"I'm not going to marry you," she shot back. "Andrew knows where we are. He can go get help if we need it."

"By the time he gets back with an able-bodied man, we'll have been up here alone for several hours."

"And I suppose you've such a high opinion of your male prowess that you think people will believe you managed to compromise me on a roof."

"Believe me," George hissed, "any man with sense would know you are thoroughly uncompromisable."

Billie's brows came together for a second of confusion. Was he complimenting her moral rectitude? But then—

Oh!

"You are despicable," she seethed. Since that was her only choice of reply. Somehow she didn't think *You have no idea how many men would like to compromise me* would earn her any points for dignity and wit.

Or honesty.

"Andrew," George called down, in that haughty *I-am-the-eldest-son* voice of his, "I will pay you one hundred pounds to take off that sling and fix the ladder into place."

One hundred pounds?

Billie turned on him with wild disbelief. "Are you *insane*?"

"I don't know," Andrew mused. "It might actually be worth one hundred pounds to watch the two of you kill each other."

"Don't be an ass," George said, flicking a furious look at him.

"You wouldn't even inherit," Billie pointed out, not that Andrew had ever wished to succeed his father as Earl of Manston. He was far too enamored of his footloose life for that sort of responsibility.

"Ah, yes, Edward," Andrew said with an exaggerated sigh, referring to the second Rokesby son, who was two years his senior. "That does throw a fly in the ointment. It'd look deuced suspicious if both of you perish in curious circumstances."

There was a moment of awkward silence as they all realized that Andrew had, perhaps, made light of something far too heavy for offhand quips. Edward Rokesby had taken the proudest route of second sons and was a captain in His Majesty's 54th Regiment of Foot. He'd been sent to the American colonies over a year earlier and had served bravely in the Battle of Quaker Hill. He'd remained in Rhode Island for several months before being transferred to British Headquarters in New York Town. News of his health and welfare came far too infrequently for anyone's comfort.

"If Edward perishes," George said stiffly, "I do not believe that the circumstances would ever be described as 'curious.'"

"Oh, come now," Andrew said, rolling his eyes at his older brother, "stop being so bloody serious all the time."

"Your brother risks his life for King and Country," George said, and truly, Billie thought, his voice was clipped and tense, even for him.

"As do I," Andrew said with a cool smile. He tipped his injured arm up toward the roof, his bent and bound limb hinging at the shoulder. "Or at least a bone or two."

Billie swallowed and looked hesitantly over at George, trying to gauge his reaction. As was common for third sons, Andrew had skipped university and gone straight into the Royal Navy as a midshipman. He had been raised to the rank of lieutenant a year earlier. Andrew didn't find himself in harm's way nearly so often as Edward, but still, he wore his uniform proudly.

George, on the other hand, had not been permitted to take a commission; as the heir to the earldom, he had been deemed far too valuable to throw himself in front of American musket balls. And Billie wondered . . . did that bother him? That his brothers served their country and he did not? Had he even wanted to fight?

Then she wondered . . . why had she never wondered about this? True, she did not devote much thought to George Rokesby unless he was standing in front of her, but the lives of the Rokesbys and Bridgertons were thoroughly intertwined. It seemed odd that she did not know this.

Her eyes moved slowly from brother to brother. They had not spoken for several moments. Andrew was still staring up with a measure of challenge in his icy blue eyes, and George was looking right back down with . . . well, it wasn't anger exactly. At least not any longer. But nor was it regret. Or pride. Or anything she could identify.

There was far more to this conversation than rose to the surface.

"Well, *I* have risked life and limb for an unappreciative feline," she declared, eager to direct the conversation back to less controversial topics. Namely, her rescue.

"Is that what happened?" Andrew murmured, bending over the ladder. "I thought you didn't like cats."

George turned to her with an expression that went somewhere beyond exasperation. "You don't even like cats?"

"Everyone likes cats," Billie said quickly.

George's eyes narrowed, and she knew there was no way he believed that her bland smile was anything but a placation, but thankfully Andrew chose that moment to let out a muffled curse, causing both of them to return their attention to his struggles with the ladder.

"Are you all right?" Billie called out.

"Splinter," Andrew bit off. He sucked on the side of his little finger. "Bloody hell."

"It's not going to kill you," George snapped.

Andrew took a moment to fix his brother with a livid glare.

George rolled his eyes. "Oh, for the love of God."

"Don't provoke him," Billie hissed.

George made an odd, growly sound, but he remained silent, crossing his arms as he stared down at his younger brother.

Billie scooted a tiny bit closer to the end for a better view of Andrew as he wedged one of his feet against the bottom of the rail and then bent over to grasp a rung. He grunted audibly as he pulled the ladder upright. The physics of the maneuver were all wrong, but there was only so much a one-armed man could do.

But at least he was a strong one-armed man, and with great exertion and not a little inappropriate language, he managed to set the ladder into place against the side of the building.

"Thank you," George breathed, although from his tone Billie wasn't sure if he was thanking his brother or the Almighty.

With Andrew to brace the ladder—and no cats underfoot—the descent was considerably simpler than their first attempt. But it hurt. By God, the pain in her ankle stole the very breath from her body. And there was nothing she could do about it. She couldn't very well hop down the rungs, so with each step she had to put some weight on her injured ankle. By the time she reached the third-to-last rung, it was all she could do to keep her tears silent.

Strong hands settled at her waist. "I've got you," George said quietly, and she let herself collapse.

Chapter 4

George had had a feeling that Billie was in more pain than she'd let on, but he didn't realize how much until they finally made their way down the ladder. He briefly considered taking her down on his back, but it seemed safer to have her follow him instead. He moved down three rungs before she set her good foot onto the ladder, then he watched as she gingerly followed with its injured companion. For a moment she stood still, probably trying to decide how best to proceed to the next rung.

"I'd lead with the good one," he said quietly, "and grip the rails hard to absorb some of your weight."

She gave a tense nod of acknowledgment and followed his instructions, her breath escaping with an agonized hiss when her good foot was solid and secure, and she was able to lift the injured one from the upper rung.

She'd been holding her breath. He didn't blame her.

He waited as she composed herself, well aware that he needed to remain only a few rungs ahead; if she fell—and she might; he could see that her ankle was very weak—he had to be close enough to stop her from tumbling all the way to the ground.

"Maybe if I try it the other way . . ." she said, breathing hard through her pain.

"I wouldn't," he replied, keeping his voice purposefully even and humble. Billie had never taken well to being told what to do. He supposed he understood this better than anyone. "You don't want your lower foot to be the weak one," he said. "Your leg could buckle—"

"Of course," she said tightly. Not angrily, just tightly. He knew that tone. It was the tone of one who had conceded a point and *really* didn't want any further elucidation on the matter.

It was one he himself used quite often.

Well, as often as he deigned to concede points.

"You can do this," he said. "I know it hurts."

"It really does," she admitted.

He smiled a little. He wasn't sure why, but he was glad she couldn't see his face. "I won't let you fall."

"Everything all right up there?" Andrew called out.

"Tell him to shut up," Billie ground out.

George laughed despite himself. "Miss Bridgerton requests that you shut the hell up," he called down.

Andrew let out a bark of laughter. "It's all good, then."

"I wouldn't say *that*," Billie grumbled, gasping her way through another step.

"You're almost halfway there," George said encouragingly.

"You're lying, but I do appreciate the show of support."

He smiled, and this time he did know why. Billie might be a right pain in the ass most of the time, but she'd always had a good sense of humor. "You're halfway to halfway, then," he said.

"Such an optimist," she muttered.

She made it down another rung without incident, and George realized that their conversation was proving an able distraction. "You can do this, Billie," he said.

"You said that already."

"It bears repeating."

"I think—" She hissed, then sucked in her breath as she moved down another rung.

He waited while she collected herself, her body quivering as she balanced for a moment on her good foot.

"I think," she said again, her voice more carefully modulated, as if she were determined to get the sentence out in an orderly manner, "that this might be the most amiable you have ever behaved in my presence."

"I could say the same," he commented.

She made it down to the halfway mark. "Touché."

"There is nothing quite so invigorating as an able opponent," he said, thinking of all the times they had crossed verbal swords. Billie had never been an easy person to best in conversation, which was why it was always so delicious when he did.

"I'm not sure that holds true on the battle—oh!"

George waited as she gritted her teeth and continued.

"—on the battlefield," she said, after a rather angry-sounding inhalation. "My God, this hurts," she muttered.

"I know," he said encouragingly.

"No you don't."

He smiled yet again. "No, I don't."

She gave a terse nod and took another step. Then, because she was Billie Bridgerton and thus fundamentally unable to allow an unfinished point to lie dormant, she said, "On the battlefield, I think I might find an able opponent inspiring."

"Inspiring?" he murmured, eager to keep her talking.

"But not invigorating."

"One would lead to the other," he said, not that he had any first-hand experience. His only battles had taken place in fencing salons and boxing rings, where the most serious risk was to one's pride. He eased down another step, giving Billie room to maneuver, then peered over his shoulder at Andrew, who appeared to be whistling while he waited.

"Can I help?" Andrew asked, catching his glance.

George shook his head, then looked back up to Billie. "You're almost to the bottom," he told her.

"Please tell me you're not lying this time."

"I'm not lying."

And he wasn't. He hopped down, skipping the last two rungs, and waited for her to draw close enough for him to grab her. A moment later she was within reach, and he swept her into his arms.

"I've got you," he murmured, and he felt her collapse a little, for once in her life allowing someone else to take charge of her.

"Well done," Andrew said cheerfully, poking his head in close. "Are you all right there, Billie-goat?"

Billie nodded, but she didn't look all right. Her jaw was still clenched, and from the way her throat worked, it was clear she was trying her damnedest not to cry.

"You little fool," George murmured, and then he knew she wasn't all right, because she let that pass without a word of protest. In fact, she apologized, which was so wholly unlike her as to be almost alarming.

"Time to go home," George said.

"Let's take a look at that foot," Andrew said, his voice still an obnoxiously bright note in the tableau. He peeled off her stocking, let out a low whistle, and said with some admiration, "Ech, Billie, what did you do to yourself? That looks brutal."

"Shut up," George said.

Andrew just shrugged. "It doesn't look broken—"

"It's not," Billie cut in.

"Still, you'll be off it for a week, at least."

"Perhaps not quite so long," George said, even though he rather thought Andrew was correct in his assessment. Still, there was no point in debating her condition. They weren't saying anything Billie didn't already know. "Shall we go?" he said.

Billie closed her eyes and nodded. "We should put the ladder away," she mumbled.

George tightened his arms around her and headed east toward Aubrey Hall, where Billie lived with her parents and three younger siblings. "We'll get it tomorrow."

She nodded. "Thank you."

"For what?"

"Everything."

"That covers quite a lot," he said in a dry voice. "Are you sure you wish to be in such debt?"

She looked up at him, her eyes tired but wise. "You're far too much of a gentleman to hold me to it."

George chuckled at that. She was right, he supposed, although he'd never treated Billie Bridgerton like any other female of his acquaintance. Hell, no one did.

"Will you still be able to come to dinner tonight?" Andrew asked, loping alongside George.

Billie turned to him distractedly. "What?"

"Surely you haven't forgotten," he said, laying one dramatic hand over his heart. "The Family Rokesby is welcoming the prodigal son—"

"You're not the prodigal son," George said. Good God.

"*A* prodigal son," Andrew corrected with good cheer. "I have been gone for months, even years."

"Not years," George said.

"Not years," Andrew agreed, "but it felt like it, didn't it?" He leaned down toward Billie, close enough to give her a little nudge. "You missed me, didn't you, Goatrix? Come now, admit it."

"Give her some room," George said irritably.

"Oh, she doesn't mind."

"Give *me* some room."

"An entirely different matter," Andrew said with a laugh.

George started to scowl, but then his head snapped up. "*What* did you just call her?"

"He frequently likens me to a goat," Billie said in the flat tone of one who has given up taking offense.

George looked at her, then looked at Andrew, then just shook his head. He'd never understood their sense of humor. Or maybe it was just that he'd never been a part of it. Growing up, he had always felt so separate from the rest of the Rokesbys and Bridgertons. Mostly by virtue of his age—five years older than Edward, who was the next one down the line—but also by his position. He was the eldest, the heir. He, as his father was quick to remind him, had responsibilities. He couldn't bloody well frolic about the countryside all day, climbing trees and breaking bones.

Edward, Mary, and Andrew Rokesby had been born in quick succession, separated from each other by barely a year. They, along with Billie, who was almost precisely Mary's age, had formed a tight little pack that did everything together. The Rokesby and Bridgerton homes were a mere three miles apart, and more often than not the children had met somewhere in the middle, at the brook that separated the estates, or in the treehouse Lord Bridgerton had had built at Billie's insistence in the ancient oak by the trout pond. Most of the time George wasn't sure what specific mischief they'd got up to, but his siblings had tended to come home filthy and hungry and in blooming good spirits.

He hadn't been jealous. Really, they were more annoying than anything else. The last thing he'd wanted to do when he came home from school was muck about with a pack of wild urchins whose average age didn't even scrape into the double digits.

But he had been occasionally wistful. What would it have been like if he'd had such a close cadre of companions? He'd not had a true friend his own age until he left for Eton at the age of twelve. There simply hadn't been anyone to befriend.

But it mattered little now. They were all grown, Edward in the army and Andrew in the navy and Mary married off to George's good friend Felix Maynard. Billie, too, had passed the age of majority, but she was still Billie, still romping around her father's property, still riding her too-spirited mount like her bones were forged of steel and flashing her wide smile around the village that adored her.

And as for George . . . he supposed he was still himself, too.

Still the heir, still preparing for responsibility even as his father re-linquished none of it, still doing absolutely nothing while his brothers took up their arms and fought for the Empire.

He looked down at his own arms, currently cradling Billie as he carried her home. It was quite possibly the most useful thing those arms had done in years.

"We should take you to Crake," Andrew said to Billie. "It's closer, and then you'll be able to stay for dinner."

"She's hurt," George reminded him.

"Pfft. When has that ever stopped her?"

"Well, she's not dressed properly," George said. He sounded like a prig and he knew it, but he was feeling unaccountably ir-ritated, and he couldn't very well take it out on Billie while she was injured.

"I'm sure she can find something to wear in Mary's wardrobe," Andrew said dismissively. "She didn't take everything with her when she got married, did she?"

"No," Billie said, her voice muffled against George's chest. It was funny, that, how one could *feel* sound through one's body. "She left quite a bit behind."

"That settles it, then," Andrew said. "You'll come for supper, you'll spend the night, and all will be right with the world."

George gave him a slow look over his shoulder.

"I'll stay for supper," Billie agreed, moving her head so that her voice slid out into the air instead of George's body, "but then I'll go home with my family. I'd much rather sleep in my own bed, if you don't mind."

George stumbled.

"You all right?" Andrew queried.

"It's nothing," George muttered. And then, for no reason he could discern, he was compelled to add, "Just one of those things when one of your legs goes weak for a moment and bends a bit."

Andrew gave him a curious look. "Just one of those things, eh?"

"Shut up."

Which only made Andrew laugh.

"I have those," Billie said, looking up at him with a little smile. "When you're tired and you don't even realize it. And your leg surprises you."

"Exactly."

She smiled again, a smile of kinship, and it occurred to him—although not, he realized with some surprise, for the first time—that she was actually rather pretty.

Her eyes were lovely—a deep shade of brown that was always warm and welcoming, no matter how much ire might lie in their depths. And her skin was remarkably fair for one who spent as much time out of doors as she did, although she did sport a light sprinkling of freckles across her nose and cheeks. George couldn't remember if they'd been there when she was young. He hadn't really been paying attention to Billie Bridgerton's freckles.

He hadn't really been paying attention to her at all, or at least he'd been trying not to. She was—and always had been—rather difficult to avoid.

"What are you looking at?" she asked.

"Your freckles." He saw no reason to lie.

"Why?"

He shrugged. "They're there."

Her lips pursed, and he thought that would be the end of the conversation. But then she said, somewhat abruptly, "I don't have very many of them."

His brows rose.

"Sixty-two," she said.

He almost stopped walking. "You counted?"

"I had nothing else to do. The weather was beastly, and I couldn't go outside."

George knew better than to inquire about embroidery, or watercolors, or any of a dozen other indoor pursuits commonly taken up by ladies of his acquaintance.

"Probably a few more now," Billie admitted. "It's been a prodigiously sunny spring."

"What are we talking about?" Andrew asked. He'd got a bit ahead of them and they'd only just caught up.

"My freckles," Billie said.

He blinked. "My God, you *are* boring."

"Or bored," Billie countered.

"Or both."

"Must be the company."

"I've always thought George was dull," Andrew said.

George rolled his eyes.

"I was talking about *you*," Billie said.

Andrew only grinned. "How's the foot?"

"It hurts," she said plainly.

"Better? Worse?"

Billie thought about that for a moment, then answered, "The same. No, better, I suppose, since I'm not putting weight on it." She looked back up at George. "Thank you," she said. "Again."

"You're welcome," he replied, but his voice was brusque. He didn't really have a place in their conversation. He never had.

The path forked, and George turned off to the right, toward Crake. It *was* closer, and with Andrew's arm in a sling, he was going to have to carry Billie the entire way.

"Am I too heavy?" she asked, sounding a touch sleepy.

"It wouldn't really matter if you were."

"*Gad*, George, no wonder you're starved for female companionship," Andrew groaned. "That was a clear invitation to say, 'Of course not. You are a delicate petal of womanhood.'"

"No, it wasn't," Billie said.

"It was," Andrew said firmly. "You just didn't realize it."

"I'm not starved for female companionship," George said. Because *really*.

"Oh, yes, of course not," Andrew said with great sarcasm. "You've got Billie in your arms."

"I think you might have just insulted me," she said.

"Not at all, m'dear. Just a statement of fact."

She scowled, her chestnut brows drawing down hard toward her eyes. "When do you go back to sea?"

Andrew gave her an arch look. "You'll miss me."

"I don't believe I will."

But they all knew she was lying.

"You'll have George, at any rate," Andrew said, reaching up and swatting a low-hanging branch. "You two make quite a pair."

"Shut up," Billie said. Which was a lot tamer than what came out of George's mouth.

Andrew chuckled, and the three of them continued on toward Crake House, walking in amiable silence as the wind whistled lightly through the newly budded tree leaves.

"You're not too heavy," George suddenly said.

Billie yawned, shifting slightly in his arms as she looked up at his face. "What did you just say?"

"You're not too heavy." He shrugged. For some reason, it had seemed important to say it.

"Oh. Well." She blinked a few times, her brown eyes equal parts puzzled and pleased. "Thank you."

Up ahead, Andrew laughed, although for the life of him, George didn't know why.

"Yes," Billie said.

"I beg your pardon?"

"Yes," she said again, answering the question he didn't think he'd asked, "he's laughing at us."

"I had a feeling."

"He's an idiot," she said, sighing into George's chest. But it was an affectionate sigh; never had the words *he's an idiot* been imbued with more love and fondness.

"It's nice to have him home, though," George said quietly. And it was. He'd spent years being annoyed by his younger brothers, Andrew most especially, but now that they were grown and pursuing a life beyond the ordinariness of Kent and London, he missed them.

Almost as much as he envied them.

"It is nice, isn't it?" Billie gave a wistful smile, then she added, "Not that I'd ever tell him so."

"Oh no. Definitely not."

Billie chuckled at their shared joke, then let out a yawn. "Sorry," she mumbled. She couldn't very well cover her mouth with her arms around his neck. "Do you mind if I close my eyes?"

Something odd and unfamiliar lurched in George's chest. Something almost protective. "Of course not," he said.

She smiled—a sleepy, happy thing—and said, "I never have trouble falling asleep."

"Never?"

She shook her head, and her hair, which had long since given up any attempt to remain confined with pins, crept up and tickled his chin. "I can sleep anywhere," she said with a yawn.

She dozed the rest of the way home, and George did not mind it at all.

Chapter 5

Billie had been born just seventeen days after Mary Rokesby, and according to their parents, they had been the best of friends from the moment they'd been placed in the same cradle when Lady Bridgerton called upon Lady Manston for their regular Thursday morning visit.

Billie wasn't sure why her mother had brought along a two-month-old baby when there had been a perfectly able nanny back at Aubrey Hall, but she suspected it had something to do with her rolling over from front to back at the improbably early age of six weeks.

The Ladies Bridgerton and Manston were devoted and loyal friends, and Billie was quite sure that each would lay down her life for the other (or for the other's children), but it had to be said, there had always been a strong element of competition in their relationship.

Billie also suspected that her stunning prowess in the art of rolling over had less to do with innate genius and more to do with the tip of her mother's forefinger against her shoulder, but as her mother pointed out, there were no witnesses.

But what *was* witnessed—by both their mothers and a housemaid—was that when Billie had been placed in Mary's spacious cradle, she had reached out and grabbed the other baby's tiny hand. And when their mothers tried to pull them apart, they both started howling like banshees.

Billie's mother told her that she had been tempted to just leave her there at Crake House overnight; it was the only way to keep both babies calm.

That first morning was surely a portent of things to come. Billie and Mary were, as their nannies like to say, two peas in a pod. Two very different peas that happened to be quite fond of each other.

Where Billie was fearless, Mary was careful. Not timid, just careful. She always looked before she leapt. Billie looked, too; she just tended to do it in a somewhat more perfunctory manner.

And then she leapt high and far, often outdoing both Edward and Andrew, who had been more or less forced to befriend her after they realized that Billie would A) follow them to the ends of the earth except that B) she'd probably get there before they did.

With Mary—after a careful consideration of the ambient danger—right at her heels.

And so they became a foursome. Three wild children and one voice of reason.

They did listen to Mary occasionally. Truly, they did. It was probably the only reason all four had reached adulthood without permanent injury.

But like all good things, it came to an end, and a few years after both Edward and Andrew left home, Mary had fallen in love, got married, and moved away. She and Billie exchanged letters regularly, but it wasn't the same. Still, Billie would always call Mary her best friend, and thus, when she found herself at Crake House with a sprained ankle and nothing to wear but men's breeches and a rather dusty shirt and coat, she had no compunction raiding her friend's wardrobe for a garment suitable for a family dinner. Most of the dresses were a few years out of fashion, but that didn't bother Billie. In all truth, she likely wouldn't have even noticed if the maid who was helping her to dress for dinner hadn't apologized for it.

And they were certainly more stylish than anything she possessed in her own closet.

Billie rather thought that the bigger problem was the length, or rather, the excess of it. Mary was taller than she was, by at least three inches. It had always irked Billie (and amused Mary) to no end; it had always *seemed* like she should be the taller of the two. But as Billie couldn't even walk, this was less of an issue than it might have been.

Mary's gowns were also a bit too large in the chest. But beggars could never be choosers, and so Billie tucked two extra fichus into the bodice and decided instead to be grateful that Mary's wardrobe had contained a relatively simple round gown in a shade of forest green that Billie liked to think flattered her complexion.

The maid was tucking a few final pins into Billie's hair when a knock sounded on the door to Mary's old room, where Billie had taken up residence.

"George," she said with surprise when she saw his strong form filling the doorway. He was elegantly dressed in a midnight blue coat that she suspected would complement his eyes if he wore it in the full light of day. Gold buttons twinkled in the candlelight, adding to his already regal mien.

"My lady," he murmured, executing a small bow. "I've come to help you down to the drawing room."

"Oh." Billie wasn't sure why she was surprised. Andrew couldn't very well do it, and her father, who was surely already downstairs, wasn't as strong as he used to be.

"If you prefer," George said, "we could summon a footman."

"No, no, of course not," Billie replied. A footman seemed most awkward. At least she *knew* George. And he had already carried her once.

He came into the room, clasping his hands behind his back when he reached her side. "How is your ankle?"

"Still quite painful," she admitted, "but I bound it with some wide ribbon, and that seems to be helping."

His lips curved, and his eyes took on an azure sparkle of amusement. "Ribbon?"

To her maid's horror, Billie hiked up her overlong skirt and stuck out her foot, revealing an ankle bound in a length of festive pink ribbon.

"Very stylish," George commented.

"I could not justify tearing up a bedsheet when this would do just as well."

"Ever practical."

"I like to think so," Billie said, her jaunty voice giving way to a slight frown when it occurred to her that this might not have been a compliment. "Well," she said, brushing an invisible speck of dust off her arm, "they're your sheets, at any rate. You should thank me."

"I'm sure I do."

Her eyes narrowed.

"Yes," he said, "I'm mocking you. But only a little."

Billie felt her chin rise an inch or so. "So long as it's only a little."

"I wouldn't dare otherwise," he replied. He leaned in, just a bit. "At least not in your presence."

Billie stole a glance at the maid. She appeared thoroughly scandalized by the exchange.

"In all seriousness, though, Billie," George said, proving that a sympathetic heart did beat somewhere in his chest, "are you certain you're well enough to dine?"

She fastened an earring. Again, Mary's. "I have to eat. I might as well do it in good company."

He smiled at that. "It has been too long since we have had everyone—well, at least as many as we have tonight—together."

Billie nodded, feeling wistful. When she was a child, the

Rokesbys and Bridgertons had dined together several times each month. With nine children between the two families, suppers—or luncheons, or whatever odd holiday they'd elected to celebrate—could not be anything but loud and boisterous affairs.

But one by one, the boys left for Eton, first George, then Edward, and then Andrew. Billie's two younger brothers, Edmund and Hugo, were boarding there now, along with the youngest Rokesby, Nicholas. Mary had found love and moved to Sussex, and now the only ones left in regular residence were Billie and her younger sister Georgiana, who at fourteen was perfectly pleasant but no bosom bow for a grown woman of three and twenty.

And George of course, but—eligible unmarried gentleman that he was—he split his time between Kent and London.

"Penny for them," George said, crossing the room to where Billie sat at the vanity.

She shook her head. "Not worth even that, I'm afraid. It's all quite maudlin, really."

"Maudlin? You? I must learn more."

She gave him a look, then said, "We are so diminished in number now. There used to be so many of us."

"There still are," he pointed out.

"I know, but we're so rarely together. It makes me sad." She could hardly believe she was speaking so frankly with George, but it had been such an odd, trying day. Perhaps it was making her less guarded.

"We shall all be together again," he said gamely. "I'm quite sure of it."

Billie lifted a brow. "Have you been assigned to cheer me up?"

"Your mother offered me three quid."

"*What?*"

"I jest."

She scowled, but with no real feeling behind it.

"Here, come now. I'll carry you down." He bent down to take her into his arms, but when he moved to the right, she moved to the left, and their heads bumped.

"Ooof, sorry," he muttered.

"No, it was my fault."

"Here, I'll . . ." He made to put his arms behind her back and under her legs, but there was something inescapably awkward about it, which was the oddest thing, since he had carried her for over a mile just a few hours earlier.

He lifted her into the air, and the maid, who had been standing at quiet attention throughout the conversation, jolted out of the way as Billie's legs swung around in an arc.

"A little less pressure on my neck, if you would," George said.

"Oh, so sorry." Billie adjusted her position. "It was just the same as this afternoon."

He moved out into the hall. "No, it wasn't."

Maybe not, Billie conceded to herself. She'd felt so at ease when he had carried her through the woods. Far more at ease than she'd had any right to in the arms of a man who was not her relation. Now it was just plain uncomfortable. She was excruciatingly aware of his nearness, of the bold heat of his body, seeping through his clothing. His coat collar was properly high, but when her finger grazed the very top of it, a little lock of his light brown hair curled down over her skin.

"Is aught amiss?" he asked as they reached the top of the staircase.

"No," she said quickly, then cleared her throat. "Why would you think so?"

"You haven't stopped fidgeting since I picked you up."

"Oh." She couldn't really think of anything to say to that. "It's just that my foot hurts." No, apparently she *could* think of something. Pity it was completely irrelevant.

He paused, gazing down at her with concern. "Are you sure you want to come to dinner?"

"I'm *sure*." She let out an exasperated snuff of air. "For heaven's sake, I'm already *here*. It would be ridiculous to quarantine myself in Mary's room."

"It's hardly a quarantine."

"It would feel like quarantine," she muttered.

He regarded her with a curious expression. "You don't like being by yourself, do you?"

"Not when the rest of the world is making merry without me," she retorted.

He was quiet for a moment, his head cocking just far enough to the side to indicate that he found her words curious. "What about the rest of the time?"

"I beg your pardon?"

"When the world isn't gathering without you," he said with a vaguely condescending tone. "Do you mind being on your own?"

She felt her brows come together as she gazed up at him. What on earth could be prompting such probing?

"It's not a difficult query," he said, something slightly provocative bringing his voice down to a murmur.

"No, of course I don't mind being alone." She pressed her lips together, feeling rather peeved. And peevish. But he was asking her questions she never even asked herself. But then, before she realized she was planning to speak, she heard herself say, "I don't like—"

"What?"

She gave her head a shake. "Never mind."

"No, tell me."

She let out a sigh. He wasn't going to let up. "I don't like being cooped up. I can spend all day in my own company if I'm out of doors. Or even down in the drawing room, where the windows are tall and let in so much light."

He nodded slowly, as if he agreed with her.

"Are you much the same way, then?" she asked.

"Not at all," he said.

Well, then, so much for her being able to interpret his gestures.

"I quite enjoy my own company," he continued.

"I'm sure you do."

His mouth managed half a smile. "I thought we weren't insulting each other tonight."

"We weren't?"

"I *am* carrying you down a flight of stairs. You'd do well to speak kindly to me."

"Point taken," she acceded.

George rounded the landing, and she thought they were done with the conversation when he said, "The other day it rained . . . all day long, unremittingly."

Billie tipped her head to the side. She knew which day he was talking about. It had been miserable. She had been planning to take her mare Argo out to inspect the fences at the southern end of her father's lands. And maybe stop at the wild strawberry patch. It was much too early in the season for fruit, but the blossoms would be starting to emerge, and she was curious as to their abundance.

"I stayed indoors, of course," George continued. "There was no reason to go out."

She wasn't quite sure where he was going with this, but obliged him by inquiring, "How did you occupy yourself?"

"I read a book." He sounded quite pleased with himself. "I sat in my study and read an entire book from start to finish, and it was quite the most pleasant day in recent memory."

"You need to get out more," she deadpanned.

He ignored that entirely. "All I'm saying is, I spent the day cooped up, as you call it, and it was delightful."

"Well. That just proves my point."

"We were making points?"

"We're always making points, George."

"And always keeping score?" he murmured.

Always. But she didn't say it out loud. It seemed childish. And petty. And worse, like she was trying too hard to be something she wasn't. Or rather, something she *was* but that society would never allow her to be. He was Lord Kennard, and she was Miss Sybilla Bridgerton, and while she'd gleefully stack her inner fortitude up against his any day of the week, she was no fool. She understood how the world worked. Here in her little corner of Kent, she was queen of her domain, but in any contest held outside the homey little circle drawn 'round Crake and Aubrey Hall . . .

George Rokesby would win. Always. Or if not, he'd give the appearance of having done so.

And there was nothing she could do about it.

"You look uncommonly serious all of a sudden," he said, stepping onto the polished parquet of the ground-floor hall.

"Thinking about *you*," she said truthfully.

"A dare if ever I heard one." He reached the open door to the drawing room, and his lips moved closer to her ear. "And one I shall not take."

Her tongue touched the top of her mouth, readying a reply, but before she could make a sound, George had stepped through the entry to Crake House's formal drawing room.

"Good evening, everyone," he said grandly.

Any hope Billie might have had at making a subtle entrance was squashed immediately when she realized they were the last to arrive. Her mother was seated next to Lady Manston on the long sofa with Georgiana in a nearby chair looking vaguely bored. The men had congregated over by the window. Lords Bridgerton and Manston were chatting with Andrew, who was happily accepting a glass of brandy from his father.

"Billie!" her mother exclaimed, practically hopping to her feet. "In your message you wrote that it was just a sprain."

"It *is* just a sprain," Billie replied. "I'll be as good as new by the end of the week."

George snorted. She ignored him.

"It's nothing, Mama," Billie assured her. "I've certainly done worse."

Andrew snorted. She ignored him, too.

"With a cane, she might have made it down on her own," George said as he set her down on the settee, "but it would have taken her thrice as long, and neither of us has the patience for that."

Billie's father, who had been standing by the window with a glass of brandy, let out a hearty guffaw.

Billie gave him a bit of an evil eye, which only made him laugh with more vigor.

"Is that one of Mary's gowns?" Lady Bridgerton asked.

Billie nodded. "I was in breeches."

Her mother sighed but made no comment. It was an endless argument between them, and their truce was maintained only by Billie's promise to always dress properly for dinner. And among guests. And at church.

There was actually a rather long list of events for which she was required to attire herself to her mother's specifications. But in the matter of Billie wearing breeches while conducting business around the estate, Lady Bridgerton had acquiesced.

To Billie, it had felt like a victory. As she had explained to her mother—repeatedly—all she really needed was permission to dress sensibly when out and about. The tenants surely called her something more colorful than eccentric, but she knew she was well-liked. And respected.

The affection had come naturally; according to Billie's mother, she'd emerged from the womb smiling, and even as a child, she'd been the tenants' favorite.

The respect, however, had been earned, and for that reason it was all the more fiercely treasured.

Billie knew that her younger brother would one day inherit Aubrey Hall and all its lands, but Edmund was still a child, eight years her junior. Most of the time he was away at school. Their father wasn't getting any younger, and someone had to learn how to properly manage such a large estate. Besides, Billie was a natural at it; everyone said so.

She'd been an only child for so many years; there had been two babies between her and Edmund's births, but neither had lived past infancy. During those years of prayers and hopes and wishing for an heir, Billie had become something of a mascot to the tenants, a living, smiling symbol of Aubrey Hall's future.

Unlike most highborn daughters, Billie had always accompanied her parents on their duties around the estate. When her mother brought baskets of food to the needy, she was right there with apples for the children. When her father was out surveying the land, she could more often than not be found at his feet, digging up worms as she explained why she thought rye would be a much better choice than barley in such a sun-starved field.

At first she'd been a source of amusement—the energetic little five-year-old who insisted upon measuring grain when the rents were collected. But eventually she became a fixture, and now it was expected that she would see to the needs of the estate. If a cottage roof was leaking, she was the one who made sure it was mended. If a harvest was lean, she went out and tried to figure out why.

She was, for all intents and purposes, her father's eldest son.

Other young ladies might read romantic poetry and Shakespearean tragedies. Billie read treatises on agricultural management. And she loved them. Honestly. They were ripping good reads.

It was difficult to imagine a life that might suit her better, but it had to be said: it was all much easier to conduct without a corset.

Much as it pained her mother.

"I was out seeing to the irrigation," Billie explained. "It would have been impractical in a frock."

"I didn't say anything," Lady Bridgerton said, even though they all knew she'd been thinking it.

"Not to mention difficult to climb that tree," Andrew put in.

That did get her mother's attention. "She was climbing a tree?"

"Saving a cat," Andrew confirmed.

"One might assume," George said, his voice purring with authority, "that had she been wearing a frock, she would not have attempted the tree."

"What happened to the cat?" Georgiana asked.

Billie looked to her sister. She'd almost forgotten she was there. And she had definitely forgotten the cat. "I don't know."

Georgiana leaned forward, her blue eyes impatient. "Well, did you save it?"

"If so," Billie said, "it was entirely against its wishes."

"It was a most ungrateful feline," George said.

Billie's father chuckled at the description and gave him a manly slap on the back. "George, m'boy, we must get you a drink. You'll need it after your trials."

Billie's mouth fell open. "*His* trials?"

George smirked, but no one else saw it, the bloody man.

"Mary's gown looks lovely on you," Lady Bridgerton said, steering the conversation back to more ladylike pursuits.

"Thank you," Billie replied. "I rather like this shade of green." Her fingers flitted to the lace along the round neckline. It was really most becoming.

Her mother stared at her in shock.

"I like pretty dresses," Billie insisted. "I just don't like wearing them when it's impractical to do so."

"The *cat*," Georgiana persisted.

Billie flicked her an impatient look. "I told you, I don't know. Honestly, it was a horrid little creature."

"Agreed," George said, raising his glass in salute.

"I can't believe you're toasting to the possible demise of a cat," Georgiana said.

"*I'm* not," Billie replied, glancing around to see if someone might bring her a drink. "But I'd like to."

"It's all right, darling," Lady Bridgerton murmured, giving her younger daughter a reassuring smile. "Don't fret so."

Billie looked back at Georgiana. If their mother used such a tone on her, she would likely go mad. But Georgiana had been sickly as a child, and Lady Bridgerton had never quite learned to treat her with anything less than solicitous concern.

"I'm sure the cat survived its ordeal," Billie told Georgiana. "He was quite a scrappy fellow. Had the look of a survivor in his eye."

Andrew loped over and leaned down near Georgiana's shoulder. "Always lands on its feet, that one."

"Oh, stop!" Georgiana batted him away, but it was clear she wasn't angry about the joke. No one was ever angry at Andrew. Not for long, at least.

"Is there any news of Edward?" Billie asked Lady Manston.

Lady Manston's eyes clouded as she shook her head. "None since the last letter. The one we received last month."

"I'm sure he's well," Billie said. "He is such a talented soldier."

"I'm not sure how much talent plays into it when someone is aiming a gun at your chest," George said darkly.

Billie turned to glare. "Don't listen to him," she said to Lady Manston. "He's never been a soldier."

Lady Manston smiled at her, an expression that was sad and sweet and loving, all at once. "I think he would like to have been," she said, peering up at her eldest. "Wouldn't you, George?"

Chapter 6

George forced his face into an impassive mask. His mother meant well; she always did. But she was a woman. She could never understand what it meant to fight for one's king and country. She could never understand what it meant *not* to do so.

"It doesn't matter what I wanted," he said gruffly. He took a large gulp of his brandy. Then he took another. "I was needed here."

"For which I am grateful," his mother declared. She turned back to the other ladies with a determined smile, but her eyes were overbright. "I don't need *all* of my sons going off to war. God willing, this nonsense will be over before Nicholas is of an age to take a commission."

At first no one spoke. Lady Manston's voice had been just a little too loud, her words just a little too shrill. It was one of those awkward moments that no one quite knew how to break. George finally took a small sip of his drink and said in a low voice, "There will always be nonsense among men."

That seemed to let some of the tension out of the air, and sure enough, Billie looked up at him with a defiant tilt to her chin. "Women would do a far better job if we were allowed to govern."

He returned her volley with a bland smile. She was trying to goad him. He refused to indulge her.

Billie's father, however, was hooked quite neatly on her bait. "I'm certain you would," he said, with enough placation in his voice for everyone to know he did not mean it.

"We would," Billie insisted. "Certainly there would be less war."

"I would have to agree with her there," Andrew said, lifting his glass in her direction.

"It's a moot point," Lord Manston said. "If God had wanted women to govern and fight, he would have made them strong enough to wield swords and muskets."

"I can shoot," Billie said.

Lord Manston looked at her and blinked. "Yes," he said, almost as if he were contemplating an odd scientific curiosity, "you probably can."

"Billie brought down a stag last winter," Lord Bridgerton said, shrugging as if this were a normal occurrence.

"Did you?" Andrew said admiringly. "Well done."

Billie smiled. "It was delicious."

"I can't believe you allow her to hunt," Lord Manston said to Lord Bridgerton.

"Do you really think I could stop her?"

"No one can stop Billie," George muttered. He turned abruptly and crossed the room to get another drink.

There was a long silence. An uncomfortable silence. George decided that this time he didn't care.

"How *is* Nicholas?" Lady Bridgerton asked. George smiled into his glass. She'd always known how to deflect a conversation from delicate topics. Sure enough, her perfect social smile was evident in her voice as she added, "Better behaved than Edmund and Hugo, I'm sure."

"I'm sure he *isn't*," Lady Manston returned with a laugh.

"Nicholas wouldn't—" Georgiana started to say.

But Billie's voice came out on top. "It's difficult to imagine anyone getting sent down more often than Andrew."

Andrew held up a hand. "I hold the record."

Georgiana's eyes grew wide. "Among Rokesbys?"

"Among everyone."

"That cannot be true," Billie scoffed.

"I assure you, it is. There's a reason I left early, you know. I reckon if I showed up for a visit, they would not let me back through the gate."

Billie gratefully accepted the glass of wine the footman finally brought over and then lifted it toward Andrew in a skeptical salute. "*That* only shows that the headmaster should be applauded for his great good sense."

"Andrew, stop your exaggerations," Lady Manston said. She rolled her eyes as she turned back to Lady Bridgerton. "He did get sent down from Eton more than once, but I assure you, he has not been banished."

"Not for want of trying," Billie quipped.

George let out a long breath and turned back to the window, peering out into the inky night. Perhaps he was an insufferable prig—an insufferable prig who, as it happened, had never been sent down from Eton *or* Cambridge—but he really didn't feel like listening to Andrew and Billie's endless banter.

It never changed. Billie would be deliciously clever, and then Andrew would play the rogue, and then Billie would say something utterly deflating, and then Andrew would laugh and twinkle, and then *everyone* would laugh and twinkle, and it was always, *always* the same damned thing.

He was just so bored of it all.

George glanced briefly at Georgiana, sitting morosely in what was, in his opinion, the least comfortable chair in the house. How was it possible that no one noticed she'd been left out of the conversation? Billie and Andrew were lighting up the room with their wit and vivacity, and poor Georgiana couldn't get a word in. Not that she appeared to be trying, but at fourteen, how could she hope to compete?

Abruptly, he crossed the room to the younger girl's side and leaned down. "I saw the cat," he said, his words disappearing into her gingery hair. "It dashed off into the woods."

It hadn't, of course. He had no idea what had become of the cat. Something involving brimstone and the wrath of the devil, if there was any justice in the world.

Georgiana started, then turned to him with a wide smile that was disconcertingly like her sister's. "Did you? Oh, *thank you* for letting me know."

George glanced over at Billie as he straightened. She was regarding him with a keen eye, silently admonishing him for lying. He returned the expression with equal insolence, his quirked brow almost daring her to call him out on it.

But she didn't. Instead she dismissed him with a one-shouldered shrug so tiny no one could possibly have noticed it but him. Then she turned back to Andrew with her usual sparkle and charm. George returned his attention to Georgiana, who was clearly a cleverer girl than he'd ever realized, because she was watching the scene with slow-rising curiosity, her eyes moving back and forth between all of them, as if they were players on a field.

He shrugged. Good for her. He was glad she had a brain in her head. She was going to need it with her family.

He took another sip of his brandy, losing himself in his thoughts until the conversation around him descended into a low hum. He felt restless tonight, unusually so. Here he was, surrounded by people he'd known and loved his entire life, and all he wanted . . .

He stared toward the window, searching for an answer. All he wanted was to . . .

He didn't know.

There was the problem. Right there. He didn't know what he wanted, just that it wasn't here.

His life, he realized, had reached a new depth of banality.

"George? George?"

He blinked. His mother was calling his name.

"Lady Frederica Fortescue-Endicott has become betrothed to the Earl of Northwick," she said to him. "Had you heard?"

Ah. So this was to be tonight's conversation. He finished his drink. "I had not."

"The Duke of Westborough's eldest daughter," his mother said to Lady Bridgerton. "Such a charming young lady."

"Oh, of course, lovely girl. Dark hair, yes?"

"And such beautiful blue eyes. Sings like a bird."

George stifled a sigh.

His father slapped him on the back. "The duke set her up with a good dowry," he said, coming straight to the point. "Twenty thousand *and* a piece of property."

"As I've missed my chance," George said with a diplomatically impassive smile, "there can be no benefit to the catalogue of her many attributes."

"Of course not," his mother said. "It's far too late for that. But if you had listened to me last spring—"

The supper gong sounded—*thank God*—and his mother must have decided that there was no use in further pressing her matchmaking points because the next words out of her mouth had to do with the evening's menu, and the apparent lack of good fish this week at market.

George made his way back to Billie's side. "Shall I?" he murmured, holding out his arms.

"Oh," she exclaimed lightly, although for the life of him, he couldn't imagine why she'd be surprised. Nothing had changed in the past quarter of an hour; who else was going to carry her into the dining room?

"How very gallant of you, George," his mother said, taking her husband's hand and allowing him to lead her across the room.

He gave her a dry smile. "I confess it's a heady feeling to have Billie Bridgerton at my mercy."

Lord Bridgerton laughed. "Enjoy it while you can, son. She doesn't like to lose, that one."

"Does anyone?" Billie retorted.

"Of course not," her father replied. "It's more of a question of how gracefully one concedes."

"I'm perfectly gr—"

George scooped her into his arms. "Are you sure you want to finish that sentence?" he murmured. Because they all knew. Billie Bridgerton was rarely graceful in defeat.

Billie clamped her mouth together.

"Two points for honesty," he said.

"What would it take to earn three?" she shot back.

He laughed.

"And anyway," Billie said to her father, fundamentally unable to let a point drop, "I didn't *lose* anything."

"You lost the cat," Georgiana said.

"And your dignity," Andrew added.

"Now *that* earns three points," George said.

"I sprained my ankle!"

"We know, dear," Lady Bridgerton said, giving her daughter a little pat on the arm. "You'll feel better soon. You said so."

Four points, George started to say, but Billie fixed him with a murderous glare.

"Don't you dare," she ground out.

"But you make it so *easy*."

"Are we mocking Billie?" Andrew asked, catching up as they entered the hall. "Because if we are, I'll have you know I'm hurt that you would begin without me."

"*Andrew*," Billie all but growled.

Andrew laid his good hand on his heart in feigned affront. "Hurt. Hurt, I say."

"Do we think we could not mock me?" Billie asked in an exasperated voice. "Just for one evening?"

"I suppose," Andrew said, "but George isn't nearly so much fun."

George started to say something, but then he caught a glance at

Billie's face. She was tired. And in pain. What Andrew had taken as customary banter was actually a plea for relief.

He brought his lips close to her ear, lowering his voice to a quiet murmur. "Are you certain you're up to supper?"

"Of course!" she replied, visibly chagrined that he'd asked. "I'm fine."

"But are you well?"

Her lips tightened. Then trembled.

George slowed his pace, allowing Andrew to amble ahead of them. "There is no shame in needing a rest, Billie."

She looked up at him, something almost rueful in her eyes. "I'm hungry," she said.

He nodded. "I can ask that a small ottoman be placed under the table so that you might elevate your leg."

Billie blinked up at him in surprise, and for a moment he could have sworn he could hear the sound of her breath passing across her lips. "That would be most welcome," she said. "Thank you."

"Consider it done." He paused. "You do look rather fetching in that gown, by the way."

"What?"

He had no idea why he'd said that. And judging from her shocked expression, neither did she.

He shrugged, wishing he had a free hand to adjust his cravat. It felt unaccountably tight. And of course he would say something complimentary about her gown; wasn't that what gentlemen did? Plus, she'd looked as if she could use a little boost. And it did suit her quite well. "It's a nice color," he improvised. He could be occasionally charming. "It, ehrm . . . brings out your eyes."

"My eyes are brown."

"It still brings them out."

She looked vaguely alarmed. "Good heavens, George. Have you ever paid a lady a compliment before?"

"Have you ever *received* one?"

Too late he realized how awful that sounded, and he stammered something that was meant to approximate an apology, but Billie was already shaking with laughter. "Oh, I'm sorry," she gasped, wiping her eyes on her shoulder since her hands were around his neck. "Oh, that was funny. Your face . . ."

Amazingly, George felt himself smile. "I was trying to ask if you'd ever *accepted* one," he was compelled to say. Then he muttered, "Obviously, you've received them."

"Oh, obviously."

He shook his head. "Truly, I'm sorry."

"You're such a gentleman," she teased.

"This surprises you?"

"Not at all. I think you would die before insulting a lady, however inadvertently."

"I'm fairly certain I've insulted you at some point in our history."

She waved that off. "I'm not sure I count."

"I will confess," he said, "you do seem more of a lady than usual this evening."

Her expression grew shrewd. "There is an insult in there somewhere, I'm sure."

"*Or* a compliment."

"No," she said, pretending to give it serious thought, "I don't think there is."

He laughed, full and throaty, and it was only when his mirth had subsided to a light chuckle that he realized how unfamiliar it had felt. It had been a long time since he had given himself over to laughter, allowing it to tickle through his body.

It was a far cry from the social titters one encountered in London.

"I *have* received a compliment before," Billie said, her voice softening when she added, "but I will own that I am not well-skilled in accepting them. At least not for the color of my gown."

George slowed his pace yet again as he turned a corner and the door to the dining room came into view. "You never did go to London for a Season, did you?"

"You know I didn't."

He wondered why. Mary had done so, and she and Billie usually did everything together. But it didn't seem polite to ask, at least not now, just as supper was about to commence.

"I didn't want to," Billie said.

George did not point out that he had not asked for an explanation.

"I'd have been dreadful at it."

"You'd have been a breath of fresh air," he lied. She *would* have been dreadful at it, and then he'd have been conscripted to be her social savior, making sure her dance card was at least halfway filled, and then defending her honor every time some brainless young lord assumed she was lax of morals because she was a bit too loud and free.

It would have been exhausting.

"Excuse me," he murmured, pausing to ask a footman to find her an ottoman. "Shall I hold you until he returns?"

"Hold me?" she echoed, as if she had suddenly lost her command of English.

"Is something wrong?" his mother asked, watching them with undisguised curiosity through the open doorway. She, Lady Bridgerton, and Georgiana had already taken their seats. The gentlemen were waiting for Billie to be set down.

"Sit," George told them, "please. I've asked a footman to bring something for under the table. So that Billie may elevate her foot."

"That's very kind of you, George," Lady Bridgerton said. "I should have thought of that."

"I've turned an ankle before," he said, carrying Billie into the room.

"And I have not," Lady Bridgerton returned, "although one would think I'd be an expert on them by now." She looked over at Georgiana. "I think you might be the only one of my children who hasn't broken a bone or twisted a joint yet."

"It's my special skill," Georgiana said in a flat voice.

"I must say," Lady Manston said, looking over at George and Billie with a deceptively placid smile, "the two of you make quite a pair."

George speared his mother with a stare. *No.* She might want to see him married, but she was not going to try *this*.

"Don't tease so," Billie said, with exactly the right amount of affectionate admonishment in her voice to put a halt to that line of thinking. "Who else would carry me if not George?"

"Alas, my fractured limb," Andrew murmured.

"How did you break it?" Georgiana asked.

He leaned forward, his eyes sparkling like the sea. "Wrestled with a shark."

Billie snorted.

"No," Georgiana said, unimpressed, "what really happened?"

Andrew shrugged. "I slipped."

There was a little beat of silence. No one had expected anything so mundane as that.

"The shark makes for a better story," Georgiana finally said.

"It does, doesn't it? The truth is rarely as glamorous as we'd like."

"I thought at the very least you'd fallen from the mast," Billie said.

"The deck was slippery," Andrew said in a matter-of-fact manner. And while everyone was pondering the utter banality of this, he added, "It gets that way. Water, you know."

The footman returned with a small tufted ottoman. It was not as tall as George would have liked, but he still thought it would be better for Billie than letting her foot dangle.

"I was surprised Admiral McClellan allowed you to recuperate at home," Lady Manston said as the footman crawled under the table to set the ottoman into place. "Not that I'm complaining. It's delightful to have you at Crake where you belong."

Andrew gave his mother a lopsided smile. "Not much use for a one-armed sailor."

"Even with all those peg-legged pirates?" Billie quipped as George set her down in her seat. "I thought it was practically a requirement to be missing a limb at sea."

Andrew tipped his head thoughtfully to the side. "Our cook is missing an ear."

"Andrew!" his mother exclaimed.

"How gruesome," Billie said, eyes aglow with macabre delight. "Were you there when it happened?"

"Billie!" her mother exclaimed.

Billie whipped her head around to face her mother, protesting, "You can't expect me to hear about an earless sailor and *not* ask."

"Nevertheless, it is not appropriate conversation at a family supper."

Gatherings between the Rokesby and Bridgerton clans were always classified as family, no matter that there wasn't a drop of shared blood between them. At least not within the last hundred years.

"I can't imagine where it would be more appropriate," Andrew said, "unless we all head out to the public inn."

"Alas," Billie said, "I'm not allowed this time of night."

Andrew flashed her a cheeky grin. "Reason seven hundred and thirty-eight why I'm glad I was not born a female."

Billie rolled her eyes.

"Are you allowed during the day?" Georgiana asked her.

"Of course," Billie said, but George noticed that her mother didn't look happy about it.

Neither did Georgiana. Her lips were pursed into a frustrated frown, and she had one hand on the table, her index finger tapping impatiently against the cloth.

"Mrs. Bucket makes the most delicious pork pie," Billie said. "Every Thursday."

"I'd forgotten," Andrew said, shuddering with delicious culinary memory.

"How on earth could you? It's heaven in a crust."

"Agreed. We shall have to sup together. Shall we say at noo—"

"Women are bloody," Georgiana blurted out.

Lady Bridgerton dropped her fork.

Billie turned to her sister with an expression of cautious surprise. "I'm sorry?"

"Women can be bloody, too," Georgiana said, her tone approaching truculence.

Billie seemed not to know what to make of that. Normally George would be enjoying her discomfiture, but the conversation had taken such a sharp turn into the bizarre that he could not bring himself to feel anything but sympathy.

And relief that he wasn't the one questioning the young girl.

"What you said earlier," Georgiana said. "About women, and how we would wage war less frequently than men. I don't think that's true."

"Oh," Billie said, looking mightily relieved. Truth was, George was relieved, too. Because the only other explanation for women being bloody was a conversation he did *not* want to have at the dining table.

Or anywhere for that matter.

"What about Queen Mary?" Georgiana continued. "No one could call her a pacifist."

"They didn't call her Bloody Mary for nothing," Andrew said.

"Exactly!" Georgiana agreed with an enthusiastic nod. "And Queen Elizabeth sank an entire armada."

"She had her *men* sink the armada," Lord Bridgerton corrected.

"*She* gave the orders," Georgiana shot back.

"Georgiana has a point," George said, happy to give credit where it was due.

Georgiana gave him a grateful look.

"Indeed," Billie said with a smile.

At that, Georgiana seemed ridiculously pleased.

"I did not mean to say that women couldn't be violent," Billie said, now that Georgiana was done with her argument. "Of course we can, given proper motivation."

"I shudder to think," Andrew murmured.

"If someone I loved was in danger," Billie said with quiet intensity, "I'm quite certain I could be moved to violence."

For years George would wonder about that moment. Something changed. Something shook and twisted. The air crackled electric, and everyone—every last Rokesby and Bridgerton at the table—

sat almost suspended in time, as if waiting for something none of them understood.

Even Billie.

George studied her face. It was not difficult to imagine her as a warrior, fierce and protective of the people she loved. Was he counted among that number? He rather thought he was. Anyone with his surname would fall beneath her protection.

No one spoke. No one even breathed until his mother let out a laugh that was really nothing more than a breath, and then declared, "Such a depressing topic."

"I disagree," George said softly. He didn't think she'd heard him. But Billie did. Her lips parted, and her dark eyes met his with curiosity and surprise. And maybe even a hint of gratitude.

"I do not understand why we are talking of such things," his mother continued, thoroughly determined to steer the conversation back to sweetness and light.

Because it's important, George thought. *Because it means something*. Because nothing had meant anything for years, not for those who had been left behind. He was sick of being useless, of pretending that he was more valuable than his brothers by virtue of his birth.

He looked down at his soup. He'd lost his appetite. And of course that was when Lady Bridgerton exclaimed, "We should have a party!"

Chapter 7

A party?

Billie carefully set down her napkin, a vague sense of alarm washing over her. "Mother?"

"A house party," her mother clarified, as if *that* had been what she'd been asking about.

"This time of year?" her father asked, his soupspoon pausing only briefly on its way to his mouth.

"Why not this time of year?"

"We usually have one in the autumn."

Billie rolled her eyes. What typically male reasoning. Not that she disagreed. The last thing she wanted right now at Aubrey Hall was a house party. All those strangers tramping around her home. Not to mention the time it would take to play the part of the dutiful daughter of the hostess. She'd be stuck in her frocks all day, unable to tend to the very real responsibilities of running the estate.

She tried to catch her father's eye. Surely he realized what a bad idea this was, no matter the season. But he was oblivious to anything but his wife. And his soup.

"Andrew won't be home in the autumn," Lady Bridgerton pointed out. "And we should celebrate now."

"I do love a party," Andrew said. It was true, but Billie had a feeling he'd said it more to smooth the tension at the table. Because it was quite tense. And it was oddly clear to her that no one knew why.

"It's settled, then," her mother said. "We shall have a house party. Just a small one."

"Define small," Billie said warily.

"Oh, I don't know. A dozen guests, perhaps?" Lady Bridgerton turned to Lady Manston. "What do you think, Helen?"

Lady Manston surprised no one when she replied, "I think it sounds delightful. But we shall have to act quickly, before Andrew is sent back to sea. The admiral was quite explicit that his leave was for the duration of his convalescence and not a moment longer."

"Of course," Lady Bridgerton murmured. "Shall we say in one week's time?"

"One week?" Billie exclaimed. "You can't possibly ready the house in one week."

"Oh, pish. Of course I can." Her mother gave her a look of amused disdain. "I was born for this sort of thing."

"That you were, my dear," her father said affectionately.

He would be no help at all, Billie realized. If she was going to put a stop to this madness, she was going to have to do it herself. "Think of the guests, Mama?" she persisted. "Surely you must give them more notice. People lead busy lives. They will have plans."

Her mother waved this away as if it were of no consequence. "I'm not planning to send invitations across the country. We've plenty of time to reach friends in the nearby counties. Or London."

"Who will you invite?" Lady Manston asked.

"You, of course. Do say you'll come and stay with us. It will be so much more fun to have everyone under one roof."

"That hardly seems necessary," George said.

"Indeed," Billie agreed. For the love of God, they lived only three miles apart.

George gave her a look.

"Oh, please," she said impatiently. "You can't possibly take offense."

"*I* can," Andrew said with a grin. "In fact I think I will, just for the fun of it."

"Mary and Felix," Lady Bridgerton said. "We cannot possibly have a celebration without them."

"It would be nice to see Mary," Billie admitted.

"What about the Westboroughs?" Lady Manston asked.

George groaned. "Surely that ship has sailed, Mother. Didn't you just tell me that Lady Frederica has become engaged?"

"Indeed." His mother paused, delicately lifting her soupspoon to her lips. "But she has a younger sister."

Billie let out a choked laugh, then quickly schooled her face into a frown when George threw her a furious scowl.

Lady Manston's smile grew positively terrifying. "And a cousin."

"Of course she does," George said under his breath.

Billie would have expressed some sort of sympathy, but of course *that* was the moment her own mother chose to say, "We shall have to find some nice young men, too."

Billie's eyes widened in horror. She should have known that her turn was coming. "Mother, *don't*," she cautioned.

Cautioned? Ordered was more like it.

Not that this had any effect on her mother's enthusiasm. "We'll be uneven if we don't," she said briskly. "Besides, you're not getting any younger."

Billie closed her eyes and counted to five. It was either that or go for her mother's throat.

"Doesn't Felix have a brother?" Lady Manston asked.

Billie bit her tongue. Lady Manston knew perfectly well that Felix had a brother. Felix Maynard was married to her only daughter.

Lady Manston had likely known the names and ages of his every first cousin before the ink was dry on the betrothal papers.

"George?" his mother prompted. "Doesn't he?"

Billie stared at Lady Manston in fascinated amazement. Her single-minded determination would do an army general proud. Was it some kind of inborn trait? Did females spring from the womb with the urge to match men and women into neat little pairs? And if so, how was it possible that *she'd* been skipped?

Because Billie had no interest in matchmaking, for herself or anyone else. If that made her some kind of strange, unfeminine freak, so be it. She would much rather be out on her horse. Or fishing at the lake. Or climbing a tree.

Or anything, really.

Not for the first time Billie wondered what her Heavenly Father had been thinking when she'd been born a girl. She was clearly the least girlish girl in the history of England. Thank heavens her parents had not forced her to make her debut in London when Mary had done so. It would have been miserable. *She* would have been a disaster.

And no one would have wanted her.

"George?" Lady Manston said again, impatience sharpening the edge of her voice.

George started, and Billie realized he'd been looking at her. She couldn't begin to imagine what he had seen on her face . . . what he'd *thought* he'd seen there.

"He does," George confirmed, turning toward his mother. "Henry. He's two years younger than Felix, but he's—"

"Excellent!" Lady Manston exclaimed, clapping her hands together.

"But he's what?" Billie asked. Or rather, pounced. Because this was her potential mortification they were talking about.

"Nearly engaged," George told her. "Or so I've heard."

"It doesn't count until it's official," his mother said airily.

Billie stared at her in disbelief. This, from the woman who had been planning Mary's wedding from the first time Felix had kissed her hand.

"Do we like Henry Maynard?" Lady Bridgerton asked.

"We do," Lady Manston confirmed.

"I thought she wasn't even sure he had a brother," Billie said.

Beside her, George chuckled, and she felt his head draw close to hers. "Ten pounds says she knew every last detail of his current courtship before she even mentioned his name," he murmured.

Billie's lips flickered with a hint of a smile. "I would not take that bet."

"Smart girl."

"Always."

George chuckled, then stopped. Billie followed his gaze across the table. Andrew was watching them with an odd expression, his head tilted at the slightest of angles and his brow pleated into a thoughtful frown.

"What?" she said, while the mothers continued their plans.

Andrew shook his head. "Nothing."

Billie scowled. She could read Andrew like the back of her hand. He was up to something. "I don't like his expression," she murmured.

"I never like his expression," George said.

She glanced at him. How odd this was, this silly little kinship with George. It was usually Andrew with whom she was sharing muttered quips. Or Edward. But not George.

Never George.

And while she supposed this was a good thing—there was no reason she and George *had* to be at constant loggerheads—it still made her feel strange. Off-balance.

Life was better when it puttered along without surprises. It really was.

Billie turned to her mother, determined to escape this growing sense of unease. "Do we really *have* to have a party? Surely Andrew can feel celebrated and adored without a twelve-course meal and archery on the lawn."

"Don't forget the fireworks and a parade," Andrew said. "And I might want to be carried in on a litter."

"You want to *encourage* this?" Billie asked, gesturing to him with an exasperated hand.

George snorted into his soup.

"Will I be permitted to attend?" Georgiana asked.

"Nothing in the evening," her mother said, "but certainly some of the afternoon entertainments."

Georgiana sat back with a cat-in-the-cream smile. "Then I think it's an excellent idea."

"*Georgie*," Billie said.

"*Billie*," Georgiana mocked.

Billie's lips parted in surprise. Was the entire world tipping on its axis? Since when did her younger sister talk back to her like *that*?

"It's settled, Billie," her mother said in a tone that brooked no dissent. "We are having a party, and you will attend. In a dress."

"Mother!" Billie cried out.

"I don't think it's an unreasonable demand," her mother said, glancing about the table for confirmation.

"I *know* how to behave at a house party." Good Lord, what did her mother think she would do? Come to dinner with riding boots under her gown? Race the hounds through the drawing room?

She knew the rules. She did. And she didn't even mind them under the right circumstances. That her own mother thought her so inept . . . and that she would say so in front of all the people Billie cared most about . . .

It hurt more than she could ever have imagined.

But then the strangest thing happened. George's hand found hers and squeezed. Under the table, where no one could see. Billie jerked her head to look at him—she couldn't help it—but he'd already let go and was saying something to his father about the price of French brandy.

Billie stared at her soup.

What a day.

Later that evening, after the men had gone off to have their port and the ladies were congregated in the drawing room, Billie stole away to the library, wanting nothing more than a spot of peace and quiet.

Although she wasn't really sure if it counted as *stealing away* when she was required to beg a footman to carry her there.

Still, she'd always liked the library at Crake House. It was smaller than the one they had at Aubrey Hall, and it felt less imposing. Almost cozy. Lord Manston had a habit of falling asleep on the soft leather sofa, and as soon as Billie settled into the cushions she understood why. With a fire in the grate and a knitted blanket thrown over her legs, it was the perfect place to rest her eyes until her parents were ready to return home.

She wasn't sleepy, though. Just weary. It had been a long day, and her entire body ached from her fall, and her mother had been spectacularly insensitive, and Andrew hadn't even noticed that she wasn't feeling well, and George *had*, and then Georgiana had gone and turned into someone she didn't recognize, and—

And, and, and. It was all *and*s this evening, and the sum of it all was exhausting.

"Billie?"

She let out a softly startled shriek as she lurched into a more upright position. George was standing in the open doorway, his expression made unreadable by the dim, flickering candlelight.

"Sorry." She squeezed her eyes shut, taking a moment to catch her breath. "You surprised me."

"My apologies. It was not my intention." He leaned against the doorjamb. "Why are you here?"

"I needed a bit of quiet." She still could not see his face clearly, but she could well imagine his bemused countenance, so she added, "Even I need quiet every now and again."

He smiled faintly. "You don't feel cooped up?"

"Not at all." She tipped her head, acknowledging the riposte.

He took a moment to consider this, then said, "Would you like me to leave you to your solitude?"

"No, it's all right," Billie said, surprising herself with her statement. George's presence was oddly calming, in a way Andrew's or her mother's or really any of the others' never were.

"You're in pain," he said, finally stepping into the room.

How had he known? Nobody else had. But then again, George had always been uncomfortably observant. "Yes," she said. There was little point pretending otherwise.

"A great deal?"

"No. But more than a little."

"You should have rested this evening."

"Perhaps. But I enjoyed myself, and I think it was worth it. It was lovely to see your mother so happy."

George's head cocked to the side. "You thought she was happy?"

"Didn't you?"

"To see Andrew, perhaps, but in some ways his presence only serves to remind her that Edward is not here."

"I suppose. I mean, of course she'd rather have two sons home, but the reminder of Edward's absence is surely outweighed by the joy of Andrew's presence."

George's lips pressed into a wry, one-sided curve. "She did have two sons home."

Billie stared at him for a moment before— "Oh! I'm so sorry. Of course she did. I was just thinking of the sons who aren't normally at home. I . . . Good God, I'm really sorry." Her face was burning. Thank heavens the candlelight hid her blush.

He shrugged. "Think nothing of it."

She couldn't, though. No matter how even his mien, she couldn't help but think she'd hurt his feelings. Which was mad; George Rokesby did not care enough for her good opinion to be bothered by anything she said.

But still, there had been something in his expression . . .

"Does it bother you?" she asked.

He came further into the room, stopping by the shelf where the good brandy was kept. "Does what bother me?"

"Being left behind." She bit her lip. There had to be a better way of saying it. "Remaining home," she amended, "when everyone else is gone."

"You're here," he pointed out.

"Yes, but I'm hardly a comfort. To you, I mean."

He chuckled. Well, not really, but he did exhale a bit through his nose, and it sounded amused.

"Even Mary's gone to Sussex," Billie said, shifting her position so that she could watch him over the back of the sofa.

George poured himself a brandy, setting the glass down as he returned the stopper to the decanter. "I can't begrudge my sister a happy marriage. To one of my closest friends, no less."

"Of course not. Nor could I. But I still miss her. And you're still the only Rokesby in regular residence."

He brought his glass to his lips, but he didn't quite take a sip. "You do have a way of cutting right to the heart of the matter, don't you?"

Billie held her tongue.

"Does it bother *you*?" he asked.

She didn't pretend to misunderstand the question. "My siblings aren't all gone. Georgiana is still home."

"And you have so much in common with her," he said in a dry voice.

"More than I used to think," Billie told him. It was true. Georgiana had been a sickly child, worried over by her parents, stuck inside while the rest of the children ran wild across the countryside.

Billie had never disliked her younger sister; but at the same time, she hadn't found her very interesting. Most of the time, she'd forgotten she was even there. There were nine years between them. Really, what could they possibly have had in common?

But then everyone else went away, and now Georgiana was finally growing close enough to adulthood to become interesting.

It was George's turn to speak, but he did not seem to have noticed this fact, and the silence stretched for long enough to be vaguely unsettling.

"George?" Billie murmured. He was looking at her in the oddest manner. As if she were a puzzle—no, not that. As if he were thinking, quite deeply, and she just happened to be in the way of his eyes.

"George?" she repeated. "Are you all—"

He looked up suddenly. "You should be nicer to her." And then, as if he hadn't just said the most appalling thing, he motioned to the brandy. "Would you like a glass?"

"Yes," Billie said, even though she was well aware that most ladies would have refused, "and what on earth do you mean, I should be nicer to her? When have I ever been unkind?"

"Never," he agreed, splashing a bit of liquid into a glass, "but you ignore her."

"I do not."

"You forget about her," he amended. "It amounts to the same thing."

"Oh, and you pay so much attention to Nicholas."

"Nicholas is at Eton. I can hardly shower him with attention from here."

He handed her a brandy. She noticed her glass was considerably less full than his had been.

"I don't ignore her," Billie muttered. She didn't like being scolded, especially by George Rokesby. Especially when he was right.

"It's all right," he said, surprising her with his sudden kindness. "I'm sure it's different when Andrew isn't home."

"What does Andrew have to do with anything?"

He turned to her with an expression that hovered somewhere between surprised and amused. "Really?"

"I don't know what you're talking about." Maddening man.

George took a long sip, and then—without even turning toward her—he managed to give her a condescending look. "He should just marry you and be done with it."

"What?" Her surprise was unfeigned. Not that she might marry

Andrew. She'd always thought she'd one day marry him. Or Edward. She didn't really care which; it was all the same to her. But that George was actually speaking of it in such a manner . . .

She didn't like it.

"I'm sure you're aware," she said, quickly regaining her composure, "that Andrew and I have no understanding."

He waved that off with a roll of his eyes. "You could do worse."

"So could he," she retorted.

George chuckled. "True enough."

"I'm not going to marry Andrew," she said. Not yet, anyway. But if he asked . . .

She would probably say yes. It was what everyone expected.

George took a sip of his brandy, watching her enigmatically over the rim of his glass.

"The last thing I'd want to do," Billie said, unable to leave the silence be, "is get engaged to someone who is going to turn around and leave."

"Oh, I don't know," George said with a thoughtful frown. "Many military wives follow their husbands. And you're more adventurous than most."

"I like it here."

"In my father's library?" he quipped.

"In Kent," she said pertly. "At Aubrey Hall. I'm needed."

He made a patronizing sound.

"I am!"

"I'm sure you are."

Her spine stiffened. If her ankle weren't throbbing, she'd have probably jumped to her feet. "You have no idea all I do."

"Please don't tell me."

"What?"

He made a dismissive motion with his hand. "You have that look about you."

"What loo—"

"The one that says you're about to launch into a very long speech."

Her lips parted with shock. Of all the condescending, supercilious . . . Then she saw his face. He was enjoying himself!

Of course he was. He lived to get under her skin. Like a needle. A dull, rusty needle.

"Oh, for heaven's sake, Billie," he said, leaning against a bookcase as he chuckled. "Can't you take a ribbing? I know you help your father from time to time."

From time to time? She ran the bloody place. Aubrey Hall would fall apart without her direction. Her father had all but ceded the ledgers to her, and the steward had long since given up protesting about having to answer to a woman. Billie had, for all intents and purposes, been raised as her father's eldest son. Except that she couldn't inherit anything. And eventually Edmund would grow up, take his rightful place. Her younger brother wasn't stupid; he'd learn what to do quickly enough, and when he did . . . when Edmund showed all of Aubrey how capable he was, everyone would breathe a sigh of relief and say something about natural order being restored.

Billie would be superfluous.

Replaced.

The ledgers would be quietly removed from her purview. No one would ask her to inspect the cottages or settle disputes. Edmund would become lord of the manor, and she'd be his long-toothed older sister, the one people quietly pitied and mocked.

God, maybe she *should* marry Andrew.

"Are you sure you're not unwell?" George asked.

"I'm fine," she said curtly.

He shrugged. "You looked rather ill all of a sudden."

She'd felt rather ill all of a sudden. Her future had finally danced before her, and there was nothing bright and beautiful about it.

She tossed back the rest of her brandy.

"Careful there," George cautioned, but she was already coughing, unaccustomed to setting her throat on fire. "It's better to sip it slowly," he added.

"I *know*," she ground out, well aware that she sounded like an idiot.

"Of course you do," he murmured, and just like that, she felt better. George Rokesby was being a pompous ass. Everything was back to normal. Or almost normal.

Normal enough.

Chapter 8

Lady Bridgerton began planning her assault on the social Season the very next morning. Billie hobbled into the small dining room to break her fast, fully prepared to be drafted into service, but to her relief and amazement her mother said that she did not require Billie's assistance with the planning. All she asked was that Billie write a note of invitation to Mary and Felix. Billie nodded her grateful agreement. This she could do.

"Georgiana has offered to help me," Lady Bridgerton said as she signaled to a footman to prepare a breakfast plate. Billie was agile on her crutches, but even she could not fix her own meal from the sideboard while balanced on a pair of sticks.

Billie glanced at her younger sister, who appeared quite pleased at this prospect. "It will be great fun," Georgiana said.

Billie swallowed a retort. She couldn't think of much that would be *less* fun, but she did not need to insult her sister by saying so. If

Georgiana wanted to spend the afternoon penning invitations and planning menus, she was welcome to it.

Lady Bridgerton prepared a cup of tea for Billie. "How do you plan to spend your day?"

"I'm not sure," Billie said, nodding her thanks to the footman as he set her plate in front of her. She gazed wistfully out the window. The sun was just beginning to break through the clouds, and within an hour the morning dew would have evaporated. A perfect day to be out of doors. On horseback. Being useful.

And she had so much to do. One of the tenants was rethatching the roof of his cottage, and even though his neighbors knew they were expected to offer their aid, Billie still suspected that John and Harry Williamson would try to weasel out of it. Someone needed to make sure that the brothers did their share, just like someone needed to make sure that the western fields were being planted properly and the rose garden had been pruned to her mother's exact specifications.

Someone needed to do all that, and Billie had no idea who that would be if not her.

But no, she was stuck inside with a stupid swollen foot, and it wasn't even her fault. All right, maybe it was a little bit her fault, but certainly more the cat's fault, and the bloody thing hurt like the devil—her foot, that was, not the cat, although she was small-minded enough to hope that the beastly little creature also had reason to limp.

She paused to consider that. When it came right down to it . . .

"Billie?" her mother murmured, eyeing her above the rim of her bone china teacup.

"I think I'm not a very nice person," Billie mused.

Lady Bridgerton choked so hard tea came out her nose. It was quite a sight, really, and not one Billie had ever expected to see in her lifetime.

"I could have told you *that*," Georgiana said.

Billie flashed a scowl at her sister that was, all things considered, rather immature.

"Sybilla Bridgerton," came her mother's brook-no-dissent voice. "You are a perfectly nice person."

Billie opened her mouth to speak, not that she had anything intelligent to say.

"If you're not," her mother continued, her voice leaping into the moment with a *don't-you-dare-think-of-contradicting-me* punch of volume, "it reflects badly upon *me*, and I refuse to believe I am so derelict a mother as that."

"Of course not," Billie said quickly. Very quickly.

"Therefore I will repeat my question," her mother said. She took a delicate sip of her tea and gazed upon her elder daughter with remarkable impassivity. "What do you plan to do today?"

"Well," Billie stalled. She glanced over at her sister, but Georgiana was no help. She just lifted her shoulders in a helpless little shrug that could have meant anything from *I-have-no-idea-what's-got-into-her* to *I-am-enjoying-your-discomfort-immensely.*

Billie scowled. Wouldn't it be lovely if people just said what they thought?

Billie turned back to her mother, who was still regarding her with a deceptively placid expression. "Well," she stalled again. "I might read a book?"

"A book," her mother repeated. She dabbed at the corner of her mouth with her napkin. "How delightful."

Billie eyed her cautiously. Any number of sarcastic retorts sprang to mind, but despite her mother's serene demeanor, there was a gleam in her eye that told Billie she'd be wise to keep her mouth shut.

Lady Bridgerton reached for the teapot. She always drank more tea at breakfast than the rest of the family combined. "I could recommend something, if you like," she said to Billie. She also generally read more books than the rest of the family combined.

"No, that's all right," Billie replied, cutting her sausage into rounds. "Father bought the latest volume of *Prescott's Encyclopaedia of Agriculture* when he was in London last month. I should have already started it, but the weather has been so fine I haven't had the chance."

"You could read outside," Georgiana suggested. "We could put down a blanket. Or drag out a chaise."

Billie nodded absently as she stabbed a sausage disc. "It would be better than remaining in, I suppose."

"You could help me plan the entertainments for the house party," Georgiana said.

Billie gave her a condescending look. "I don't think so."

"Why not, darling?" Lady Bridgerton put in. "It might be fun."

"You just told me I didn't have to take part in the planning."

"Only because I didn't think you wanted to."

"I don't want to."

"Of course not," her mother said smoothly, "but you *do* want to spend time with your sister."

Oh, hell. Her mother was *good*. Billie pasted a smile on her face. "Can't Georgie and I do something else?"

"If you can convince her to read your agricultural treatise over your shoulder," her mother said, her hand flitting delicately through the air.

Delicately like a bullet, Billie thought. "I'll help with *some* of the planning," she conceded.

"Oh, that will be marvelous!" Georgiana exclaimed. "And so very helpful. You'll have much more experience with this sort of thing than I."

"Not really," Billie said frankly.

"But you've *been* to house parties."

"Well, yes, but . . ." Billie didn't bother finishing her sentence. Georgiana looked so happy. It would be like kicking a puppy to tell Georgiana that she had hated being dragged to house parties with their mother. Or if *hate* was too strong a word, she certainly hadn't enjoyed herself. She really didn't like traveling. She'd learned that much about herself.

And she did not enjoy the company of strangers. She wasn't shy; not at all. She just preferred being among people she knew.

People who knew *her*.

Life was so much easier that way.

"Look at it this way," Lady Bridgerton said to Billie. "You don't want a house party. You don't like house parties. But I am your mother, and I have decided to host one. Therefore, you have no choice but to attend. Why not take the opportunity to mold this gathering into something you might actually enjoy?"

"But I'm not going to enjoy it."

"You certainly won't if you approach it with that attitude."

Billie took a moment to compose herself. And to hold down the urge to argue her point and defend herself and tell her mother that she would not be spoken to as if she was a child . . .

"I would be delighted to assist Georgiana," Billie said tightly, "as long as I get some time to read my book."

"I wouldn't dream of pulling you away from *Prescott's*," her mother murmured.

Billie glared at her. "You shouldn't mock it. It's exactly that sort of book that has enabled me to increase productivity at Aubrey Hall by a full ten percent. Not to mention the improvements to the tenant farms. They are all eating better now that—"

She cut herself off. Swallowed. She'd just done exactly what she'd told herself not to do.

Argue her point.

Defend herself.

Act like a child.

She shoveled as much of her breakfast into her mouth as she could manage in thirty seconds, then stood and grabbed her crutches, which were leaning against the table. "I will be in the library if anyone needs me." To Georgiana she added, "Let me know when the ground is dry enough to spread a blanket."

Georgiana nodded.

"Mother," Billie said to Lady Bridgerton with a nod to replace the normal bob of a curtsy she gave when she took her leave. Yet another thing one couldn't manage on crutches.

"Billie," her mother said, her voice conciliatory. And perhaps a little frustrated. "I wish you wouldn't . . ."

Billie waited for her to finish her sentence, but her mother just shook her head.

"Never mind," she said.

Billie nodded again, pressing a crutch into the ground for balance as she pivoted on her good foot. She *thunked* the crutches on the ground, then swung her body between them, her shoulders held tight and straight as she repeated the motion all the way to the door.

It was bloody hard to make a dignified exit on crutches.

George still wasn't sure how Andrew had talked him into accompanying him to Aubrey Hall for a late morning visit, but here he was, standing in the grand entry as he handed his hat to Thamesly, butler to the Bridgertons since before he was born.

"You're doing a good deed, old man," Andrew said, slapping George's shoulder with surely more force than was necessary.

"Don't call me old man." God, he hated that.

But this only made Andrew laugh. Of course. "Whomever you might be, you're still doing a good deed. Billie will be out of her mind with boredom."

"She could use a little boredom in her life," George muttered.

"True enough," Andrew conceded, "but my concern was for her family. God only knows what madness she'll inflict upon them if no one shows up to entertain her."

"You talk as if she's a child."

"A child?" Andrew turned to look at him, his face taking on an enigmatic serenity that George knew well enough to find suspicious in the extreme. "Not at all."

"Miss Bridgerton is in the library," Thamesly informed them. "If you will wait in the drawing room, I will alert her to your presence."

"No need," Andrew said cheerily. "We will join her in the library. The last thing we want is to force Miss Bridgerton to hobble about more than is necessary."

"Very kind of you, sir," Thamesly murmured.

"Is she in a great deal of pain?" George inquired.

"I would not know," the butler said diplomatically, "but it may be worth noting that the weather is very fine, and Miss Bridgerton is in the library."

"So she's miserable, then."

"Very much so, my lord."

George supposed *this* was why he'd allowed Andrew to drag him away from his weekly meeting with their father's steward. He'd known Billie's ankle could not have been much improved. It had been grotesquely swollen the night before, no matter how festively she'd wrapped it with that ridiculous pink ribbon. Injuries like that did not resolve themselves overnight.

And while he and Billie had never been friends, precisely, he felt a strange responsibility for her well-being, at least as pertained to her current situation. What was that old Chinese proverb? If you saved a life, you were responsible for it forever? He certainly had not saved Billie's life, but he had been stuck up on a roof with her, and . . .

And bloody hell, he had no idea what any of this meant, just that he thought he ought to make sure she was feeling at least somewhat better. Even though she was the *most* exasperating female, and she bloody well set his teeth on edge half the time.

It was still the right thing to do. That was all.

"Oh, Billie . . ." Andrew called as they made their way to the back of the house. "We've come to rescue you . . ."

George shook his head. How his brother survived in the navy he would never know. Andrew had not a serious bone in his body.

"Billie . . ." he called again, his voice warbling into a ridiculous singsong. "Where aaaaaarrrrrre you?"

"In the library," George reminded him.

"Well, of course she is," Andrew said with a blinding grin, "but isn't this more fun?"

Naturally, he did not wait for an answer.

"Billie!" he called again. "Oh, *Billiebilliebilliebill*—"

"For heaven's sake!" Billie's head popped out of the doorway to the library. Her chestnut hair had been pulled back into the loose coiffure of a lady with no plans to socialize. "You're loud enough to wake the dead. What are you doing here?"

"Is that any way to greet an old friend?"

"I saw you last night."

"So you did." Andrew leaned down and dropped a brotherly kiss on her cheek. "But you had to go without for so very long. You need to stock up."

"On your company?" Billie asked dubiously.

Andrew patted her arm. "We are so fortunate that you have this opportunity."

George leaned to the right so that he could see her from behind his brother. "Shall I strangle him or will you?"

She rewarded him with a devious smile. "Oh, it must be a joint endeavor, don't you think?"

"So that you may share the blame?" Andrew quipped.

"So that we may share the joy," Billie corrected.

"You wound me."

"Happily, I assure you." She hopped to the left and looked at George. "What brings you here this fine morning, Lord Kennard?"

He gave her a bit of a look at her use of his title. The Bridgertons and Rokesbys never stood on occasion when it was just the two families. Even now, no one so much as blinked at Billie being alone with two unmarried gentlemen in the library. It wasn't the sort of thing that would be permitted during the upcoming house party, though. They were all well aware that their relaxed manners would not stand in extended company.

"Dragged along by my brother, I'm afraid," George admitted. "There was some fear for your family's safety."

Her eyes narrowed. "Really."

"Now, now, Billie," Andrew said. "We all know you don't do well trapped indoors."

"I came for *his* safety," George said with a jerk of his head toward Andrew. "Although it is my belief that any injury you might do to him would be entirely justified."

Billie threw back her head and laughed. "Come, join me in the library. I need to sit back down."

While George was recovering from the unexpectedly marvelous sight of Billie in full joy, she hopped back to the nearest reading table, holding her light blue skirts above her ankles for easier motion.

"You should use your crutches," he told her.

"Not worth it for such a short trip," she replied, settling back down into her chair. "Besides, they tipped over and it was far too much trouble to retrieve them."

George followed her gaze to where the crutches lay askew on the ground, one slightly atop the other. He leaned down and picked them up, setting them gently against the side of the library table. "If you need help," he said in a quiet voice, "you should ask for it."

She looked at him and blinked. "I didn't need help."

George started to tell her not to be so defensive, but then he realized she *hadn't* been defensive. She was merely stating a fact. A fact as *she* saw it.

He shook his head. Billie could be so bloody literal.

"What was that?" she asked.

He shrugged. He had no idea what she was about.

"What were you going to say?" she demanded.

"Nothing."

Her mouth tightened at the corners. "That's not true. You were definitely going to say something."

Literal *and* tenacious. It was a frightening combination. "Did you sleep well?" he asked politely.

"Of course," she said, with just enough of an arch to her brows to tell him that she was well aware that he'd changed the subject. "I told you yesterday. I never have trouble sleeping."

"You said you never have trouble falling asleep," he corrected, somewhat surprised that he recalled the distinction.

She shrugged. "It's much the same thing."

"The pain did not wake you up?"

She glanced down at her foot as if she'd quite forgotten it was there. "Apparently not."

"If I might interrupt," Andrew said, bowing to Billie with a ridiculous sweep of his arm, "we are here to offer our assistance and succor in any way you deem necessary."

She gave Andrew the sort of look George normally reserved for small, recalcitrant children. "Are you sure you want to make such a sweeping promise?"

George leaned down until his lips were at the same latitude as her ear. "Pray remember that he uses 'we' as a grandiose gesture, not as a plural pronoun."

She grinned. "In other words, you want no part of it?"

"None whatsoever."

"You insult the lady," Andrew said without a hint of protest in his voice. He sprawled in one of the Bridgertons' fine wingback chairs, his long legs stretched out so that the heels of his boots rested against the carpet.

Billie gave him an exasperated glance before turning back to George. "Why *are* you here?"

George took a seat at the table across from her. "What he said, but without the hyperbole. We thought you might need company."

"Oh." She drew back a touch, clearly surprised by his frankness. "Thank you. That's very kind of you."

"*Thank you, that's very kind of you?*" Andrew echoed. "Who *are* you?"

She whipped her head to face him. "Was I supposed to curtsy?"

"It would have been nice," he demurred.

"Impossible on crutches."

"Well, if *that's* the case . . ."

Billie turned back to George. "He's an idiot."

He held up his hands. "You will find no argument here."

"The plight of the younger son," Andrew said with a sigh.

Billie rolled her eyes, tipping her head toward Andrew as she said to George, "Don't encoura*g*e him."

"To be ganged up upon," Andrew went on, "never respected . . ."

George craned his neck, trying to read the title of Billie's book. "What are you reading?"

"And," Andrew continued, "apparently ignored as well."

Billie rotated her book so that the gold leaf lettering faced George. "*Prescott's Encyclopaedia of Agriculture.*"

"Volume four," he said approvingly. He had volumes one through three in his own personal library.

"Yes, it was only recently published," Billie confirmed.

"It must have been very recently, or I would have purchased it when I was last in London."

"My father brought it back from his most recent trip. You can read it when I'm done if you wish."

"Oh, no, I'm sure I'll need a copy of my own."

"As a reference," she said with an approving nod.

"This might be the dullest conversation I have ever beheld," Andrew said from behind them.

They ignored him.

"Do you often read such tomes?" George asked, nodding at the Prescott book. He'd always thought ladies preferred slim volumes of poetry or plays by Shakespeare and Marlowe. It was what his sister and mother seemed to enjoy reading.

"Of course," she replied, scowling as if he'd insulted her with the very question.

"Billie helps her father with the land management," Andrew said, apparently bored of making fun of them. He pushed himself to his feet and wandered over to the wall of shelves, selecting a book seemingly at random. He leafed through a few pages, frowned, and put it back.

"Yes, you mentioned you'd been assisting him," George said. He looked at Billie. "Very singular of you."

Her eyes narrowed.

"That was not meant as an insult," he got in before she could open her rash little mouth, "just an observation."

She did not look convinced.

"You will concede," he said smoothly, "that most young ladies do not assist their fathers in such a manner. Hence, your singularity."

"I swear, George," Andrew said, glancing up from the book he was paging through, "you even give your compliments like a conceited ass."

"I'm going to kill him," George muttered.

"You'll have to form a line," Billie remarked. But then she lowered her voice. "It's a little bit true, though."

He drew back. "I beg your pardon?"

"You did sound a little . . ." She waved her hand in the air as a substitute for actually finishing her sentence.

"Like an ass?" George supplied.

"No!" She said this with enough speed and conviction for him to believe her. "Just a little bit . . ."

He waited.

"Are you talking about me?" Andrew asked, settling back in his chair with a book in his hand.

"No," they said in unison.

"I don't mind if it's complimentary," he murmured.

George ignored him, keeping his eyes on Billie. She was frowning. Two small lines formed between her brows, curving against each other like an hourglass, and her lips tightened into a curious pucker, almost as if she were anticipating a kiss.

He'd never watched her think, he realized.

Then he realized what a staggeringly odd observation *that* was.

"You did sound a *little* conceited," Billie finally said. Her voice was quiet, meant for their ears only. "But I think that's understandable?"

Understandable? He leaned forward. "Why are you saying that like it's a question?"

"I don't know."

He sat back and crossed his arms, quirking one brow to indicate that he was waiting for her to continue.

"Fine," she said, less than graciously. "You're the eldest, the heir.

You're the brilliant, the handsome, oh, and we must not forget, the *eligible* Viscount of Kennard."

George felt a slow smile spread across his face. "You think I'm handsome?"

"This is exactly what I'm talking about!"

"Brilliant, too," George murmured. "I had no idea."

"You're acting like Andrew," Billie muttered.

For some reason, this made him chuckle.

Billie's eyes narrowed into a glare.

George's smile stretched into a full-fledged grin. By God, it was fun to needle her.

She leaned forward, and in that moment he realized just how well people could speak through clenched teeth. "I was trying to be considerate," she ground out.

"I'm sorry," George said immediately.

Her lips pressed together. "You asked me a question. I was trying to give you an honest, thoughtful answer. I thought you deserved as much."

Well, *now* he felt like an ass.

"I'm sorry," he said again, and this time it was more than an ingrained bit of polite manners.

Billie let out a breath, and she caught the inside of her lower lip between her teeth. She was thinking again, George realized. How remarkable it was to see another person think. Was everyone this expressive as they pondered their ideas?

"It's how you were brought up," she finally said. "You're no more to blame than . . ." She exhaled again, but George was patient. She would find the right words.

And after a few moments, she did. "You've been raised—" But this time she stopped herself quite suddenly.

"To be conceited?" he said softly.

"To be confident," she corrected, but he had a feeling that his statement was a lot closer to what she had been about to say. "It's not your fault," she added.

"Now who's being patronizing?"

She gave him a wry smile. "Me, I'm sure. But it's true. You can't help it any more than I can help being a . . ." She waved her hands again, which was apparently her all-purpose gesture for things that were too awkward to say aloud.

"What I am," she finally finished.

"What you are." He said it softly. He said it because he had to say it, even if he didn't know why.

She looked up at him, but only with her eyes. Her face remained tipped slightly down, and he had the oddest notion that if he did not meet her gaze, if he did not hold it with his own, she would return hers to her tightly clutched hands, and the moment would be lost forever.

"What are you?" he whispered.

She shook her head. "I have no idea."

"Is anyone hungry?" Andrew suddenly asked.

George blinked, trying to snap himself out of whatever spell had been cast over him.

"Because I am," Andrew continued. "Famished. Utterly. I ate only one breakfast this morning."

"*One* breakfast?" Billie started to say, but Andrew was already on his feet, bounding over to her side.

He set his hands on the table, leaning down to murmur, "I was hoping I'd be invited to tea."

"Of course you're invited to tea," Billie said, but she sounded just as off-balance as George felt. She frowned. "It's a little early, though."

"It's never too early for tea," Andrew declared. "Not if your cook has been making shortbread." He turned to George. "I don't know what she puts in it, but it's divine."

"Butter," Billie said absently. "Quite a lot of it."

Andrew cocked his head to the side. "Well, that makes sense. Everything tastes better with quite a lot of butter."

"We should ask Georgiana to join us," Billie said, reaching for her crutches. "I'm meant to be helping her plan the entertainments for the house party." She rolled her eyes. "My mother's orders."

Andrew let out a bark of laughter. "Does your mother even *know* you?"

Billie threw an irritated look at him over her shoulder.

"Seriously, Billie-goat, what will you have us do? Head out to the south lawn to plant barley?"

"Stop," George said.

Andrew swung around. "What was that?"

"Leave her alone."

Andrew stared at him for so long George could not help but wonder if he'd been speaking in tongues.

"It's Billie," Andrew finally said.

"I know. And you should leave her alone."

"I can fight my own battles, George," Billie said.

He glanced over at her. "Of course you can."

Her lips parted, but she seemed not to know how to respond to that.

Andrew looked back and forth between the two of them before offering Billie a small bow. "My apologies."

Billie nodded awkwardly.

"Perhaps I might help in the planning," Andrew suggested.

"You'll certainly be better at it than I am," Billie said.

"Well, *that* goes without saying."

She poked him in the leg with one of her crutches.

And just like that, George realized, all was back to normal.

Except it wasn't. Not for him.

Chapter 9

Four days later

It was remarkable—no, *inspirational*—Billie decided, how quickly she'd weaned herself from her crutches. Clearly, it was all in the mind.

Strength. Fortitude.

Determination.

Also, the ability to ignore pain was helpful.

It didn't hurt *that* much, she reasoned. Just a twinge. Or maybe something closer to a nail being hammered into her ankle at intervals corresponding to the speed at which she took her steps.

But not a very big nail. Just a little one. A pin, really.

She was made of stern stuff. Everybody said so.

At any rate, the pain in her ankle wasn't nearly as bad as the chafing under her arms from the crutches. And she wasn't planning to go for a five-mile hike. She just wanted to be able to get about the house on her own two feet.

Nevertheless, her pace was considerably slower than her usual stride as she headed toward the drawing room a few hours after breakfast. Andrew was waiting for her, Thamesly had informed her. This was not terribly surprising; Andrew had called upon her every day since her injury.

It was really quite sweet of him.

They'd been building card houses, a characteristically perverse choice for Andrew, whose dominant arm was still immobilized in a sling. He'd said that as long as he was coming over to keep her company, he might as well do something useful.

Billie didn't bother pointing out that building a house of cards might very well be the definition of *not* useful.

As for his having only one working arm, he needed help getting the first few cards balanced, but after that, he could set up the rest just as well as she could.

Or better, really. She'd forgotten how freakishly good he was at building card houses—*and* how freakishly obsessed he became during the process. The day before had been the worst. As soon as they'd completed the first level he'd banned her from construction. Then he banned her from the entire area, claiming that she breathed too hard.

Which of course left her with no choice but to sneeze.

She might also have kicked the table.

There had been a fleeting moment of regret when it had all come down in a spectacular earthquake of destruction, but the look on Andrew's face had been worth it, even if he had gone home immediately following the collapse.

But that was yesterday, and knowing Andrew, he'd want to start again, bigger and better the fifth time around. So Billie had collected another two decks on her way to the drawing room. It should be enough for him to add another story or two to his next architectural masterpiece.

"Good morning," she said as she entered the drawing room. He was standing over by a plate of biscuits someone had left out on the table that ran behind the sofa. A maid, probably. One of the sillier ones. They were always giggling over him.

"You've jettisoned the crutches," he said with an approving nod. "Congratulations."

"Thank you." She glanced about the room. Still no George. He had not visited since that first morning in the library. Not that she had expected him to. She and George were not friends.

They weren't *enemies*, of course. Just not friends. They never had been. Although maybe they were a little bit . . . now.

"What's wrong?" Andrew asked.

Billie blinked. "Nothing's wrong."

"You're scowling."

"I'm not scowling."

His expression turned condescending. "You can see your own face?"

"And you're here to cheer me up," she drawled.

"Gad no, I'm here for the shortbread." He reached out and took some of the playing cards from her. "And maybe to build a house."

"At last, some honesty."

Andrew laughed and flopped down on the sofa. "I have hardly been hiding my motives."

Billie acknowledged this with a flick of her eyes. He had eaten a prodigious amount of shortbread in the past few days.

"You'd be kinder to me," he continued, "if you knew how horrid the food is on a ship."

"Scale of one to ten?"

"Twelve."

"I'm so sorry," she said with a grimace. She knew how Andrew liked his sweets.

"I knew what I was getting into." He paused, frowning with thought. "No, actually I don't think I did."

"You wouldn't have entered the navy if you'd realized there would be no biscuits?"

Andrew sighed dramatically. "Sometimes a man must make his own biscuits."

Several playing cards slid from her grasp. "*What*?"

"I believe he's substituting biscuits for destiny," came a voice from the door.

"George!" Billie exclaimed. With surprise? With delight? What *was* that in her voice? And why couldn't she, of all people, figure it out?

"Billie," he murmured, offering a polite bow.

She stared. "What are you doing here?"

His mouth moved into a dry expression that in all honesty could not be called a smile. "Ever the model of gentility."

"Well"—she bent down to gather the cards she'd dropped, trying not to trip on the lace trim of her skirt—"you haven't visited for four days."

Now he did smile. "You've missed me, then."

"No!" She glared at him, reaching out to snatch up the knave of hearts. The annoying little rascal had slid halfway under the sofa. "Don't be ridiculous. Thamesly said nothing about your being here. He mentioned only Andrew."

"I was seeing to the horses," George said.

She immediately looked to Andrew, surprise coloring her features. "Did you ride?"

"Well, I tried," he admitted.

"We went very slowly," George confirmed. Then his eyes narrowed. "Where are your crutches?"

"Gone," she replied, smiling proudly.

"I can *see* that." His brow pulled down into a scowling vee. "Who told you you were allowed to stop using them?"

"No one," she bristled. Who the devil did he think he was? Her father? No, definitely not her father. That was just . . .

Ugh.

"I rose from bed," she said with exaggerated patience, "took a step, and decided for myself."

George snorted.

She drew back. "What is that supposed to mean?"

"Allow me to translate," Andrew said from the sofa, where he was still stretched out in a boyish sprawl.

"I *know* what it meant," Billie snapped.

"Oh, Billie," Andrew sighed.

She swung around to glare at him.

"You need to get out of the house," he said.

Please, as if she didn't know *that*. She turned back to George. "Pray, excuse my impoliteness. I wasn't expecting you."

His brows arched, but he accepted her apology with a nod and took a seat when she did.

"We need to feed him," Billie said, tilting her head toward Andrew.

"Water him, too?" George murmured, as if Andrew were a horse.

"I'm right here!" Andrew protested.

George motioned to the day-old copy of the *London Times*, which lay freshly ironed on the table next to him. "Do you mind if I read?"

"Not at all," Billie said. Far be it from her to expect him to entertain her. Even if that had been his implied purpose in stopping by. She leaned forward, giving Andrew a little tap on his shoulder. "Would you like me to get you started?"

"Please," he said, "and then don't touch it."

Billie looked at George. The newspaper was still folded in his lap, and he was watching the two of them with amused curiosity.

"In the center of the table," Andrew said.

Billie gave him a bit of a look. "Autocratic as always."

"I am an artist."

"Architect," George said.

Andrew looked up, as if he'd forgotten his brother was there. "Yes," he murmured. "Quite."

Billie slid from her chair and knelt in front of the low table, adjusting her weight so as not to put pressure on her bad foot. She selected two cards from the messy pile near the table's edge and balanced them into the shape of a *T*. Carefully, she released her fingers and waited to see if it was secure.

"Nicely done," George murmured.

Billie smiled, absurdly pleased by his compliment. "Thank you."

Andrew rolled his eyes.

"I swear, Andrew," Billie said, using a third card to transform the *T* into an *H*, "you turn into the *most* annoying person when you're doing this."

"But I get the job done."

Billie heard George chuckle, followed by the crinkling sound of the newspaper opening and then folding into a readable shape. She shook her head, decided that Andrew was extraordinarily fortunate she was his friend, and set a few more cards into place. "Will that be enough to get you started?" she asked Andrew.

"Yes, thank you. Mind the table when you get up."

"Is this what you're like at sea?" Billie asked, limping across the room to get her book before settling back down. "It's a wonder anyone puts up with you."

Andrew narrowed his eyes—at the card structure, not at her—and placed a card into position. "I get the job done," he repeated.

Billie turned back to George. He was watching Andrew with a peculiar expression on his face. His brow was furrowed, but he wasn't precisely frowning. His eyes were far too bright and curious for that. Every time he blinked, his lashes swept down like a fan, graceful and—

"Billie?"

Oh, God, he'd caught her looking at him.

Wait, *why* was she looking at him?

"Sorry," she mumbled. "Lost in thought."

"I hope it was something interesting."

She choked on her breath before answering, "Not really." Then she felt kind of terrible, insulting him without his even knowing it.

And without her really meaning to.

"He's like a different person," she said, motioning to Andrew. "I find it very disconcerting."

"You've never seen him like this before?"

"No, I have." She looked from the chair to the sofa and decided on the sofa. Andrew was now on the floor, and he wasn't likely to want his spot back anytime soon. She sat down, leaning against the arm and stretching her legs out in front of her. Without really thinking about what she was doing she reached for the blanket that lay folded over the back and spread it over her legs. "I still find it disconcerting."

"He is unexpectedly precise," George said.

Billie considered that. "Unexpected because . . . ?"

George shrugged and motioned to his brother. "Who would think it of him?"

Billie thought for a moment, then decided she agreed with him. "There's an odd sort of sense to that."

"I can still hear you, you know," Andrew said. He'd got about a dozen more cards into place and had pulled back a few inches to examine the house from several angles.

"I don't believe we were aiming for stealth," George said mildly.

Billie smiled to herself and slid her finger into the correct spot in her book. It was one of those volumes that came with an attached ribbon to use as a bookmark.

"Just so you are aware," Andrew said, moving to the other side of the table, "I will kill you if you knock this down."

"Brother," George said with impressive gravity, "I am barely breathing."

Billie stifled a giggle. She rarely saw this side of George, teasing and dry. Usually he was so irritated by the rest of them that he was left entirely without humor.

"Is that *Prescott's*?" George asked.

Billie turned to look at him over her shoulder. "Yes."

"You're making good progress."

"Despite myself, I assure you. It's very dry."

Andrew didn't look up, but he did say, "You're reading an encyclopedia of agriculture and you're complaining that it's dry?"

"The last volume was brilliant," Billie protested. "I could hardly put it down."

Even from the back of his head, it was obvious that Andrew was rolling his eyes.

Billie returned her attention to George, who, it had to be said, had not once maligned her for her reading choices. "It must be the subject matter. He seems terribly stuck on mulch this time."

"Mulch is important," George said, his eyes twinkling in what was an impressively somber face.

She met his gaze with equal seriousness. And perhaps just the littlest twitch of her lips. "Mulch is mulch."

"God," Andrew grunted, "the two of you are enough to make me want to tear my hair out."

Billie tapped him on the shoulder. "But you love us."

"Don't touch me," he warned.

She looked back over at George. "He's very touchy."

"Bad pun, Billie," Andrew growled.

She let out a light laugh and returned to the book in her hands. "Back to the mulch."

She tried to read. She really did. But *Prescott's* seemed so dull this time around, and every time George moved, his newspaper crinkled and then she *had* to look up.

But then *he* would look up. And then she'd have to pretend she'd been watching Andrew. And then she really *was* watching Andrew, because it was bizarrely riveting to watch a one-armed man build a house of cards.

Back to *Prescott's*, she admonished herself. As dull as mulch was, she had to get through it. And she did, somehow. An hour drifted by in companionable silence, she on the sofa with her book, George in his chair with the newspaper, and Andrew on the floor with his cards. She got through the straw mulch, and she got through the peat mulch, but when she got to sour mulch, she just couldn't do it any longer.

She sighed, and not elegantly. "I am so bored."

"Just the sort of thing one says to company," Andrew quipped.

She gave him the side eye. "You don't count as company."

"Does George?"

George looked up from his newspaper.

She shrugged. "I suppose not."

"I count," he said.

Billie blinked. She had not realized he'd even been listening.

"I count," he said again, and if Billie hadn't been looking at him she would have missed it. She would have missed the blaze of fire in his eyes, hot and intense, burning for less than a second before he banked it and returned his attention to his newspaper.

"You treat Andrew like a brother," he said, turning a page with slow, deliberate movements.

"And I treat you . . ."

He looked at her. "Not like a brother."

Billie's lips parted. She couldn't look away. And then she *had* to look away, because she felt very strange, and it was suddenly imperative that she get back to the sour mulch.

But then George made a noise, or maybe he just breathed, and she couldn't stop herself, she was looking at him again.

He had nice hair, she decided. She was glad he didn't powder it, at least not for everyday. It was thick, with just a hint of a wave, and it looked like it would curl if he grew it long. She gave a little snort. Wouldn't her maid love hair like that? Billie usually just tied her hair back in a queue, but sometimes she had to fancify herself. They had tried everything with her hair—hot tongs, wet ribbons—but it just wouldn't take a curl.

She liked the color of George's hair, too. It was like caramel, rich and sweet, tipped with strands of gold. She would wager he sometimes forgot to wear his hat in the sun. She was the same way.

It was interesting how all the Rokesbys had the exact same color eyes, but their hair ran the gamut of browns. No one was blond, and no one ginger, but even though they were all brunet, no one had quite the same coloring.

"Billie?" George asked, his voice somewhere between confused and amused.

Oh, bloody hell, he'd caught her looking at him again. She

winced out a smile. "I was just thinking how you and Andrew resemble each other," she said. It was sort of the truth.

Andrew glanced up at that. "Do you really think so?"

No, she thought, but she said, "Well, you both have blue eyes."

"As does half of England," Andrew said dryly. He shrugged and got back to work, his tongue catching between his teeth as he pondered his next move.

"My mother has always said that we have the same ears," George commented.

"*Ears*?" Billie's jaw fell about an inch. "I've never heard of anyone comparing ears."

"As far as I know, no one does, aside from my mother."

"Dangling lobes," Andrew put in. He didn't look at her, but he did use his good hand to tweak his lobe. "Hers are attached."

Billie touched her own earlobe. There was no way *not* to, now. "I didn't even realize there was more than one kind."

"Yours are also attached," Andrew said without looking up.

"You know this?"

"I notice ears," he said unapologetically. "I can't help it now."

"Nor can I," George admitted. "I blame Mother."

Billie blinked a few times, still pinching her lobe between her fingers. "I just don't . . ." She frowned and swung her legs off the sofa.

"Watch out!" Andrew snapped.

She shot him a look of great irritation, not that he was paying attention to her, and bent forward.

Andrew turned slowly. "Are you examining my ears?"

"I'm just trying to see what the difference is. I told you, I didn't even realize there was more than one type."

He flicked his hand toward his brother. "Go look at George's if you must. You're too close to the table here."

"I vow, Andrew," she said, carefully edging herself sideways until she was out of the space between the sofa and the table, "this is like a disease with you."

"Some men turn to drink," he said archly.

George stood, having seen that Billie had come to her feet. "Or cards," he said with a sly half-smile.

Billie snorted a laugh.

"How many levels do you think he's laid down?" George asked.

Billie leaned to the right; Andrew was blocking her view. One, two, three, four . . .

"Six," she told him.

"That's remarkable."

Billie quirked a smile. "Is this what it takes to impress you?"

"Quite possibly."

"Stop talking," Andrew snapped.

"We move the air with our breath," Billie explained, giving the statement gravity it absolutely didn't deserve.

"I see."

"Yesterday I sneezed."

George turned to her with full admiration. "Well done."

"I need more cards," Andrew said. He backed up from the table very slowly, scooting along the carpet like a crab until he was far enough away to rise without risking knocking into anything.

"I don't have any," Billie said. "I mean, I'm sure we do, but I wouldn't know where to find them. I brought you the last two decks from the game room earlier."

"This won't do," Andrew muttered.

"You could ask Thamesly," she suggested. "If anyone would know, it would be he."

Andrew nodded slowly, as if he were working it all out in his head. Then he turned and said, "You'll have to move."

She stared at him. "I beg your pardon."

"You can't stand there. You're too close."

"Andrew," she said plainly, "you've gone mad."

"You're going to knock it down."

"Just go," Billie said.

"If you—"

"Go!" she and George yelled together.

Andrew threw an evil eye at them both and left the room.

Billie looked at George. He looked at her.

They burst into laughter.

"I don't know about you," Billie said, "but I'm moving to the other side of the room."

"Ah, but then you are admitting defeat."

She tossed him a glance over her shoulder as she walked away. "I prefer to think of it as self-preservation."

George chuckled and followed her to the bank of windows. "The irony," he said, "is that he's terrible at cards."

"He is?" She wrinkled her nose. It was odd, really, but she didn't think she and Andrew had ever played cards.

"All games of chance, actually," George went on. "If you ever need some money, he's your man."

"Alas, I don't gamble."

"With cards," he countered.

She had a feeling he'd meant to sound droll, but to her ears it was patronizing in the extreme. She scowled. "What do you mean by that?"

He looked at her as if he were mildly surprised by her question. "Just that you gamble quite happily with your life all the time."

She felt her chin draw back. "That's absurd."

"Billie, you fell out of a tree."

"Onto a *roof*."

He almost laughed. "This counters my argument *how*?"

"You would have done the exact same thing I did," she insisted. "In fact, you did."

"Oh, really."

"I went up the tree to save a cat." She jabbed him in the shoulder with her index finger. "You went up to save me."

"First of all," he shot back, "I did not go up the tree. And secondly, you're comparing yourself to a cat?"

"Yes. No!" For the first time she was grateful she'd injured her foot. She might have stamped it, otherwise.

"What would you have done if I hadn't come along?" he demanded. "Truly, Billie. What would you have done?"

"I'd have been fine."

"I'm sure you would have. You've the devil's own luck. But your family would have been frantic, and likely the entire village would have been called out to search for you."

He was right, damn it, and that just made it worse. "Do you think I'm not aware of that?" she demanded, her voice dropping to a low hiss.

He regarded her for just long enough to make her uncomfortable. "No," he said, "I don't."

She sucked in her breath. "Everything I do, I do for the people here. My whole life . . . everything. I'm reading a bloody encyclopedia of agriculture," she said, her arm jerking back toward the book in question. "Volume *four*. Who else do you know who—" Her words came to a choking halt, and several moments passed before she was able to continue. "Do you really believe me to be so uncaring?"

"No." His voice was devastatingly low and even. "I believe you to be unthinking."

She lurched back. "I can't believe I thought we were starting to be friends."

He didn't say anything.

"You're a terrible person, George Rokesby. You are impatient and intolerant and—"

He grabbed her arm. "Stop this."

Billie yanked back, but his fingers were too firmly wrapped around her flesh. "Why did you even come here this morning? You only look at me to find fault."

"Don't be absurd," he scoffed.

"It's true," she shot back. "You don't see yourself when you're near me. All you do is frown and scold and—and—everything about you. Your manner, your expressions. You are so disapproving."

"You're being ridiculous."

She shook her head. She felt almost revelatory. "You disapprove of everything about me."

He stepped toward her, his hand tightening on her arm. "That is so far from the truth as to be laughable."

Billie's mouth fell open.

Then she realized that George looked as shocked by his words as she did.

And that he was standing very close.

Her chin tipped up, bringing her eyes to his.

She stopped breathing.

"Billie," he whispered, and his hand rose, as if to touch her cheek.

Chapter 10

He almost kissed her.

Dear God, he almost kissed Billie Bridgerton.

He had to get out of here.

"It's late," George blurted.

"What?"

"It's late. I need to go."

"It's not late," she said, blinking rapidly. She looked confused. "What are you talking about?"

I don't know, he almost said.

He'd almost kissed her. His eyes had dropped to her mouth and he heard the tiny rush of her breath across her lips, and he'd felt himself leaning, wanting . . .

Burning.

He prayed she hadn't realized. Surely she'd never been kissed before. She wouldn't have known what was happening.

But he'd wanted her. By God, he'd wanted her. It had hit him like a swell, sneaking up and then washing over him so fast and hard he'd barely been able to think straight.

He still wanted her.

"George?" she said. "Is something wrong?"

His lips parted. He needed to breathe.

She was watching him with an almost wary curiosity. "You were scolding me," she reminded him.

He was fairly certain his brain had not resumed its normal workings. He blinked, trying to absorb her words. "Did you want me to continue?"

She shook her head slowly. "Not particularly."

He raked a hand through his hair and tried to smile. It was the best he could do.

Billie's brow knitted with concern. "Are you sure you're well? You look very pale."

Pale? He felt like he was on *fire*. "Forgive me," he said. "I think I'm somewhat—" What? Somewhat *what*? Tired? Hungry? He cleared his throat and decided on: "Light-headed."

She did not look as if she believed him. "Lightheaded?"

"It came on suddenly," he said. That much was true.

She motioned toward the bellpull. "Shall I get you something to eat? Do you want to sit down?"

"No, no," he said stupidly. "I'm fine."

"You're fine," she repeated, her lack of belief in this statement practically radiating from her.

He gave a nod.

"No longer light-headed."

"Not at all."

She was staring at him as if he'd gone mad. Which was quite possible. He couldn't think of any other explanation.

"I should go," he said. He turned, striding to the door. He could not get out of there fast enough.

"George, wait!"

So close. But he stopped. He had to. He could no more leave the room when a gentlewoman was calling his name than spit in the face of the King. It had been bred into his bones.

When he turned around he saw that she'd moved several steps closer. "Don't you think you should wait for Andrew?" she asked.

He exhaled. Andrew. Of course.

"He'll need help, won't he? With his mount?"

Bloody hell. George exhaled. "I will wait."

Billie caught her lower lip between her teeth. The right side. She only ever worried the right side, he realized.

"I can't imagine what is taking him so long," she said, glancing at the door.

George shrugged.

"Maybe he couldn't find Thamesly."

He shrugged again.

"Or perhaps my mother waylaid him. She can be a nuisance that way."

He started to shrug for a third time, realized how inane he looked and instead opted for a *who-can-guess* sort of smile.

"Well," Billie said, apparently out of suggestions. "Hmmm."

George clasped his hands behind his back. Looked at the window. At the wall. But not at Billie. Anywhere but Billie.

He still wanted to kiss her.

She coughed. He managed to look at her feet.

This was awkward.

Insane.

"Mary and Felix arrive in two days," she said.

He gave a shove to the part of his brain that knew how to make conversation. "Doesn't everyone arrive in two days?"

"Well, of course," Billie replied, sounding somewhat relieved to have an actual question to answer, "but they're the only ones I care about."

George smiled despite himself. How like her to throw a party and hate every minute of it. Although in truth she hadn't had much choice; they all knew that the house party had been Lady Bridgerton's idea.

"Has the guest list been finalized?" he asked. He knew the answer, of course; the guest list had been drawn up for days, and the invitations had gone out with swift messengers with orders to wait for replies.

But this was a silence that needed filling. She was no longer on the sofa with her book and he in the chair with the newspaper. They had no props, nothing but themselves, and every time he looked at her, his eyes fell to her lips, and nothing—*nothing* could have been more wrong.

Billie wandered aimlessly toward a writing desk and tapped her hand on the table. "The Duchess of Westborough is coming," she said. "Mother is very pleased that she has accepted our invitation. I'm told it's a coup."

"A duchess is always a coup," he said wryly, "and usually also a great bother."

She turned and looked back at him. "Do you know her?"

"We've been introduced."

Her expression turned rueful. "I imagine you've been introduced to everyone."

He thought about that. "Probably," he said. "Everyone who comes to London, at least." Like most men of his station, George spent several months each year in the capital. He generally enjoyed it. He saw friends, he kept himself up-to-date on affairs of the state. Lately he'd been eyeing prospective brides; it had been a far more tedious endeavor than he had anticipated.

Billie caught her lip between her teeth. "Is she very grand?"

"The duchess?"

She nodded.

"No grander than any other duchess."

"George! You know that's not what I'm asking."

"Yes," he said, taking pity on her, "she's quite grand. But you will—" He stopped, looked at her. Really looked at her, and finally caught the way her eyes lacked their usual sparkle. "Are you nervous?"

She picked a piece of lint off her sleeve. "Don't be silly."

"Because—"

"Of course I'm nervous."

That drew him up short. She was nervous? *Billie*?

"What?" she demanded, seeing the incredulity on his face.

He shook his head. For Billie to admit to nerves after all the things she'd done . . . all the things she'd done with a mad grin on her face . . . it was inconceivable.

"You jumped out of a tree," he finally said.

"I fell out of a tree," she returned pertly, "and what has that to do with the Duchess of Westborough?"

"Nothing," he admitted, "except that it's difficult to imagine you nervous about . . ." He felt his head shaking, slow, tiny movements, and a reluctant admiration rose within him. She was fearless. She had always been fearless. "About anything," he finished.

Her lips pressed together. "Have you ever danced with me?"

He gaped at her. "What?"

"Have you ever danced with me?" she repeated, her voice edging toward impatience.

"Yes?" The word was drawn out, a question.

"No," she said, "you haven't."

"That can't be possible," he said. Of course he'd danced with her. He'd known her all of her life.

She crossed her arms.

"You can't dance?" he asked.

She shot him a look of pure irritation. "Of course I can dance."

He was going to kill her.

"I'm not very good," she continued, "but I'm good enough, I suppose. That's not the point."

George was fairly certain they had reached the point where there *was* no point.

"The point is," Billie went on, "you have never danced with me because I don't *go* to dances."

"Perhaps you should."

She scowled mightily. "I don't glide when I walk, and I don't know how to flirt, and the last time I tried to use a fan I poked someone in the eye." She crossed her arms. "I certainly don't know how to make a gentleman feel clever and strong and better than me."

He chuckled. "I'm fairly certain the Duchess of Westborough is a lady."

"George!"

He drew back, surprised. She was truly upset. "Forgive me," he said, and he watched her carefully, warily even. She looked hesitant, picking nervously at the folds of her skirt. Her brow was knit not into a frown but into a rueful wrinkle. He had never seen her like this.

He did not know this girl.

"I don't do well in polite company," Billie said in a low voice. "I don't—I'm not good at it."

George knew better than to make another joke, but he did not know what sort of words she needed. How did one comfort a whirlwind? Reassure the girl who did everything well and then did it all backwards for fun? "You do perfectly well when you dine at Crake," he said, even though he knew this wasn't what she was talking about.

"That doesn't count," she said impatiently.

"When you're in the village . . ."

"Really? You're going to compare the villagers to a *duchess*? Besides, I've known the villagers all my life. They know *me*."

He cleared his throat. "Billie, you are the most confident, competent woman I know."

"I drive you mad," she said plainly.

"True," he agreed, although that madness had been taking on a disturbingly different hue lately. "But," he continued, trying to get his words in the proper order, "you are a Bridgerton. The daughter of a viscount. There is no reason why you cannot hold your head high in any room in the land."

She let out a dismissive snort. "You don't understand."

"Then make me." To his great surprise, he realized that he meant it.

She didn't answer right away. She wasn't even looking at him. She was still leaning on the table, and her eyes seemed locked on her hands. She glanced up, briefly, and it occurred to him that she was trying to determine if he was sincere.

He was outraged, and then he wasn't. He wasn't used to having his sincerity questioned, but then again, this was Billie. They had a long history of needling one another, of searching for the perfect weak spot, tiny and undefended.

But it was changing. It *had* changed, just over this past week. He didn't know why; neither of *them* had changed.

His respect for her was no longer so grudging. Oh, he still thought she was beyond headstrong and reckless in the extreme, but underneath all that, her heart was true.

He supposed he'd always known that. He'd just been too busy being aggravated by her to notice.

"Billie?" He spoke softly, his voice a gentle prod.

She looked up, one corner of her mouth twisting forlornly. "It's not a case of holding my head high."

He made sure to keep any hint of impatience out of his voice when he asked, "Then what is the problem?"

She looked at him for a long moment, lips pressed together, before saying, "Did you know that I was presented at court?"

"I thought you didn't have a Season."

"I didn't"—Billie cleared her throat—"after that."

He winced. "What happened?"

She did not quite look at him when she said, "I may have set someone's dress on fire."

He nearly lost his footing. "*You set someone's dress on fire?*"

She waited with exaggerated patience, as if she'd been through this conversation before and knew exactly how long it was going to take to get through it.

He stared at her, dumbfounded. "You set someone's dress on fire."

"It wasn't on purpose," she snipped.

"Well," he said, impressed despite himself, "I suppose if anyone was going to—"

"Don't say it," she warned.

"How did I not hear of this?" he wondered.

"It was a very small fire," she said, somewhat primly.

"But still . . ."

"Really?" she demanded. "I set someone's dress on fire, and your biggest question is how you missed the gossip?"

"I apologize," he said immediately, but then he could not help but ask (somewhat gingerly), "Are you inviting me to inquire *how* you set this dress on fire?"

"No," she said irritably, "and it's not why I brought it up."

His first inclination was to tease her further, but then she sighed, and the sound was so tired and disconsolate that his mirth slid away. "Billie," he said, his voice as gentle as it was sympathetic, "you can't—"

But she did not let him finish. "I don't fit the mold, George."

No, she didn't. And hadn't he been thinking the same thing just a few days earlier? If Billie had gone to London for a Season with his sister it would have been an unmitigated disaster. All the things that made her wonderful and strong would have been her downfall in the rarefied world of the *ton.*

They would have used her for target practice.

They weren't *all* cruel, the lords and ladies of high society. But the ones who were . . . their words were their weapons, and they wielded them like bayonets.

"Why are you telling me this?" he suddenly asked.

Her lips parted, and a flash of pain shot through her eyes.

"I mean, why me?" he said quickly, lest she think he didn't care enough to listen. "Why not Andrew?"

She didn't say anything. Not right away. And then— "I don't know. I don't . . . Andrew and I don't talk about such things."

"Mary will be here soon," he said helpfully.

"For the love of God, George," she nearly spat, "if you don't want to talk to me, you can just say so."

"No," he said, grabbing her wrist before she could whirl away. "That's not what I meant. I'm happy to talk with you," he assured her. "I'm happy to listen. I just thought you'd rather have someone who . . ."

She stared at him, waiting. But he could not bring himself to say the words that had been on the tip of his tongue.

Someone who cares.

Because it was hurtful. And it was petty. And most of all, it wasn't true.

He did care.

He cared . . . quite a lot.

"I will . . ." The word trailed off, lost in his turbulent thoughts, and all he could do was watch her. Watch her watching him as he tried to remember how to speak his mother tongue, as he tried to figure out which words were right, which words were reassuring. Because she looked sad. And she looked anxious. And he hated that.

"If you wish," he said, slowly enough to allow him to pick over his thoughts as he spoke, "I will watch out for you."

She eyed him cautiously. "What do you mean?"

"Make sure you . . ." He made an air motion with his hands, not that either one of them knew what it meant. "That you're . . . well."

"That I'm well?" she echoed.

"I don't know," he said, frustrated with his inability to put together a complete thought, much less translate it into actual sentences. "Just that if you need a friend, I will be there."

Her lips parted, and he saw movement in her throat, all her words trapped there, all her emotions in check.

"Thank you," she said. "That's . . ."

"Don't say it's kind of me," he ordered.

"Why not?"

"Because it's not kindness. It's . . . I don't know what it is," he said helplessly. "But it's not kindness."

Her lips quivered into a smile. A mischievous smile. "Very well," she said. "You're not kind."

"Never."

"May I call you selfish?"

"That would be going too far."

"Conceited?"

He took a step in her direction. "You're pushing your luck, Billie."

"Arrogant." She ran around the table, laughing as she put it between them. "Come now, George. You cannot deny arrogant."

Something devilish rose up within him. Something devilish and hot. "What do I get to call you?"

"Brilliant?"

He moved closer. "How about maddening?"

"Ah, but that's in the eye of the beholder."

"Reckless," he said.

She feinted left when he feinted right. "It's not recklessness if you know what you're doing."

"You fell onto a *roof*," he reminded her.

She grinned wickedly. "I thought you said I jumped."

He growled her name and lunged, chasing her as she shrieked, "I was trying to save the cat! I was being noble!"

"I'll show you noble . . ."

She yelped and jumped back.

Straight into the house of cards.

It did not fall gracefully.

Neither did Billie, to tell the truth. When the dust had settled, she was sitting squarely on the table, the wreckage of Andrew's masterpiece scattered around like a Chinese firecracker had been lit beneath it.

She looked up and said in a very small voice, "I don't suppose the two of us can put it back together."

Mutely, he shook his head.

She swallowed. "I think I might have reinjured my ankle."

"Badly?"

"No."

"In that case," he told her, "I'd advise you to lead with *that* when Andrew returns."

And of course that was when he walked through the door.

"I hurt my ankle," Billie all but yelled. "It really hurts."

George had to turn away. It was the only way to keep from laughing.

Andrew just stared. "Again," he finally said. "You did it again."

"It was a very nice house," she said weakly.

"I suppose it's a talent," Andrew said.

"Oh, indeed," Billie said brightly. "You're brilliant at it."

"No, I meant you."

"Oh." She swallowed—her pride, most likely—and stretched out a smile. "Well, yes. There's no point in doing something if you're not going to do it well, wouldn't you agree?"

Andrew said nothing. George had the urge to clap his hands in front of his face. Just to make sure he wasn't sleepwalking.

"I'm truly sorry," Billie said. "I'll make it up to you." She pushed herself off the table and limped her way upright. "Although I don't really know how."

"It was my fault," George said suddenly.

She turned to him. "You don't need to take the blame."

He held up his hands in supplication. "I was chasing you."

That snapped Andrew out of his daze. "You were chasing her?"

Damn. He had not thought that one through. "Not in so many words," George said.

Andrew turned to Billie. "He was chasing you?"

She didn't blush, but her expression turned most sheepish. "I might have been somewhat provoking . . ."

"Provoking?" George said with a snort. "You?"

"It's really the cat's fault," she returned. "I would never have fallen if my ankle wasn't so weak." She frowned thoughtfully. "I may blame everything on that mangy beast from now on."

"What is happening here?" Andrew asked, his face turning

slowly from Billie to George and back again. "Why aren't you killing each other?"

"The small matter of the gallows," George murmured.

"Not to mention your mother would be very displeased," Billie added.

Andrew just stared at them, his mouth slack. "I'm going home," he finally said.

Billie giggled.

And George . . . his breath caught. Because he'd heard Billie giggle before. A thousand times he'd heard her giggle. But this time was different. It sounded exactly the same, but when the light laugh reached his ears . . .

It was the loveliest sound he'd ever heard.

And quite possibly the most terrifying. Because he had a feeling he knew what it meant. And if there was one person in this world he was *not* going to fall in love with, it was Billie Bridgerton.

Chapter 11

Billie wasn't exactly certain what she'd done to her ankle when she crashed into Andrew's house of cards, but it felt only a little bit worse than before, so on the last day before the house party she decided that she was well enough to ride, as long as she did so sidesaddle.

She really didn't have any choice. Honestly, if she didn't get out to the west fields to monitor the progress of the barley crops, she had no idea who would. But dismounting was difficult, which meant she'd had to take a groom with her. Which neither of them enjoyed. The last thing the groom wanted was to inspect barley, and the last thing Billie wanted was to be watched by a groom while she inspected barley.

Her mare was in bad spirits as well, just to round out the cranky triumvirate. It had been a long time since Billie had sat in a sidesaddle, and Argo didn't like it one bit.

Neither did Billie. She had not forgotten how much she hated riding sidesaddle, but she *had* forgotten how much it hurt the next day when one was out of practice. With every step her right hip and thigh groaned with pain. Factor in her ankle, which was still twinging like mad, and it was a wonder she wasn't lurching around the house like a drunken sailor.

Or maybe she was. The servants gave her very odd looks when she made her way down the next morning to break her fast.

She supposed it was for the best that she was too sore to get back in the saddle. Her mother had made it explicitly clear that Billie was to remain at Aubrey Hall throughout the day. There were four Bridgertons currently in residence, she said, and there would be four Bridgertons standing in the drive to greet each and every guest.

And so Billie stood between her mother and Georgiana at one o'clock, when the Duchess of Westborough arrived in her grand coach and four, accompanied by her daughters (one engaged, one not) and niece.

Billie stood between her mother and Georgiana at half two, when Henry Maynard drove up in his racy little curricle with his good friend Sir Reginald McVie.

And she stood between her mother and Georgiana at twenty minutes past three, when Felix and Mary arrived with their neighbors Edward and Niall Berbrooke, who were both of good family and, it just so happened, of marriageable age.

"Finally," Lord Bridgerton grumbled, stretching a crick from his neck as they waited in their neat little row for Felix and Mary's carriage to come to a halt, "someone I know."

"You know the Berbrookes?" Georgiana asked, leaning forward to speak to him past her sister and mother.

"I know Felix and Mary," he replied. He looked at his wife. "When do the Rokesbys arrive?"

"An hour before supper," she said without turning her head. The carriage had come to a stop, and, consummate hostess that she was, her eyes were on the door, awaiting her guests.

"Remind me why they're sleeping over?" he asked.

"Because it will be infinitely more festive."

Lord Bridgerton frowned, but he very wisely chose not to question her further.

Billie, however, showed no such restraint. "If it were me," she said, tugging on the sleeve of her printed cotton dress, "I would want to sleep in my own bed."

"It's not you," her mother replied tartly, "and stop fidgeting."

"I can't help it. It's itchy."

"I think it looks lovely on you," Georgiana said.

"Thank you," Billie said, momentarily nonplussed. "I'm not so sure about the front." She looked down. The bodice draped in a crisscross fashion, rather like a shawl. She'd never worn anything quite like it, although her mother assured her it had been in style for several years.

Was she revealing too much décolletage? She reached for the pin that secured the linen near her waist. It looked like she could adjust it with a little—

"Stop it," her mother hissed.

Billie sighed.

The carriage finally came to a complete stop, and Felix alighted first, holding out his hand to assist his wife. Mary Maynard (née Rokesby) wore a chintz traveling jacket and shawl that even Billie could tell was the height of fashion. It looked absolutely perfect on her, Billie realized. Mary looked happy and jaunty from her light brown curls right down to the tips of her elegantly shod feet.

"Mary!" Lady Bridgerton gushed, striding forward with outstretched arms. "You are blooming!"

Georgiana elbowed Billie. "Does that mean what I think it means?"

Billie gave her a lopsided grimace and a shrug—code universal for *I-haven't-a-clue*. Was Mary pregnant? And if so, why on earth did her mother know this before she did?

Georgiana leaned slightly in, whispering out the corner of her mouth. "She doesn't *look*—"

"Well, if she *is*," Billie cut in, whispering out the corner of *her* mouth, "she can't be very far along."

"Billie!" Mary exclaimed, hurrying over to greet her good friend with a hug.

Billie leaned forward, speaking in a low voice. "Is there something you need to tell me?"

Mary didn't even pretend to misunderstand. "I don't know how your mother knows," she said.

"Did you inform *your* mother?"

"Yes."

"Well, there's your answer."

Mary laughed, her Rokesby-blue eyes crinkling just the way George's did when he—

Billie blinked. Just one moment . . . What the devil was *that* about? Since when did George have the right to plague her thoughts? Perhaps they were getting on somewhat better than they had done in the past, but still, he was not a welcome distraction.

Mary, she reminded herself. She was talking to Mary. Or rather, Mary was talking to her.

"It is *so* good to see you," Mary was saying. She clasped both of Billie's hands in her own.

Billie felt something warm and tingly behind her eyes. She'd known she was missing Mary, but she hadn't realized how very *much* until now. "I agree," she said, working hard to keep the choke of emotion out of her voice. It wouldn't do to turn into a watering pot in the front drive.

It wouldn't do to turn into a watering pot, period. Goodness, her mother would probably send for the *physician* before the first tear reached her chin. Billie Bridgerton was *not* a crier.

She did not cry. What could be the use of it?

She swallowed, and somehow this reclaimed her equilibrium enough to smile at Mary and say, "Letters just aren't the same."

Mary rolled her eyes. "Especially with *you* as a correspondent."

"What?" Billie's mouth fell open. "That's not true. I am a brilliant letter-writer."

"When you write," Mary retorted.

"I send you a letter every two—"

"Every three."

"—every three weeks," Billie finished, keeping her voice filled with enough outrage to masque the fact that she had changed her story. "Without fail."

"You really should come to visit," Mary said.

"You know I can't," Billie replied. Mary had been inviting her for a visit for over a year, but it was so difficult for Billie to get away. There was always something that needed to be done around the estate. And truly, didn't it make more sense for Mary to come to Kent, where she already knew everyone?

"You *can*," Mary insisted, "you just won't."

"Perhaps in the winter," Billie said, "when there isn't as much to do in the fields."

Mary's brows rose doubtfully.

"I would have visited last winter," Billie insisted, "but there was no point. You had already decided to come home for Christmas."

Mary's dubious expression did not alter in the least, and she gave Billie's hand one final squeeze before turning to Georgiana. "My goodness," she said, "I think you've grown three inches since I last saw you."

"Unlikely," Georgiana replied with a smile. "You were just here in December."

Mary glanced from sister to sister. "I think you're going to be taller than Billie."

"Stop saying that," Billie ordered.

"But it's true." Mary grinned, fully enjoying Billie's scowl. "We are *all* going to be taller than you." She turned back toward her husband, who was introducing the Berbrooke brothers to Lord and Lady Bridgerton. "Darling," she called out, "don't you think Georgiana has grown tremendously since we last saw her?"

Billie bit back a smile as she watched a flash of utter incomprehension cross Felix's face before he carefully schooled his features into indulgent affection.

"I have no idea," he said, "but if you say it, it must be true."

"I hate when he does that," Mary said to Billie.

Billie didn't bother to hide her smile that time.

"Billie," Felix said as he stepped forward to greet them. "And Georgiana. It is so good to see you both again."

Billie bobbed a curtsy.

"Allow me to introduce Mr. Niall Berbrooke and Mr. Edward Berbrooke," Felix continued, motioning to the two sandy-haired gentlemen at his side. "They live just a few miles away from us in Sussex. Niall, Ned, this is Miss Sybilla Bridgerton and Miss Georgiana Bridgerton, childhood friends of Mary's."

"Miss Bridgerton," one of the Berbrookes said, bowing over her hand. "Miss Georgiana."

The second Berbrooke repeated his brother's felicitations, then straightened and gave a somewhat eager smile. He reminded her of a puppy, Billie decided, with nothing but endless good cheer.

"Have my parents arrived?" Mary asked.

"Not yet," Lady Bridgerton told her. "We expect them just before dinner. Your mother preferred to dress at home."

"And my brothers?"

"Coming with your parents."

"I suppose that makes sense," Mary said with a bit of grumble, "but you would think Andrew could have ridden ahead to say hello. I haven't seen him for ages."

"He's not riding much right now," Billie said offhandedly. "His arm, you know."

"That must be driving him mad."

"I think it would do, were he not so proficient at milking the injury for all it's worth."

Mary laughed and linked her arm through Billie's. "Let us go inside and catch up. Oh, you're limping!"

"A silly accident," Billie said with a wave of her hand. "It's nearly healed."

"Well, you must have loads to tell me."

"Actually, I don't," Billie said as they ascended the portico stairs. "Nothing has changed around here. Not really."

Mary gave her a curious look. "Nothing?"

"Other than Andrew being home, it's all just as it ever was." Billie shrugged, wondering if she ought to be disappointed in all the sameness. She supposed she had been spending a little more time with George, but that hardly counted as an event.

"Your mother's not trying to marry you off to the new vicar?" Mary teased.

"We don't have a new vicar, and I believe she's trying to marry me off to Felix's brother." She tipped her head. "Or one of the Berbrookes."

"Henry is practically engaged," Mary said authoritatively, "and you do *not* want to marry one of the Berbrookes. Trust me."

Billie gave her a sideways glance. "Do tell."

"Stop that," Mary admonished. "It's nothing salacious. Or even interesting. They're lovely, both of them, but they're dull as sticks."

"Here, let's go up to my room," Billie said, steering them toward the main staircase. "And you know," she added, mostly to be contrary, "some sticks are actually quite pointy."

"Not the Berbrookes."

"Why did you offer to bring them, then?"

"Your mother begged! She sent me a three-page letter."

"*My* mother?" Billie echoed.

"Yes. With an addendum from mine."

Billie winced. The collective might of the Ladies Rokesby and Bridgerton was not easily ignored.

"She needed more gentlemen," Mary continued. "I don't think she was anticipating that the Duchess of Westborough would bring both of her daughters *and* her niece. And anyway, Niall and Ned are both very good-natured. They will make lovely husbands for someone." She gave Billie a pointed look. "But not for you."

Billie decided there was no point taking affront. "You don't see me marrying someone good-natured?"

"I don't see you marrying someone who can barely read his name."

"Oh, come now."

"Fine. I exaggerate. But this is important." Mary stopped in the middle of the upstairs hall, forcing Billie to a halt beside her. "You know I know you better than anyone."

Billie waited while Mary fixed her with a serious stare. Mary liked to dispense advice. Billie didn't ordinarily like to receive it, but it had been so long since she'd had the company of her closest friend. Just this once she could be patient. Placid, even.

"Billie, listen to me," Mary said with an odd urgency. "You cannot treat your future so flippantly. Eventually you are going to have to choose a husband, and you will go mad if you do not marry a man of at least equal intelligence to yourself."

"That presupposes that I marry anyone." Or, Billie did not add, that she might actually have a *choice* of husbands.

Mary drew back. "Don't say such a thing! Of course you will get married. You need only to find the right gentleman."

Billie rolled her eyes. Mary had long since succumbed to that sickness that seemed to afflict all recently married individuals: the fever to see everyone else blissful and wed. "I'll probably just marry Andrew," Billie said with a shrug. "Or Edward."

Mary stared at her.

"What?" Billie finally asked.

"If you can say it like *that*," Mary said with hot disbelief, "like you don't care *which* Rokesby you meet at the altar, you have no business marrying either one of them."

"Well, I *don't* care. I love them both."

"As *brothers*. Goodness, if you're going to take that view of it, you might as well marry George."

Billie stopped short. "Don't be daft."

She, marry George? It was ludicrous.

"Honestly, Mary," she said with a stern little hiss to her voice. "That's not even something to joke about."

"You said that one Rokesby brother would be as good as another."

"No, *you* said that. I said *either* Edward or Andrew would do." Really, she did not understand why Mary was so upset. Marriage to either brother would have the same effect. Billie would become a Rokesby, and she and Mary would be sisters in truth. Billie thought it sounded rather lovely.

Mary clapped her hand to her forehead and groaned. "You are so unromantic."

"I don't necessarily see that as a flaw."

"No," Mary grumbled, "you wouldn't."

She'd meant it as criticism, but Billie just laughed. "Some of us need to view the world with practicality and sense."

"But not at the price of your happiness."

For the longest moment, Billie said nothing. She felt her head tipping slightly to the side, her eyes narrowing with thought as she watched Mary's face. Mary wanted what was best for her; she understood that. But Mary didn't know. How could she know?

"Who are you," Billie asked softly, "to decide what constitutes another person's happiness?" She made sure to keep her words gentle, her tone without edge. She did not want Mary to feel attacked by the question; she did not *mean* the question as such. But she did want Mary to think about this, to stop for one moment and try to understand that despite their deep friendship, they were fundamentally different people.

Mary looked up with stricken eyes. "I didn't mean—"

"I know you didn't," Billie assured her. Mary had always longed for love and marriage. She'd pined for Felix since the moment she'd first met him—at the age of twelve! When Billie was twelve all she'd been concerned about was the litter of puppies in the barn and whether she could climb the old oak tree faster than Andrew.

Truth be told, she was still concerned about this. It would be a massive blow if he could make it to the top branch before she could. Not that they'd be conducting a test anytime soon, what with his arm and her ankle. But still, these things were *important*.

Not that Mary would ever see them as such.

"I'm sorry," Mary said, but her smile was a little too tight. "I've no call to be so grave when I've only just arrived."

Billie almost asked her if that meant she had plans for later in the visit. But she didn't.

Such restraint. When had she developed such maturity?

"Why are you smiling?" Mary asked.

"What? I'm not smiling."

"Oh, you are."

And because Mary was her best friend, even when she was trying to tell her how to live her life, Billie laughed and linked their arms back together. "If you must know," she said, "I was congratulating myself on not making a smart comment at you."

"Such restraint," Mary said, echoing Billie's thoughts precisely.

"I know. It's so unlike me." Billie tipped her head toward the end of the hall. "Can we continue on to my bedroom? My foot hurts."

"Of course. How did you injure it?"

Billie smiled wryly as she resumed walking. "You're never going to believe who ended up being my hero . . ."

Chapter 12

At dinner that night, it became quickly apparent to George that one side of the table was the "fun" side.

He was not seated on that side.

To his left was Lady Frederica Fortescue-Endicott, who spoke incessantly of her new fiancé, the Earl of Northwick. To his right was Lady Frederica's younger sister, Lady Alexandra.

Who also spoke incessantly about the Earl of Northwick.

George was not quite sure what to make of this. For Lady Alexandra's sake, he hoped Northwick had a brother.

Billie was seated directly across from George, not that he could see her over the elaborate fruited epergne that graced the center of table. But he could hear her laughter, rich and deep, inevitably followed by Andrew's guffaw and then some asinine *bon mot* delivered by the absurdly handsome Sir Reginald McVie.

Sir *Reggie*, as he had instructed everyone to call him.

George disliked him intensely.

Never mind that they had been introduced only one hour earlier; sometimes an hour was all it took. In this case, a minute had been enough. Sir Reggie had sauntered up to George and Billie, who were enjoying a private laugh about something entirely inconsequential (but nonetheless private), and then he'd flashed a smile that was positively blinding.

The man's teeth were so straight they might have been laid into place with a yardstick. Really, who had teeth like that? It was unnatural.

Then the lout had taken Billie's hand and kissed it like some French count, proclaiming her a beauty beyond the sea, sand, stars, and skies (in French, no less, despite the loss of alliteration).

It was beyond ridiculous; George had been sure that Billie would burst out laughing. But no, she blushed.

She blushed!

And then she had batted her eyelashes. It was quite possibly the least Billie Bridgerton–like thing he'd ever seen.

All for a set of freakishly straight teeth. And she didn't even speak French!

Of *course* they had been seated next to each other at dinner. Lady Bridgerton had eyes like an eagle when it came to the marriage prospects of her eldest daughter; George did not doubt she had noticed Sir Reggie flirting with Billie within seconds of the first pearly white grin. If Billie hadn't been seated next to him earlier that day, she would be by the dinner gong.

With Andrew on Billie's other side, there was no stopping her. Laughter rang like church bells as *that* side of the table ate, drank, and made merry.

George's side continued to extoll the many virtues of the Earl of Northwick.

The many, many virtues.

By the time the soup was removed, George was ready to put the man forth for a sainthood. To hear the Ladies Frederica and Alexandra tell it, nothing less would do him justice. The two ladies were regaling him with some nonsense involving Northwick and a parasol he had held for the both of them on a particularly rainy day, and George was just about to comment that it all sounded very crowded, when yet another peal of laughter rang out from the other side of the table.

George glowered, not that Billie could see him. She wouldn't have seen him even if they didn't have that damned fruit bowl between them. She was far too busy being the life of the party. The girl was a veritable shining star. Honestly, he wouldn't have been surprised if she was *literally* sparkling.

And he'd offered to watch out for her.

Please. She was doing quite well on her own.

"What do you suppose they are talking about?" Lady Alexandra queried after a particularly loud burst of merriment.

"Teeth," George muttered.

"What did you say?"

He turned with a bland smile. "I have no idea."

"They seem to be enjoying themselves a great deal," Lady Frederica said with a thoughtful frown.

George shrugged.

"Northie is such a wonderful conversationalist," she said.

"Is he?" George murmured, stabbing a piece of roasted beef.

"Oh, yes. Surely you know him?"

George nodded absently. Lord Northwick was a few years his senior, but they had crossed paths at both Eton and Cambridge. George couldn't remember much about him other than his shock of violently blond hair.

"Then you know," Lady Frederica said with an adoring smile, "he's perfectly droll."

"Perfectly," George echoed.

Lady Alexandra leaned forward. "Are you talking about Lord Northwick?"

"Er, yes," George replied.

"He is so delightful at a house party," Lady Alexandra concurred. "I wonder why you did not invite him."

"Strictly speaking," George reminded her, "I did not draw up the guest list."

"Oh, yes, of course. I'd quite forgotten that you are not a member of the family. You seem so at home at Aubrey Hall."

"The Bridgertons and Rokesbys have long been amiable neighbors," he told her.

"Miss Sybilla is practically his sister," Lady Frederica said, leaning forward to keep herself in the conversation.

Billie? His sister? George frowned. That wasn't right. "I wouldn't say . . ." he began.

But Lady Alexandra was already talking again. "Lady Mary said as much earlier this evening. She told *the* most amusing tales. I do so adore your sister."

George had a mouthful of food, so he nodded and hoped she'd take that as a thank-you.

Lady Alexandra leaned forward. "Lady Mary said the lot of you ran wild together as children. It sounded dreadfully exciting."

"I was a bit older," he said. "I rarely—"

"—and then it *ran off*!" Andrew chortled from across the table, loudly enough to put a (thankful) halt to George's conversation with the two Fortescue-Endicott ladies.

Lady Frederica peered at them through the fruit display. "What do you think they are talking about?" she inquired.

"Lord Northwick," George said firmly.

Her entire face lit up. "Really?"

"But Mr. Rokesby said 'it,'" Lady Alexandra pointed out. "Surely he would not refer to Northie as an it."

"I'm sure you misheard," George lied. "My brother very much admires Lord Northwick."

"He does?" She leaned forward, far enough to attract her sister's attention. "Frederica, did you hear that? Lord Kennard said that his brother admires Lord Northwick."

Lady Frederica blushed prettily.

George wanted to plant his face in his potatoes.

". . . ungrateful feline!" Billie's voice wafted over the asparagus terrine. More laughter ensued, followed by: "I was furious!"

George sighed. He never thought he would yearn for Billie Bridgerton, but her smile was bright, her laughter infectious, and he was quite sure that if he had to endure another moment seated between the Ladies Frederica and Alexandra his brain was going to start washing out his ears.

Billie must have caught him moping, because she moved just a bit to the side. "We're talking about the cat," she said.

"Yes, I'd gathered."

She smiled—a rather encouraging and pleasant smile that had the effect of making him feel rather discouraged.

And unpleasant.

"Do you know what she meant?" Lady Alexandra asked. "I believe she said something about a cat."

"Northie adores cats," Lady Frederica said.

"I can't stand them myself," George said with a renewed sense of affability. The statement wasn't precisely true, but one couldn't discount the pleasure to be found in being contrary.

Lady Frederica blinked with surprise. "Everybody likes cats."

"Not me!"

Both Fortescue-Endicott sisters stared at him in shock. George supposed he couldn't blame them; his tone had been downright gleeful. But as he was finally starting to enjoy himself, he decided he didn't care. "I prefer dogs," he said.

"Well, of course everyone likes dogs," Lady Frederica said. But she sounded hesitant.

"And badgers," George said cheerfully, popping a bit of bread into his mouth.

"Badgers," she repeated.

"And moles." He grinned. She was now regarding him with visible unease. George congratulated himself on a job well done. A few more minutes of this, and she would surely think him insane.

He couldn't recall the last time he'd had so much fun at a formal dinner.

He looked over at Billie, suddenly eager to tell her about his conversation. It was exactly the sort of thing she'd find amusing. They would have such a good laugh over it.

But she was busy with Sir Reginald, who was now gazing at her as if she were a rare creature.

Which she was, George thought violently. She just wasn't *his* rare creature.

George had a sudden urge to leap across the table and rearrange Sir Reggie's perfect teeth into something far more abstract.

For the love of God, who was born with teeth like that? The man's parents had clearly sold their souls to the devil.

"Oh, Lord Kennard," Lady Alexandra said, "do you plan to observe the ladies' archery tournament tomorrow?"

"I wasn't aware there was one," he replied.

"Oh yes. Frederica and I both plan to take part. We've practiced extensively."

"With Lord Northwick?" he could not help but ask.

"Of course not," she said. "Why on earth would you think that?"

He shrugged helplessly. Dear God, how much longer would this meal last?

She laid her hand on his arm. "I do hope you will come to watch."

He glanced down at her hand. It looked so *very* wrong on his sleeve. But he had a feeling she misinterpreted his gesture, because if anything her fingers tightened. He couldn't help but wonder what had happened to Lord Northwick. God help him if he'd replaced the earl in her affections.

George wanted to shake her off, but there was that damned gentlemanly nature of his, so instead he gave a tight smile and said, "I will of a certain come to watch."

Lady Frederica leaned forward and beamed. "Lord Northwick very much enjoys observing archery, too."

"Of course he does," George said under his breath.

"Did you say something?" Lady Alexandra asked.

"Merely that Miss Bridgerton is a very accomplished archer," he said. It was the truth, even if that hadn't been what he'd said.

He looked over at Billie, intending to motion to her with his head, but she was already staring at him with a ferocious expression.

He leaned to the right to see her better.

Her mouth tightened.

He cocked his head.

She rolled her eyes and turned back to Sir Reginald.

George blinked. What the hell had that been about?

And honestly, why did he care?

Billie was having a marvelous time. Truly, she wasn't quite certain just what she'd been so nervous about. Andrew was always an amusing dinner companion, and Sir Reggie was so kind and handsome; he'd put her right at ease even if he had started speaking in French when they had been introduced.

She hadn't understood a word of it, but she'd figured it must be complimentary, so she'd nodded and smiled, and even blinked a few times the way she'd seen other ladies do when they were trying to act particularly feminine.

No one could say she wasn't trying her best.

The one fly in the proverbial ointment was George. Or rather George's predicament. She felt desperately sorry for him.

Lady Alexandra had seemed like a perfectly pleasant sort of lady when they had been introduced in the drive, but the moment she arrived in the drawing room for pre-dinner drinks, the little shrew had latched on to George like a barnacle.

Billie was appalled. She knew the man was rich and handsome and going to be an earl, but did the grasping little wench need to be quite so obvious about it?

Poor George. Was this what he'd had to contend with every time he went to London? Perhaps she ought to have had more compassion for him. At the very least she should have taken a peek into the dining room before the guests filed in to check on the seating arrangement. She could have saved him from a full evening of Lady Alexandra Four-handed-Endicott.

Blergh. She could come up with something better than that.

Formidable . . . For-heaven's-sake . . . For-the-last-time . . .

Fine. She couldn't come up with something better. But really, the woman might as well have had four hands with the way she kept clutching on to George in the drawing room.

At dinner she was even worse. It was difficult to see George across the table with her mother's monstrous fruit epergne blocking the way, but she had a clear view of Lady Alexandra, and it had to be said—the lady was displaying a highly impractical expanse of bosom.

Billie wouldn't have been surprised if she had an entire tea service hiding down there.

And then. And then! She'd put her hand on George's forearm like she *owned* it. Even Billie wouldn't have dared such a familiar gesture in such a formal setting. She leaned in her chair, trying to get a look at George's face. He could not be happy about this.

"Are you all right?"

She turned. Andrew was regarding her with an expression that hovered somewhere between suspicion and concern.

"I'm fine," she said in a clipped voice. "Why?"

"You're about to fall in my lap."

She lurched upright. "Don't be absurd."

"Has Sir Reginald broken wind?" Andrew murmured.

"Andrew!"

He gave her an unrepentant smirk. "It was either that or you've developed a new fondness for me."

She glared at him.

"I do love you, Billie," he drawled, "but not that way."

She rolled her eyes because . . . well, because. Andrew was a wretch. He had always been a wretch. And she didn't love him that way, either.

But he didn't have to be quite so mean-spirited about it.

"What do you think of Lady Alexandra?" she whispered.

"Which one is she?"

"The one who is crawling over your brother," she said impatiently.

"Oh, that one." Andrew sounded like he was trying not to laugh.

"He looks very unhappy."

Andrew tipped his head as he regarded his brother. Unlike Billie, he did not have a gargantuan fruit display to contend with. "I don't know," he mused. "He doesn't look like he minds."

"Are you blind?" Billie hissed.

"Not that I'm aware."

"He— Oh, never mind. You're of no use."

Billie leaned again, this time toward Sir Reggie. He was talking with the woman on his left, so hopefully he wouldn't notice.

Lady Alexandra's hand was *still* on George's arm.

Billie's jaw clenched. He could not be happy about this. George was a very private person. She looked up, trying to catch a glimpse of his face, but he was saying something to Lady Alexandra, something perfectly pleasant and polite.

He didn't look the least bit perturbed.

She fumed.

And then he looked up. He must have caught her looking at him because he leaned to his right just far enough to catch her eye.

His brows rose.

She flicked her gaze toward the ceiling and turned back to Sir Reggie, even though he was still speaking to the duchess's niece.

She waited for a moment, but he seemed in no rush to return his attention to her, so she picked up her fork and knife and cut her meat into ever-tinier pieces.

Maybe George *liked* Lady Alexandra. Maybe he'd court her, and maybe they'd get married and have a flock of little Rokesby babies, all blue-eyed and plump-cheeked.

If that was what George wanted, that was what he should do.

But why did it seem so very wrong? And why did it hurt so much just to think about it?

Chapter 13

By one o'clock the following afternoon, George was remembering why he disliked house parties. Or rather, he was remembering *that* he disliked house parties.

Or maybe he just disliked *this* house party. Between the Northwick-besotted Fortescue-Endicott girls, Lord Reggie of the snow white teeth, and Ned Berbrooke, who had accidentally spilled port all over George's boots the previous night, he was ready to *crawl* back to Crake House.

It was only three miles away. He could do it.

He'd skipped the midday meal—the only way to avoid Lady Alexandra, who seemed to have decided he was the next best thing to Northwick—and now he was in a very bad mood. He was hungry and he was tired, twin demons guaranteed to reduce a grown man's disposition to that of a querulous three-year-old.

The previous night's sleep had been . . .

Unsatisfying.

Yes, that seemed the most appropriate word. Desperately inadequate, but appropriate.

The Bridgertons had put all of the Rokesbys in the family wing, and George had sat in the cushioned chair by his fireplace, listening to the regular, ordinary sounds of a family ending the day—the maids attending the ladies, doors opening and closing . . .

It should have been of no consequence. They were all the same noises one heard at Crake. But somehow, here at Aubrey Hall it felt too intimate, almost as if he were eavesdropping.

With every soft and sleepy sound, his imagination took flight. He knew he couldn't hear Billie moving about; her bedroom was across the hall and three doors down. But it *felt* like he heard her. In the silence of the night he sensed her feet lightly padding across her carpet. He felt the whisper of her breath as she blew out a candle. And when she settled into her bed, he was sure he could hear the rustling of her sheets.

She'd said she fell asleep immediately—but what then? Was she a restless sleeper? Did she wriggle about, kicking the covers, pushing the sheets to the bottom of the bed with her feet?

Or did she lie still, sweetly on her side with her hands tucked under her cheek?

He'd wager she was a squirmer; this was Billie, after all. She'd spent her entire childhood in constant motion. Why would she sleep any other way? And if she shared a bed with someone . . .

His brandy nightcap turned into three, but when he'd finally laid his head against his pillow, it had taken him hours to fall asleep. And then when he did, he'd dreamed of her.

And the dream . . . oh, the dream.

He shuddered, the memory washing over him anew. If he'd ever thought of Billie as a sister . . .

He certainly didn't now.

It had started in the library, in the moonlit dark, and he didn't know what she'd been wearing—just that it wasn't like anything he'd ever seen her in before. It had to have been a nightgown . . . white and diaphanous. With every breeze it molded to her body, revealing perfectly lush curves designed to fit his hands.

Never mind that they were in the library, and there was no logical reason for a breeze. It was his dream, and it was breezy, and then it didn't matter anyway because when he took her hand and pulled her hard against him they were suddenly in his bedroom. Not the one here at Aubrey Hall but back at Crake, with his mahogany four-poster bed, the mattress large and square, with room for all sorts of reckless abandon.

She didn't say a word, which he had to admit was very unlike her, but then again, it *was* a dream. When she smiled, though, it was pure Billie—wide and free—and when he laid her on the bed, her eyes met his, and it was as if she had been born for that moment.

As if *he* had been born for that moment.

His hands opened the folds of her gown, and she arched beneath him, her perfect breasts thrusting toward him like an offering.

It was mad. It was madness. He shouldn't know what her breasts looked like. He shouldn't even be able to imagine it.

But he did, and in his dream, he worshipped them. He cupped them, squeezed them, pushed them together until that intoxicatingly feminine valley formed between them. Then he bent down and took her nipple between his teeth, teasing and tempting until she moaned with delight.

But it didn't end there. He slid his hands to the junction of her legs and her hips and he pushed her thighs open, his thumbs coming torturously close to her center.

And then he stroked . . . closer . . . closer . . . until he could sense the wet heat of her, and he knew that their joining was inevitable. She would be his, and it would be glorious. His clothes melted away, and he positioned himself at her opening . . .

And woke up.

Bloody goddamn bleeding *bollocks.*

He woke up.

Life was spectacularly unfair.

The following morning was the ladies' archery competition, and if George had felt a bit of irony while watching, surely he could be forgiven. There was Billie with a stiff, pointy thing, and there was he, *still* with a stiff, pointy thing, and it had to be said: only one of them was having any fun.

It had taken a full hour of very icy thoughts before he was able to move from his carefully cross-legged position in the chairs that had been set up at the edge of the field. Every other gentleman had got up at some point to inspect the targets, but not George. He'd smiled, and he'd laughed, and he made up some sort of nonsense about enjoying the sun. Which was ridiculous, because the one spot of blue in the sky was about the size of his thumbnail.

Desperate for a moment of his own company, he made for the library immediately after the tournament. No one in the party struck him as much of a reader; surely he could find some peace and quiet.

Which he did, for all of ten minutes before Billie and Andrew came squabbling through the door.

"George!" Billie exclaimed, limping in his direction. She looked glowingly well-rested.

She never had difficulty falling asleep, George thought irritably. *She* probably dreamed of roses and rainbows.

"Just the person I'd hoped to find," she said with a smile.

"Words to strike terror in his heart," Andrew drawled.

So true, George thought, although not for the reasons Andrew supposed.

"Stop." Billie scowled at him before turning back to George. "We need you to settle a point."

"If it's who can climb a tree faster, it's Billie," George said without missing a beat. "If it's who can shoot with more accuracy, it's Andrew."

"It's neither," Billie said with a light frown. "It's got to do with Pall Mall."

"Then God help us all," George muttered, getting up and heading for the door. He'd played Pall Mall with his brother and Billie;

it was a vicious, bloodthirsty sport involving wooden balls, heavy mallets, and the constant risk of grievous head injury. Definitely not something for Lady Bridgerton's gentle house party.

"Andrew accused me of cheating," Billie said.

"When?" George asked, honestly perplexed. As far as he knew, the entire morning had been taken up by the ladies' archery tournament. (Billie had won, not that anyone named Rokesby or Bridgerton was surprised.)

"Last April," Billie said.

"And you're arguing about it now?"

"It's the principle of the matter," Andrew said.

George looked at Billie. "Did you cheat?"

"Of course not! I don't need to cheat to beat Andrew. Edward maybe," she allowed with a flick of her eyes, "but not Andrew."

"Uncalled for, Billie," Andrew scolded.

"But true," she returned.

"I'm leaving," George said. Neither was listening, but it seemed only polite to announce his departure. Besides, he wasn't sure it was a good idea for him to be in the same room as Billie just then. His pulse had already begun a slow, inexorable acceleration and he knew he didn't want to be near her when it reached its crescendo.

This way lies ruin, his mind was screaming. Miraculously, his legs didn't put up any resistance, and he made it all the way to the door before Billie said, "Oh, don't go. It's just about to get interesting."

He managed a small but exhausted smile as he turned around. "With you it's always about to get interesting."

"Do you think so?" she asked delightedly.

Andrew gave her a look of pure disbelief. "That wasn't a compliment, Billie."

Billie looked at George.

"I have no idea what it was," he admitted.

Billie just chuckled, then jerked her head toward Andrew. "I'm calling him out."

George knew better—oh, he definitely knew better—but he

couldn't stop himself from turning the rest of the way around to gape at her.

"You're calling me out?" Andrew repeated.

"Mallets at dawn," she said with flair. Then she shrugged. "Or this afternoon. I'd rather avoid getting up early, wouldn't you?"

Andrew raised one brow. "You'd challenge a one-armed man to a game of Pall Mall?"

"I'd challenge *you.*"

He leaned in, blue eyes glittering. "I'll still beat you, you know."

"George!" Billie yelled.

Damn it. He'd almost escaped. "Yes?" he murmured, poking his head back through the doorway.

"We need you."

"No you don't. You need a nanny. You can barely walk."

"I can walk perfectly well." She limped a few steps. "See? I can't even feel it."

George looked at Andrew, not that he expected him to exhibit anything remotely approaching sense.

"I have a broken arm," Andrew said, which George supposed was meant to serve as an explanation. Or an excuse.

"You're idiots. The both of you."

"Idiots who need more players," Billie said. "It doesn't work with only two."

Technically that was true. The Pall Mall set was meant to be played with six, although anything over three would do in a pinch. But George had played this scene before; the rest of them were bit players to Andrew and Billie's tragic, vicious leads. For the two of them, the game was less about winning than it was making sure the other didn't. George was expected merely to move his ball along in their fray.

"You still don't have enough players," George said.

"Georgiana!" Billie yelled.

"Georgiana?" Andrew echoed. "You know your mother doesn't let her play."

"For the love of heaven, she hasn't been ill for years. It's time we stopped coddling her."

Georgiana came skidding around the corner. "Stop bellowing, Billie. You're going to give Mama a palpitation, and then *I'll* have to be the one to deal with her."

"We're playing Pall Mall," Billie told her.

"Oh. That's nice. I'll—" Georgiana's words tumbled to a halt, and her blue eyes went wide. "Wait, I get to play, too?"

"Of course," Billie said, almost dismissively. "You're a Bridgerton."

"Oh, brilliant!" Georgiana practically leapt into the air. "Can I be orange? No, green. I wish to be green."

"Anything you want," Andrew said.

Georgiana turned to George. "Are you playing, as well?"

"I suppose I must."

"Don't sound so resigned," Billie said. "You'll have a splendid time of it. You know you will."

"We still need more players," Andrew said.

"Perhaps Sir Reggie?" Georgiana asked.

"No!" came George's instant reply.

Three heads swiveled in his direction.

In retrospect, he might have been a bit forceful in his objection.

"He doesn't strike me as the sort of gentleman to enjoy such a rough-and-tumble game," George said with a haphazard shrug. He glanced down at his fingernails since he couldn't possibly look anyone in the eye when he said, "His teeth, you know."

"His teeth?" Billie echoed.

George didn't need to see her face to know that she was staring at him as if she were afraid he'd lost his mind.

"I suppose he does have a very elegant smile," Billie said, apparently prepared to concede the point. "And I suppose we did knock out one of Edward's teeth that one summer." She looked over at Andrew. "Do you remember? I think he was six."

"Precisely," George said, although in truth he did not recollect the incident. It must have been a milk tooth; Edward was no Sir Reginald McVie, but as far as George knew, his brother's smile was fully populated.

"We can't ask Mary," Billie went on. "She spent the entire morning hunched over a chamber pot."

"I really didn't need to know that," Andrew said.

Billie ignored him. "And besides, Felix would never permit it."

"Then ask Felix," George suggested.

"That would be unfair to Mary."

Andrew rolled his eyes. "Who cares?"

Billie crossed her arms. "If she can't play, he shouldn't, either."

"Lady Frederica went to the village with her mother and cousin," Georgiana said. "But I saw Lady Alexandra in the drawing room. She didn't seem to be doing anything important."

George was not keen to spend the afternoon listening to more tales of Lord Northwick, but after his vehement refusal of Sir Reginald, he did not think he could reasonably lodge another objection. "Lady Alexandra would make a fine addition to the game," he said diplomatically. "Provided, of course, that she wishes to play."

"Oh, she'll play," Billie said ominously.

Georgiana looked perplexed.

Billie looked at her sister but jerked her head in George's direction. "Tell her that Lord Kennard will be among the players. She'll be here with bells on her toes."

"Oh, for God's sake, Billie," George muttered.

Billie let out a self-righteous huff. "She was talking to you all night!"

"She was sitting next to me," George retorted. "She could hardly have done otherwise."

"Not true. Felix's brother was on her left. He's a perfectly acceptable conversationalist. She could have spoken with him about any number of things."

Andrew stepped between them. "Are the two of you going to snipe like jealous lovers or are we going to play?"

Billie glared.

George glared.

Andrew looked quite pleased with himself.

"You're an idiot," Billie said to him before turning back to Georgiana. "I suppose it will have to be Lady Alexandra. Get her and whomever else you can find. A gentleman if at all possible so we've equal numbers."

Georgiana nodded. "But not Sir Reginald?"

"George is too worried about his teeth."

Andrew made a choking sound.

Which came to a halt when George elbowed him in the ribs.

"Shall I meet you here?" Georgiana asked.

Billie thought for a moment, then said, "No, it will be quicker if we meet you on the west lawn." She turned back to George and Andrew. "I'll see to getting the set pulled out."

She and Georgiana exited the room, leaving George alone with his younger brother.

"His teeth, eh?" Andrew murmured.

George glowered at him.

Andrew leaned in, just far enough to be annoying. "I'd wager he has very good oral hygiene."

"Shut up."

Andrew laughed, then leaned in with what was clearly meant to be an expression of concern. "You've got a little something . . ." He motioned to his teeth.

George rolled his eyes and shoved past him.

Andrew hopped to attention, caught up, and then overtook him, tossing a grin over his shoulder as he loped down the hall. "Ladies do love a dazzling smile."

He was going to kill his brother, George decided as he followed him outside. And he was going to use a mallet.

Chapter 14

Ten minutes later George, Andrew, and Billie were standing on the lawn, watching as a footman plodded toward them, dragging the Pall Mall set behind them.

"I love Pall Mall," Billie announced, rubbing her hands together in the brisk afternoon air. "This is a brilliant idea."

"It was your idea," George pointed out.

"Of course it was," she said merrily. "Oh, look, here comes Georgiana."

George shaded his eyes as he peered across the lawn. Sure enough, she was leading Lady Alexandra in their direction. And, if he wasn't mistaken, one of the Berbrooke brothers.

"Thank you, William," Billie said as the footman brought the set into place.

He nodded. "Milady."

"Wait a moment," Andrew said. "Didn't we break one of the mallets last year?"

"Father commissioned a new set," Billie informed him.

"Same colors?"

She shook her head. "We're not having red this time around."

George turned to look at her. "Why not?"

"Well," she stalled, looking slightly sheepish, "we've had very bad luck with red. The balls keep ending up in the lake."

"And you think a different color might rectify the problem?"

"No," she said, "but I'm hoping yellow will be easier to spot beneath the surface."

A few moments later, Georgiana and her little band of players arrived on the scene. George took an instinctive step toward Billie, but he was too slow. Lady Alexandra had already taken hold of his sleeve.

"Lord Kennard," she said. "What a delight it will be to play Pall Mall. Thank you for inviting me."

"It was Miss Georgiana, actually," he said.

She smiled knowingly. "At your behest, I'm sure."

Billie looked as if she might gag.

"And Lieutenant Rokesby," Lady Alexandra continued, her hand a tight little claw on George's arm even as she turned to Andrew. "We hardly had a chance to speak last night."

Andrew bowed with all due chivalry.

"Are you acquainted with Lord Northwick?" she asked.

George desperately tried to catch his brother's eye. This was not an avenue of conversation any of them wished to pursue.

Luckily for all, the footman had just pulled the cover off the Pall Mall set, and Billie was taking efficient charge.

"Here we are," she said, pulling one of the mallets from its position. "Andrew already promised Georgiana the green, so let's see, Mr. Berbrooke will take blue, Lady Alexandra can have pink, I'll be yellow, Lieutenant Rokesby will be purple, and Lord Kennard will be black."

"Can't I be purple?" Lady Alexandra asked.

Billie looked at her as if she'd asked to have the Magna Carta revised.

"I like purple," Lady Alexandra said coolly.

Billie's back stiffened. "Take it up with Lieutenant Rokesby. It makes no difference to me."

Andrew gave Billie a curious look, then offered his mallet to Lady Alexandra with a gallant bow. "As the lady wishes . . ."

Lady Alexandra nodded graciously.

"Very well," Billie said with a sniff, "Georgiana is green, Mr. Berbrooke is blue, Lieutenant Rokesby is pink, I'm yellow, Lord Kennard is black, and Lady Alexandra is"—she gave her the side eye—"purple."

George was coming to realize that Billie *really* did not like Lady Alexandra.

"I've never played this before," Mr. Berbrooke said. He swung his mallet a few times, narrowly missing George's leg. "It looks like jolly good fun."

"Right," Billie said briskly. "The rules are quite simple. The first person to hit his ball through all the wickets in the correct order wins."

Lady Alexandra looked at the collection of wickets currently hooked onto the set. "How will we know the correct order?"

"Just ask me," Billie said. "Or Lieutenant Rokesby. We've done this a million times."

"Which one of you usually wins?" Mr. Berbrooke asked.

"Me," they both said.

"Neither," George said firmly. "They rarely manage to finish a game. You'd all do well to watch your feet. This may turn vicious."

"I can't wait," Georgiana said, practically thrumming with excitement. She turned to Lady Alexandra. "You've also got to hit the pole at the end. Billie didn't mention that."

"She likes to leave out some of the rules," Andrew said. "So she can penalize you later if you're winning."

"That is not true!" Billie protested. "At least half the times I've beaten you I've done so without cheating."

"Should you ever play Pall Mall again," George advised Lady

Alexandra, "I would ask for a full recitation of the rules and regulations. Nothing you learn here will be the least bit applicable."

"I *have* played before, you know," Lady Alexandra said. "Lord Northwick has a set."

Georgiana turned to her with a puzzled expression. "I thought Lord Northwick was engaged to your sister."

"He is," Lady Alexandra replied.

"Oh. I thought . . ." Georgiana paused, her mouth open for a second or two before she finally settled on, "You speak of him so often."

"He has no sisters of his own," Lady Alexandra said crisply. "Naturally, we have become quite devoted."

"I have a sister," Mr. Berbrooke piped up.

This was met with a beat of silence, and then Georgiana said, "That's wonderful."

"Nellie," he confirmed. "Short for Eleanor. She's very tall."

No one seemed quite to know what to say to that.

"Well then," Andrew said, breaking the now decidedly awkward moment. "It's time to set the wickets out."

"Can't the footman do it?" Lady Alexandra inquired.

Billie and Andrew both turned on her as if she'd gone mad.

George took pity, stepping forward to murmur, "They can be somewhat particular about the placement."

Lady Alexandra's chin rose an inch. "Lord Northwick always says the wickets should be laid out in the shape of a cross."

"Lord Northwick's not here," Billie snapped.

Lady Alexandra gasped.

"Well, he's not," Billie protested, looking to the rest of the group for affirmation.

George narrowed his eyes, the visual translation of an elbow in the ribs, and Billie must have realized that she had crossed a line—an absurd line, but a line nonetheless. She was the hostess, and she needed to behave as such.

It was fascinating to watch, though. Billie was a born competitor, and she had never been known for an abundance of patience. And she certainly was not inclined to acknowledge Lady Alexandra's suggestion. Still, she straightened her shoulders and fixed an almost pleasant smile on her face as she turned back to her guest.

"I think you will like it this way," she said primly. "And if you don't, you can tell Lord Northwick all about it, and then you will know for certain that his layout is superior."

George snorted.

Billie ignored him.

"The wickets," Andrew reminded everyone.

"George and I will do it," Billie said, grabbing them from Andrew's proffered hand.

George looked at her with some indulgence. "Oh we will, will we?"

"Lord Kennard," she said through clenched teeth, "will you be so kind as to help me set out the wickets?"

He glanced down at her injured ankle. "What, you mean because you cannot walk?"

She gave him an over-sweet smile. "Because I delight in your company."

He almost laughed.

"Andrew can't do it," she went on, "and no one else knows where they go."

"If we played in the shape of a cross," Lady Alexandra said to Mr. Berbrooke, "any one of us could set the wickets out."

Mr. Berbrooke nodded.

"We would start at the nave," Lady Alexandra instructed, "then move on to the transept and then the altar."

Mr. Berbrooke looked down at his mallet and frowned. "Doesn't seem like a very churchy game."

"It could be," Lady Alexandra replied.

"But we don't want it to be," Billie said sharply.

George grabbed her arm. "The wickets," he said, pulling her away before the two ladies came to blows.

"I really don't like that woman," she grumbled once they were out of earshot.

"Really?" George murmured. "I would never have known."

"Just help me with the wickets," she said, turning toward a large oak at the edge of the clearing. "Follow me."

He watched her for a few steps. She was still limping, but it was different somehow. More awkward. "Did you hurt yourself again?"

"Hmmm? Oh, that." She let out an irritated snort. "It was the sidesaddle."

"I beg your pardon?"

She shrugged. "I can't put my bad foot in a stirrup. So I had to ride sidesaddle."

"And you needed to ride because . . ."

She looked at him as if he were an idiot. Which he was fairly certain he was not.

"Billie," he said, grabbing her by the wrist so they were both yanked to a halt, "what was so important that you had to ride with an injured ankle?"

"The barley," she said plainly.

He must have misheard. "What?"

"Someone had to make sure it was being planted properly," she said, deftly pulling her hand free.

He was going to kill her. Or rather he *would*, except that she would probably end up doing it herself first. He took a breath, then asked, as patiently as he could, "Isn't that the job of your steward?"

Her brows pulled together. "I don't know what you think I do all day when I'm not flitting away at house parties, but I am an extremely busy person." Something changed in her expression; something George could not quite name, and then she said, "I am a useful person."

"I can't imagine anyone would think otherwise," George said, although he had a feeling he'd thought otherwise, and not too long ago.

"What the devil are you two doing over there?" Andrew bellowed.

"I am going to massacre him," Billie seethed.

"The wickets," George said. "Just tell me where you want them."

Billie separated one from the bunch and held it out. "Over there. Under the tree. But over the root. Make sure you put it over the root. Otherwise it will be too easy."

George very nearly saluted her.

When he returned from his task, she was already a ways down the field, jamming another wicket into place. She'd left the rest in a pile, so he leaned down and scooped them up.

She looked up as she secured the wicket. "What have you against Sir Reginald?"

George gritted his teeth. He should have known he wouldn't get off so easily. "Nothing," he lied. "I simply did not think he would enjoy the game."

She stood. "You can't know that."

"He spent the entire archery competition lounging on a lawn chair and complaining of the heat."

"*You* didn't get up."

"I was enjoying the sun." It hadn't been sunny, but he wasn't about to tell her the real reason he'd been stuck in his chair.

"Very well," Billie acceded, "Sir Reggie is probably not the best candidate for Pall Mall. But I still maintain that we could have done better than Lady Alexandra."

"I agree."

"She—" She blinked. "You do?"

"Of course. I had to spend all last night talking with her, as you so eloquently pointed out."

Billie looked about ready to throw her arms up in frustration. "Then why didn't you say something when Georgiana suggested her?"

"She's not evil, merely annoying."

Billie muttered something under her breath.

George could not stem the amused smile that spread across his face. "You really don't like her, do you?"

"I really don't."

He chuckled.

"Stop that."

"Laughing, you mean?"

She jammed a wicket into the ground. "You're just as bad as I am. One would think Sir Reggie had committed treason with the way you were carrying on."

Carrying on? George planted his hands on his hips. "That's entirely different."

She glanced up from her work. "How is that?"

"He is a buffoon."

Billie snorted out a laugh. It was not particularly feminine, but on her it was charming. She leaned toward him, her expression pure dare. "I think you're jealous."

George felt his stomach flip. Surely she didn't realize . . . *No.* These thoughts he'd been having about her . . . temporary madness. Brought on by proximity. That had to be it. He'd spent more time with her in the past week than he had in years. "Don't be ridiculous," he said scornfully.

"I don't know," Billie teased. "All the ladies are flocking to his side. You said yourself he has a handsome smile."

"I *said*," George bit out before realizing he didn't remember precisely what he'd said. Luckily for him, Billie had already interrupted him.

"The only lady who hasn't fallen under his spell is the illustrious Lady Alexandra." She tossed him a look over her shoulder. "Probably because she's so busy trying to gain *your* favor."

"Are *you* jealous?" he countered.

"Please," she scoffed, moving on to the next spot.

He followed, one step behind. "You didn't say no . . ."

"*No*," she said with great emphasis. "Of course I'm not jealous. I think she's touched in the head quite honestly."

"Because she's trying to gain my favor?" he could not help but ask.

She held her hand out for another wicket. "Of course not. That's probably the most sensible thing she's ever done."

He paused. "Why does that sound like an insult?"

"It's not," Billie assured him. "I would never be so ambiguous."

"No, that's true," he murmured. "You insult with pure transparency."

She rolled her eyes before returning to the topic of Lady Alexandra. "I was talking about her obsession with Lord Northwick. He's engaged to her sister, for heaven's sake."

"Ah, that."

"Ah, that," she mimicked, shoving another wicket into the ground. "*What* is wrong with her?"

George was saved from answering by Andrew, who was bellowing their names again, along with a rather vehement exhortation to hurry along.

Billie snorted. "I can't believe he thinks he can beat me with a broken arm."

"You do realize that if you win—"

"When I win."

"*Should* you win, you will look the worst sort of champion, taking advantage of the weakness of others."

She looked at him with wide, innocent eyes. "I can barely walk myself."

"You, Miss Bridgerton, have a convenient grasp on reality."

She grinned. "Convenient for me, yes."

He shook his head, smiling despite himself.

"Now then," she said, lowering her voice even though no one was within earshot, "you're on my team, are you not?"

George narrowed his eyes. "Since when are there teams?"

"Since today." She leaned closer. "We must *crush* Andrew."

"You're beginning to frighten me, Billie."

"Don't be silly, you're just as competitive as I am."

"Do you know, I don't think I am."

"Of course you are. You just show it differently."

He thought she might elucidate, but of course she did not.

"You don't want Andrew to win, do you?" she asked.

"I'm not certain how much I care."

She drew back.

He laughed. He couldn't help it. She looked so affronted. "No, of course I don't want him to win," he said. "He's my brother. But at the same time, I'm not sure I feel the need to resort to espionage to ensure the outcome."

She stared at him with heavy, disappointed eyes.

"Oh, fine," he gave in. "Who's on Andrew's team, then?"

She brightened up immediately. "No one. That's the beauty of it. He won't know that we've formed an alliance."

"There is no way this ends well," he said, sending the words out to the world at large.

He was fairly certain the world was not listening.

Billie set the last wicket into place. "This one's evil," she told him. "Overshoot and you're in the rosebushes."

"I shall take that under advisement."

"Do." She smiled, and his breath caught. No one smiled like Billie. No one ever had. He'd known this for years and yet . . . it was only now . . .

He indulged in a mental curse. This had to be the most inconvenient attraction in the history of man. *Billie Bridgerton*, for God's sake. She was everything he'd never wanted in a woman. She was headstrong, stupidly reckless, and if she'd ever had a mysterious, feminine moment in her life, he'd never seen it.

And yet . . .

He swallowed.

He wanted her. He wanted her like he'd never wanted anything in his life. He wanted her smile, and he wanted it exclusively. He wanted her in his arms, beneath his body . . . because somehow he knew that in his bed, she would be everything mysterious and feminine.

He also knew that every single one of these delightful activities required that he marry her, which was so patently ludicrous that—

"Oh, for God's sake," Billie muttered.

George snapped back to attention.

"Andrew's coming over," she said. "Hold your horses!" she bellowed. "I swear," she said to George, "he is so impatient."

"Said the—"

"*Don't* call me a kettle." She started marching back to the beginning of the course. As best as she could; she really did look ridiculous with her two-part limp.

He waited for a moment, grinning at her back. "Are you sure you don't want the black mallet?"

"I hate you!" she called.

He couldn't help but smile. It was quite the merriest declaration of hate he'd ever heard.

"I hate you, too," he murmured.

But he didn't mean it, either.

Chapter 15

Billie was humming quite happily by the time she reached the beginning of the Pall Mall course. She was in a remarkably cheerful mood, all things considered. Andrew was still being abominably impatient, and Lady Alexandra was still the most awful person in the history of the world, but none of that seemed to matter.

She peeked over her shoulder at George. He'd been following her the whole way, trading insults with a wolfish smile.

"What are you so happy about?" Andrew demanded.

She smiled enigmatically. Let him stew for a bit. Besides, she wasn't sure *why* she was so happy. She just was.

"Who plays first?" Lady Alexandra asked.

Billie opened her mouth to reply, but Andrew beat her to it.

"We usually play youngest to oldest," he said, "but it does seem somewhat rude to inquire . . ."

"I am certainly first, then," Georgiana announced, plopping the green ball down near the starting stick. "No question about it."

"I should think I am second," Lady Alexandra said, sending a pitying glance over at Billie.

Billie ignored her. "Mr. Berbrooke, might we inquire as to your age?"

"What? Oh, I'm twenty-five." He smiled broadly. He did that a lot. "Quarter of a century, you know."

"Very well, then," Billie said, "the order of play shall be Georgiana, Lady Alexandra . . . *we assume*, Andrew, me, Mr. Berbrooke, and George."

"Don't you mean Lord Kennard?" Lady Alexandra asked.

"No, I'm quite sure I mean George," Billie snipped. Good God but that woman grated on her.

"I rather like playing with the black ball," George said, smoothly changing the subject. But Billie had been watching him; she couldn't be positive, but she *thought* she'd seen him hiding a smile.

Good.

"It's a very manly color," Lady Alexandra confirmed.

Billie nearly gagged.

"It's the color of death," Andrew said, rolling his eyes.

"The Mallet of Death," George said thoughtfully. He swung it back and forth a few times, like a macabre pendulum. "It has quite a ring to it."

Andrew snorted.

"You laugh," George dared, "but you know you want it."

Billie rang out with laughter that only grew in volume when Andrew leveled a peevish glare in her direction. "Oh, come now, Andrew, you know it's the truth," she said.

Georgiana looked up from her position at the starting pole. "Who would want the Mallet of Peonies and Petunias when one could have the Mallet of Death?" she put in, tipping her head toward Andrew's pink equipment.

Billie smiled approvingly. When had her sister got so witty?

"My peonies and petunias shall triumph," Andrew said with a wiggle of his brows. "Just you watch."

"Your peonies and petunias are missing a vital petal," Billie countered, motioning toward his injured arm.

"I don't think I know what we're talking about," Mr. Berbrooke admitted.

"It's just silly fun," Georgiana told him as she readied for her first swing. "Billie and Andrew love to tease one another. They always have." She gave her ball a whack, and it shot through the two starting wickets. It didn't go much farther but she didn't seem to mind.

Lady Alexandra stepped up, setting her ball into place. "Lieutenant Rokesby plays after me, yes?" she confirmed. She glanced up at Billie with a deceptively placid expression. "I did not realize that you were older than he is, Miss Bridgerton."

"I am older than a great many people," Billie said coolly.

Lady Alexandra sniffed and slammed her mallet against her ball, sending it hurtling across the lawn.

"Well done!" Mr. Berbrooke cheered. "I say, you *have* played this before."

Lady Alexandra smiled modestly. "As I mentioned, Lord Northwick has a set."

"And he plays in the shape of a holy cross," Billie said under her breath.

George elbowed her.

"My turn," Andrew announced.

"Petunias ahoy!" Billie said jauntily.

Beside her she heard George chuckle. It was ridiculously satisfying, making him laugh.

Andrew ignored her completely. He dropped the pink ball, then nudged it into place with his foot.

"I still don't understand how you're going to play with a broken arm," Georgiana said.

"Watch and learn, my dear girl," he murmured. And then, after several practice swings—one of which included a full three-hundred-and-sixty-degree rotation—he whacked his ball rather impressively through the starting wickets and across the lawn.

"Almost as far as Lady Alexandra," Georgiana said admiringly.

"I do have a broken arm," he demurred.

Billie walked to the starting spot and set down her ball. "How did that happen again?" she asked innocently.

"Shark attack," he said without missing a beat.

"No!" Lady Alexandra gasped.

"A shark?" Mr. Berbrooke said. "Isn't that one of those toothy fish things?"

"Extremely toothy," Andrew confirmed.

"I shouldn't like to come across one myself," Mr. Berbrooke said.

"Has Lord Northwick ever been bitten by a shark?" Billie asked sweetly.

George made a choking sound.

Lady Alexandra's eyes narrowed. "I can't say that he has."

"Pity." Billie smacked her mallet against her ball with thundering force. It went flying across the lawn, well past the others.

"Well done!" Mr. Berbrooke again exclaimed. "Jolly good at this, you are, Miss Bridgerton."

It was impossible to remain unmoved in the face of his relentless good cheer. Billie offered him a friendly smile as she said, "I've played quite a bit over the years."

"She often cheats," Andrew said in passing.

"Only with you."

"I suppose I'd better have a go," Mr. Berbrooke said, crouching down to set the blue ball next to the starting pole.

George took a cautionary step back.

Mr. Berbrooke frowned down at the ball, testing out his mallet a few times before finally swinging. The ball went flying, but unfortunately so did one of the wickets.

"Oh! Terribly sorry," he said.

"It's no trouble," Georgiana said. "We can put it back into place."

The course was reset, and George took his turn. His black ball ended up somewhere between Lady Alexandra and Billie.

"Mallet of Death indeed," Andrew mocked.

"It's a strategic sort of assassination," George replied with an enigmatic smile. "I'm taking the longitudinal view."

"My turn!" Georgiana called out. She didn't have far to walk to reach her ball. This time she hit it much harder, and it went sailing across the field toward the next wicket, stopping about five yards short of its destination.

"Well done!" Mr. Berbrooke exclaimed.

Georgiana beamed. "Thank you. I do believe I might be getting the hang of this."

"By the end of the game you shall be trouncing us all," he pronounced.

Lady Alexandra was already in place near the purple ball. She took nearly a minute to adjust her aim, then gave it a careful tap. The ball rolled forward, stopping directly in front of the wicket.

Billie made a noise deep in her throat. Lady Alexandra was actually quite skilled.

"Did you just growl?" George asked.

She nearly jumped. She hadn't realized he was so close. He was standing almost right behind her, and she could not see him unless she turned her head away from the play.

But she could feel him. He might not be touching her, but he was so close . . . Her skin tingled, and she could feel her heart beating, low and insistent in her chest.

"I have to ask," he said, his voice intoxicatingly close to her ear, "how exactly are we meant to work as a team?"

"I'm not sure," Billie admitted, watching Andrew take his turn. "I expect that it will become obvious as we go along."

"Your turn, Billie!" Andrew yelled.

"Excuse me," Billie said to George, suddenly eager to put some space between them. She felt almost light-headed when he was standing so close.

"What are you going to do, Billie?" Georgiana asked as she approached the ball.

Billie frowned. She wasn't far from the wicket, but Lady Alexandra's purple ball was squarely in her way.

"A difficult shot," Andrew said.

"Shut up."

"You could use blunt force." He looked up at the crowd. "Her usual *modus operandi*." His voice dropped to a confidential undertone. "In Pall Mall and in life."

Billie briefly considered giving up the game right then and there and slamming the ball toward his feet.

"Wouldn't that put Lady Alexandra through the wicket?" Georgiana asked.

Andrew shrugged as if to say—*C'est la vie.*

Billie focused on her ball.

"Or she could be patient," Andrew continued, "and queue up for the wicket after Lady Alexandra. But we all know that's not like her."

Billie made a noise. This time it was definitely a growl.

"A third option—"

"Andrew!" she ground out.

He grinned.

Billie lined up her mallet. There was no way to get through the wicket without knocking Lady Alexandra through, but if she edged it on the side . . .

She let fly.

Billie's yellow ball careened toward the wicket and smacked the purple one left of center. They all watched as Lady Alexandra's ball rolled to the right, settling into position at such an angle that she couldn't possibly hope to make it through the wicket on the next turn.

Billie's ball now sat almost precisely where Lady Alexandra's had been.

"You did that on purpose!" Lady Alexandra accused.

"Of course I did." Billie looked at her disparagingly. Honestly, what had she expected? "That's how one plays."

"That's not how *I* play."

"Well, we're not on a cross," Billie snapped, losing patience. Gad, the woman was awful.

Someone made a choking sound.

"What is that supposed to mean?" Lady Alexandra demanded.

"I think," Mr. Berbrooke said thoughtfully, "that she means that she would play more piously if the game were a religious endeavor. Which I don't think it is."

Billie gave him an approving glance. Maybe he was cleverer than he seemed.

"Lord Kennard," Lady Alexandra said, turning to George. "Surely you do not approve of such underhanded tactics."

George gave a shrug. "It's how they play, I'm afraid."

"But not how *you* play," Lady Alexandra persisted.

Billie gave him a stare, waiting for his answer.

He did not disappoint. "It's how I play when I play with them."

Lady Alexandra drew back with a huff.

"Don't worry," Georgiana said, jumping into the breach. "You'll get the hang of it."

"It's not in my nature," Lady Alexandra sniffed.

"It's in everyone's nature," Andrew barked. "Whose turn is it?"

Mr. Berbrooke gave a jump. "Oh, mine I think." He walked back to his ball. "Am I allowed to aim for Miss Bridgerton?"

"Absolutely," Andrew replied, "but you might want to—"

Mr. Berbrooke whacked his ball without waiting for the rest of Andrew's instructions, which surely would have been *not* to hit her ball dead-on, which was exactly what he did.

The yellow ball went through the wicket and beyond, making it an additional three feet before coming to a stop. The blue ball also rolled through the wicket, but, having transferred its force to the yellow ball, it came to a stop only directly on the other side.

"Well done, Mr. Berbrooke!" Billie cheered.

He turned to her with a wide smile. "Thank you!"

"Oh for heaven's sake," Lady Alexandra snapped. "She doesn't mean it. She's only happy you knocked *her* through the wicket."

"I take everything back," Billie murmured to George. "Forget Andrew. It's *her* we must crush."

Mr. Berbrooke appealed to the rest of the crowd. "Miss Bridgerton would have gone through on the next turn, anyway, wouldn't she?"

"I would," Billie confirmed. "You really didn't set me too far ahead, I promise."

"And you got yourself through the wicket," Georgiana added. "That puts you in second place."

"It does, doesn't it?" Mr. Berbrooke said, looking inordinately pleased with this development.

"*And*," Billie added with great flair, "look how you're blocking everyone else. Well done, you."

Lady Alexandra let out a loud huff. "Whose turn is it?"

"Minc, I believe," George said smoothly.

Billie smiled to herself. She loved the way he said so much with nothing but a polite murmur. Lady Alexandra would hear a gentleman making a casual comment, but Billie knew him better. She knew him better than that pompous duke's daughter ever would.

She heard his smile. He was amused by the entire exchange, even if he was too well-bred to show it.

She heard his salute. Billie had won this round; he was congratulating her.

And she heard his gentle scolding, a warning of sorts. He was cautioning her not to carry this too far.

Which she probably would. He knew her every bit as well as she knew him.

"Take your turn, George," Andrew said.

Billie watched as George stepped forward and set up his play. He squinted as he aimed. It was kind of adorable.

What a thought. George Rokesby, adorable? It was just the most ridiculous thing.

She let out a little chuckle, just as George hit his ball. It was a good shot, landing him directly in front of the wicket.

"Oh, my goodness," Georgiana said, blinking at the field. "Now we'll never get through."

She was right. The black and blue balls were mere inches apart, flanking both sides of the wicket. Anyone who attempted the wicket would just add to the jam.

George stepped back toward Billie, clearing the way for the next few players. He leaned toward her, his mouth drawing close to her ear. "Were you laughing at me?" he murmured.

"Just a little bit," she replied, watching Georgiana trying to figure out her shot.

"Why?"

Her lips parted before she realized she couldn't possibly give him an honest reply. She turned to look at him, and again he was closer than she'd expected, closer than he ought to have dared.

She was suddenly *aware*.

Of his breath, warm across her skin.

Of his eyes, so blue and so magnetically fastened upon her own.

Of his lips, fine, full, and carrying a hint of a smile.

Of *him*. Simply of him.

She whispered his name.

He cocked his head to the side in question, and she realized she had no idea why she'd beckoned, just that there was something so right about standing here with him, and when he looked at her like that, like he thought she was remarkable, she *felt* remarkable.

She felt beautiful.

She knew it couldn't be true, because he'd never thought of her that way. And she didn't want him to.

Or did she?

She gasped.

"Something wrong?" he murmured.

She shook her head. *Everything* was wrong.

"Billie?"

She wanted to kiss him. She wanted to kiss *George*. She'd reached the age of three-and-twenty without wanting to even so much as flirt with a gentleman and now she wanted George *Rokesby*?

Oh, this was wrong. This was very, very wrong. This was panic-inducing, world-flipping, heart-stopping wrong.

"Billie, is something wrong?"

She snapped to attention, then remembered to breathe. "Nothing," she said, rather too brightly. "Nothing at all."

But what would he do? How would he react if she marched up to him, grabbed him by the back of his head, and dragged his mouth down to hers?

He'd tell her she was raving mad, that's what he'd do. To say nothing of the four other Pall Mall players not twenty yards away.

But what if no one else were here? What if the rest of the world fell away, and there was no one to witness her insanity? Would she do it?

And would he kiss her back?

"Billie? *Billie?*"

She turned, dazed, toward the sound of his voice.

"Billie, what is wrong with you?"

She blinked, bringing his face into focus. He looked concerned. She almost laughed. He ought to be concerned.

"Billie . . ."

"I'm fine," she said quickly. "Really. It's . . . ah . . . are you warm?" She fanned herself with her hand. "I'm very warm."

He didn't answer. He didn't need to. It wasn't the least bit warm.

"I think it's my turn!" she blurted.

She had no idea if it was her turn.

"No," George said, "Andrew's still going. I daresay Lady Alexandra is in for trouble."

"Is she," she murmured, her thoughts still on her imaginary kiss.

"Damn it, Billie, now I know something is wrong." He scowled. "I thought you wanted to crush her."

"I do," she said, slowly regaining possession of her brain. Dear heavens, she could not let herself get so discomfited. George wasn't stupid. If she descended into idiocy every time he looked at her he was going to realize that something was amiss. And if he realized that she might possibly be just a little bit *infatuated* . . .

No. He could never know.

"Your turn, Billie!" Andrew bellowed.

"Right," she said. "Right, right, right." She looked over at George without actually looking at him. "Excuse me." She hurried over to her ball, gave the field a cursory examination, and whacked it toward the next wicket.

"I do believe you've overshot," Lady Alexandra said, sidling up next to her.

Billie forced a smile, trying to look enigmatic.

"Watch out!" someone yelled.

She jumped back just before the blue ball slammed into her toes. Lady Alexandra was equally nimble, and they both watched as Mr. Berbrooke's ball settled a few feet away from the wicket.

"I suppose it would serve us both right if that idiot won the game," Lady Alexandra said.

Billie stared at her in surprise. It was one thing to trade insults with her; she could certainly give as good as she got. But to disparage Mr. Berbrooke, who was quite possibly the most genial man she'd ever met . . .

Honestly, the woman was a monster.

Billie glanced back up the course. The purple ball was still firmly fixed behind the first wicket. "It's almost your turn," she said sweetly.

Lady Alexandra narrowed her eyes and made a surprisingly unpleasant sound before stalking off.

"What did you say to her?" George asked a moment later. He'd just taken his turn and was presently well-situated to take the second wicket.

"She is a terrible person," Billie muttered.

"Not what I asked," George said, glancing back at the lady in question, "but probably answer enough."

"She— Oh, never mind." Billie gave her head a shake. "She's not worth my breath."

"Certainly not," George agreed.

Billie's heart did a flip at the compliment, and she turned. "George, have you—" She frowned, cocking her head to the side. "Is that Felix coming toward us?"

George shaded his eyes as he peered in the direction she was pointing. "I believe so, yes."

"He's moving very quickly. I hope nothing is amiss."

They watched as Felix approached Andrew, who was closer than they were to the house. They spoke for a few moments and then Andrew took off at a full sprint.

"Something's wrong," George said. Mallet still in hand, he started walking toward Felix, picking up speed with every step.

Billie hurried after him as best she could, half-limping, half-hopping, the rest of their Pall Mall equipment forgotten on the lawn. Frustrated with her lack of speed, she hiked up her skirts and just ran, pain be damned. She caught up with George moments after he reached Felix.

"There was a messenger," Felix was saying.

George's eyes searched his face. "Edward?"

Billie's hand flew to her mouth. *Not Edward. Oh, please, not Edward.*

Felix nodded grimly. "He's gone missing."

Chapter 16

George was already halfway to Aubrey Hall before he realized that Billie was scurrying alongside him, forced to run just to keep up with his long, swift stride.

Running. She was running.

On her ankle.

He stopped short. "What are you—"

But then it occurred to him, without even pausing for thought. This was Billie. Of course she was going to run on her injured ankle. She was headstrong. She was reckless.

She *cared*.

He did not say another word. He simply scooped her into his arms and continued on toward the house, his pace only fractionally slower than before.

"You didn't have to carry me," she said.

He heard the pain in her voice. "Yes," he said. "I did."

"Thank you," she whispered, her words melting into his shirt.

But he couldn't respond. He was beyond words now, at least beyond meaningless platitudes. He didn't need to say anything for Billie to know that he'd heard her. She would understand. She would know that his head was somewhere else, somewhere far beyond *please* and *you're welcome*.

"They're in the private drawing room," Felix said when they reached the house. George could only assume that *they* meant the rest of his family. And maybe the Bridgertons, as well.

They were family, too, he realized. They'd always been family.

When he reached the drawing room, the sight that awaited him was one to make any grown man blanch. His mother was on the sofa, sobbing in Lady Bridgerton's arms. Andrew looked to be in shock. And his father . . .

His father was crying.

Lord Manston stood removed from the rest of the group, not quite facing them but not turned entirely away. His arms were sticks at his sides, and his eyes were squeezed tightly shut, as if that might possibly halt the slow trickle of tears down his cheeks. As if maybe, if he could not see the world around him, then none of this would have happened.

George had never seen his father cry. He had not imagined it even possible. He tried not to stare, but the sight was so stunning, so soul-altering, that he could not quite look away.

His father was The Earl of Manston, solid and stern. Since George was a child he had led the Rokesby family with a firm but fair hand. He was a pillar; he was strength. He was unquestionably in charge. He treated his children with scrupulous fairness, which occasionally meant that no one was satisfied with his judgments, but he was always obeyed.

In his father George saw what it meant to lead a family. And in his father's tears, he saw his own future.

Soon, it would be time for George to lead.

"Dear heavens," Lady Bridgerton exclaimed, finally noticing them in the doorway. "What happened to Billie?"

George just stared for a moment. He'd forgotten he was holding her. "Here," he said, setting Billie down near her mother. He looked around the room. He didn't know to whom he should apply for information. Where was the messenger? Was he even still here?

"George," he heard Felix say. He looked up and saw his friend holding out a sheet of paper. Wordlessly, he took it.

To the Earl of Manston,
I regret to inform you that Captain the Hon. Edward Rokesby went missing on 22 March 1779 in Connecticut Colony. We are making every effort to recover him safely.
God bless and Godspeed,
Brigadier General Geo. Garth

"Missing," George said, looking helplessly around the room. "What does that even mean?"

No one had an answer.

George stared down at the paper in his hands, his eyes taking in every last loop of the script. The message was spectacular in its lack of information. Why was Edward in Connecticut Colony? The last they'd heard he was in New York Town, boarded at a loyalist tavern while keeping an eye on General Washington's troops across the Hudson River.

"If he's missing . . ." he said, thinking out loud. "They have to know."

"Know what?" Billie asked. She was looking up at him from her position on the sofa, probably the only person close enough to hear his words.

He shook his head, still trying to make sense of it. From the (admittedly sparse) wording of the missive, it seemed that the army was certain that Edward was still alive. Which meant that the general had at least some idea where he was.

If that were the case, why didn't he just say so?

George raked his fingers through his hair, the ball of his hand rubbing hard against his forehead. "How can a decorated soldier go missing?" he asked, turning back to the rest of the room. "Was he kidnapped? Is that what they are trying to tell us?"

"I'm not sure they know," Felix said quietly.

"Oh, they bloody well know," George nearly spat. "They just don't want—"

But Andrew cut him off. "It's not like here," he said, his voice hollow and dull.

George shot him an irritated glance. "I know, but what—"

"It's not like here," Andrew said again, this time with rising anger. "The villages arc far apart. The farms don't even border each other. There are giant swaths of land that nobody owns."

Everyone stared at him.

George stepped closer, trying to block his mother's view of Andrew's tortured face. "This is not the time," he said in a harsh whisper. His brother might be in shock, but so were they all. It was time for Andrew to grow up and bloody well take hold of his emotions before he shattered what little composure remained in the room.

But Andrew's tongue remained loose and indiscreet. "It would be easy to go missing there."

"You haven't been there," George snapped.

"I've heard."

"You've *heard*."

"Stop," someone said. "Stop it now."

The two men were now nearly nose to nose.

"There are men on my ship who fought in the colonies," Andrew bit off.

"Oh, and *that's* going to help us recover Edward," George practically spat.

"I know more about it than you do."

George nearly flinched. He hated this. He hated this so much. The impotence. The worthlessness. He'd been outside playing bloody Pall Mall and his brother was missing in some godforsaken colonial wilderness.

"I am still your older brother," he hissed, "and I will be head of this family—"

"Well, you're not now."

He might as well have been. George cast a fleeting glance at his father, who had not said a word.

"Oh, that was subtle," Andrew jeered.

"Shut up. Just shut—"

"Stop!" Hands came between them and forcibly pushed them apart, and when George finally looked down he realized they belonged to Billie.

"This isn't helping," she said, practically shoving Andrew into a chair.

George blinked, trying to regain his equilibrium. He didn't know why he was yelling at Andrew. He looked at Billie, still standing between them like a tiny warrior. "You shouldn't be on that foot," he said.

Her mouth fell open. "*That's* what you want to say?"

"You've probably reinjured it."

She stared at him. George knew he sounded a fool, but her ankle was the one bloody thing he actually could do something about.

"You should sit down," she said softly.

He shook his head. He didn't want to sit down. He wanted to act, to *do* something, anything that might bring his brother safely home. But he was tied here, he'd always been tied here, to this land, to these people.

"I can go," Andrew choked out.

They all turned to look at him. He was still in the chair that Billie had forced him into. He looked terrible. Thunderstruck. Andrew looked, George had a feeling, rather like he himself felt.

But with one massive difference. Andrew at least believed that he could help.

"Go where?" someone finally asked.

"To the colonies." Andrew looked up, the bleak desperation in his face slowly giving way to hard determination. "I will ask to be assigned to a different ship. There's probably one leaving in the next month."

"No," Lady Manston cried. She sounded like a wounded animal. She sounded like nothing George had ever heard.

Andrew rose to his feet. "Mother—"

"No," she said again, this time with fortitude as she pulled herself from Lady Bridgerton's comforting arms. "I will not permit it. I won't lose another son."

Andrew stood stiffly, looking more like a soldier than George had ever seen him. "It's no more dangerous than serving where I do now."

George closed his eyes. *Wrong thing to say, Andrew.*

"You can't," Lady Manston said, struggling to her feet. "You can't."

Her voice began to break again, and George silently cursed Andrew for his lack of tact. He stepped forward. "Mother . . ."

"He can't," she choked out, her tortured eyes coming to rest on George's face. "You must tell him . . . he can't."

George pulled his mother into his arms, meeting Andrew's eyes over her head before murmuring, "We can discuss it later."

"You're just saying that."

"I think you should lie down."

"We should go home," Lord Manston said.

They all turned. It was the first he had spoken since the terrible message had been delivered.

"We need to be at home," he said.

It was Billie who sprang into action. "Of course," she said, going quickly to his side. "You will be more comfortable there." She looked over at George. "The last thing you need is this house party."

George nearly groaned. He'd forgot all about the other guests. The thought of having to actually converse with any of them was excruciating. There would be questions, and condolences, never mind that none of them knew the first thing about Edward.

God, it was all so insignificant. This. The party. Everything but the people in this room.

He looked at Billie. She was still watching him, concern evident in every line of her face. "Has anyone told Mary?" she asked.

"I will do so now," Felix said. "We will join you at Crake, if that suits. I'm sure she will wish to be with her family. We have no need to go back to Sussex immediately."

"What will we do?" Lady Manston said in a lost voice.

George looked to his father. It was his right to decide.

But the earl looked lost. He'd said they should go home; apparently that was all he could manage.

George turned back to the rest of the room and took a breath. "We will take a moment," he said firmly. "We will pause to collect ourselves and decide how best to proceed."

Andrew opened his mouth to speak, but George had had enough. With a hard stare, he added, "Time is of the essence, but we are too far removed from the military theater for one day to make a difference."

"He's right," Billie said.

Several pairs of eyes turned to her in surprise, George's included.

"None of us is in a state to make a proper decision just now." She turned to George. "Go home. Be with your family. I will call tomorrow to see how I may help."

"But what can you do?" Lady Bridgerton asked.

Billie looked at her with quiet, steely grace. "Anything that is required."

George swallowed, surprised by the rush of emotion behind his eyes. His brother was missing; his father was shattered, and *now* he thought he might cry?

He ought to tell her that they did not need help, that her offer was appreciated but unnecessary.

That was the polite thing to do. It was what he would have said, to anyone else.

But to Billie he said, "Thank you."

Billie drove herself to Crake House the following day, taking a simple one-horse buggy. She wasn't sure how her mother had managed it, but the house party had been cut short by several days, and everyone had either left or was planning to do so by the following morning.

It had taken her a ridiculous amount of time to decide what to wear. Breeches were most certainly out. Despite what her mother thought, Billie did know how and when to dress appropriately, and she would never don her work clothes for a social call.

But this was no ordinary social call. Bright colors would not do. But she could not wear black. Or lavender or gray or anything that even hinted of mourning. Edward was *not* dead, she told herself fiercely.

In the end she settled on a comfortable day dress she'd got the year before. Her mother had picked out the pattern—a spring-like floral with greens and pinks and oranges set against cream muslin—but Billie had loved it from the first. It made her think of a garden on a cloudy day, which somehow seemed exactly right for calling upon the Rokesbys.

Crake was quiet when she arrived. It felt wrong. It was an enormous house; like Aubrey Hall, one could theoretically go days without seeing another member of the family. But even so, it always seemed vibrant, alive. Some Rokesby or another was always about, ever happy, ever busy.

Crake House was huge, but it was a home.

Right now, however, it felt subdued. Even the servants, who normally worked with diligence and discretion, were quieter than usual. No one smiled, no one spoke.

It was almost heartbreaking.

Billie was directed to the sitting room, but before she exited the hall George appeared, obviously having been alerted to her arrival.

"Billie," he said, bowing his head in greeting. "It is good to see you."

Her first impulse was to ask if there had been any news, but of course there would not be. There would be no swift rider, down from London with a report. Edward was far too far away. It would likely be months before they learned his fate.

"How is your mother?" she asked.

He smiled sadly. "As well as can be expected."

Billie nodded, following him into the sitting room. "And your father?"

George paused, but he did not turn to face her. "He sits in his study and stares out the window."

Billie swallowed, her heart breaking at George's bleak posture. She did not need to see his face to know his pain. He loved Edward, just as she did. Just as they all did.

"He is useless," George said.

Billie's lips parted in surprise at such harsh words, but then she realized that George had not meant them as scorn.

"He is incapacitated," he clarified. "The grief . . ."

"I don't think any of us knows how we will react to a crisis until we are forced into one."

He turned, one corner of his mouth tipping up. "When did you grow so wise?"

"It isn't wisdom to repeat platitudes."

"It is wisdom to know which ones bear repeating."

To her great surprise, Billie felt a bubble of humor rising within. "You are determined to compliment me."

"It's the only bloody bright spot in the day," George muttered.

It was the sort of comment that would normally make her heart leap, but like the rest of them, she was too blunted by pain and worry. Edward was missing, and George was hurting—

She took a breath. This wasn't about George. George was *fine*. He was here, right in front of her, healthy and hale.

No, this wasn't about George.

It couldn't be about George.

Except . . . lately it seemed as if everything was about George. She thought about him constantly, and heaven above, was it just the day before that they'd been playing Pall Mall and she'd practically *kissed* him?

She'd wanted to. Dear God, she'd wanted to, and if he'd shown any interest—and if there hadn't been four other people milling about with Pall Mall mallets—she'd have done it. She'd never kissed anyone before, but when had that ever stopped her? She'd jumped her first fence when she was six. She'd never so much as jumped a shrub before that, but she'd taken one look at that five-foot fence and known that she had to take it. So she'd just hopped on her mare, and she'd done it. Because she'd wanted to.

And also because Edward had dared her. But she wouldn't have tried it if she hadn't thought she could do it.

And known she would love it.

She'd known even then that she wasn't like other girls. She didn't want to play the pianoforte or pick at her sewing. She wanted to be outside, to fly through the air on the back of her horse, sunlight dancing across her skin as her heart skipped and raced with the wind.

She wanted to soar.

She still did.

If she kissed George . . . if he kissed her . . . would it feel the same way?

She trailed her fingers along the back of the sofa, trying to fill the moment with idle movement. But then she made the mistake of looking up . . .

He was staring at her, his eyes fierce and curious and something else, too, something she could not precisely name.

But whatever it was . . . she felt it. Her heart leapt, and her breath quickened, and she realized it was just like when she raced on her mare. Breathless and giddy and determined and wild . . . It was all there within her, bursting to get free.

All because he'd looked at her.

Dear God, if he actually *kissed* her she might fall apart.

She tapped nervous fingers on the edge of the sofa, then gestured stupidly to a chair. "I should sit."

"If you wish."

But her feet wouldn't move. "I seem not to know what to do with myself," she admitted.

"Join the club," he muttered.

"Oh, George . . ."

"Do you want a drink?" he asked suddenly.

"Now?" It was barely past eleven.

His shrug bordered on insolence. Billie could only wonder at how much he'd already had.

But he didn't head for the brandy decanter. Instead he stood by the window, staring out over the garden. It had started to rain; a light misty drizzle that made the air thick and gray.

She waited for several moments, but he did not turn around. His hands were clasped behind his back—the classic stance of a gentleman. But it wasn't quite right. There was a certain harshness to his pose, a tension in his shoulders that she wasn't used to seeing there.

He was brittle. Bleak.

"What will you do?" she finally forced herself to ask. She did not think she could bear the silence for another moment.

His posture changed, a slight movement in his neck maybe, and then he turned his head to the side. But not far enough to actually look at her. Instead she was treated to his profile as he said, "Go to London, I suppose."

"To London?" she echoed.

He snorted. "There's not much else I can do."

"You don't want to go to the Colonies to look for him?"

"Of course I want to go to the Colonies," he snapped, whirling around to face her. "But that's not what I *do.*"

Billie's lips parted, but the only sound was her pulse, racing wildly through her veins. His outburst was unexpected. Unprecedented.

She had seen George lose his temper before. She could hardly have grown up alongside his younger brothers and *not* have done so. But she had never seen *this.*

There was no missing the contempt in his voice, nor the fact that it was directed entirely within.

"George," she said, trying to keep her voice calm and reasonable, "if you want to—"

He stepped forward, his eyes hard and furious. "Don't tell me I can do what I want because if you believe that, you're just as naïve as the rest of them."

"I wasn't going to—" But it was just as well that he cut her off with a mocking snort, because that was exactly what she had been about to say, and it was only now that she realized how ludicrous it would have been. He couldn't take off and go to the Colonies; they all knew that.

He would never be as free as his brothers. The order of their birth had ensured that. George would inherit the title, the house, the land. Most of the money. But with privilege came responsibility. He was tied to this place. It was in his blood, the same way Aubrey Hall was in hers.

She wanted to ask him if he minded. If given the chance, would he trade places with Andrew or Edward?

"What will you do in London?" she said instead. Because she could never have asked him what she really wanted to know. Not while Edward's fate was uncertain.

He shrugged, although not so much with his shoulders as his head and eyes. "Speak to people. Make inquiries." He laughed bitterly. "I'm very good at speaking to people and making inquiries."

"You know how to get things done," she agreed.

"I know how to get other people to do things," he said derisively.

She pressed her lips together before she could utter something inane like, "That's an important skill." But it *was* an important skill, even if she'd never demonstrated it herself. She never left anything to her father's steward; he was surely the most overpaid clerk in the land. She acted first and thought later; she always had. And she could not bear to let someone else perform a task when she could do it better herself.

And she could almost always do it better herself.

"I need a drink," George suddenly muttered. Billie didn't dare point out again that it was still rather early for spirits.

He walked over to the side table and poured himself a brandy from the decanter. He took a sip. A long one. "Do you want one?"

Billie shook her head.

"Surprising," George muttered.

There was something hard in his voice. Something almost nasty. She felt her spine grow rigid. "I beg your pardon?"

But George only laughed, his brows arching into a mocking salute. "Oh, come now, Billie. You live to shock. I can hardly believe you wouldn't take a brandy when offered."

She gritted her teeth, reminding herself that George was not himself at the moment. "It's not even noon."

He shrugged and kicked back the rest of his brandy.

"You shouldn't be drinking."

"*You* shouldn't be telling me what to do."

She held herself still, stiff even, allowing the long pause to express her disapproval. Finally, because she needed to be as brittle as he, she gave him a cool stare, and said, "Lady Alexandra sends her regards."

He gave her a look of disbelief.

"She leaves today."

"How kind of you to convey her salutations."

She felt a cutting retort rising through her throat, but at the last minute she blurted, "No! This is ridiculous. I'm not going to stand here and speak in rhymes. I came to help."

"You can't help," he bit off.

"Certainly not when you're like this," she retorted.

He slammed his glass down and stalked toward her. "What did you just say?" he demanded. His eyes were wild and furious, and she almost took a step back.

"How much have you had to drink?"

"I'm not drunk," he said in a dangerous voice. "This . . . *that*," he corrected, waving an arm back toward the glass he'd left on the sideboard, "was my first and only drink of the day."

Billie had a feeling she was supposed to apologize, but she couldn't make herself do it.

"I'd like to be drunk," he said, moving closer with the silent grace of a large cat.

"You don't mean that."

"Don't I?" He laughed stridently. "Drunk, I might not remember that my brother is lost in some godforsaken wilderness where the locals are not predisposed to favor anyone in a red coat."

"George," she tried to say, but he would not be deterred.

"Drunk," he said again, the word punching harshly through the air, "I might not have noticed that my mother has spent the entire morning weeping in her bed. But best of all"—his hands came down heavily on a side table, and he looked at her with fury-laden despair—"if I were drunk, I might somehow forget that I am at the mercy of the rest of the goddamn world. If Edward is found—"

"When he's found," Billie cut in fiercely.

"Either way, it won't be because of me."

"What do you *want* to do?" she asked quietly. Because she had a feeling he didn't know. He said he wanted to go to the Colonies, but she wasn't sure she believed him. She didn't think he'd even allowed himself to think about what he wanted to do. He was so stuck on his restrictions that he could not think clearly about what was truly in his heart.

"What do I *want* to do?" he echoed. He looked . . . not surprised, exactly, but maybe a little dumbfounded. "I want . . . I want . . ." He blinked, then brought his eyes to hers. "I want you."

The breath left her body.

"I want you," he repeated, and it was as if the entire room shifted. The dazed look left his eyes, replaced by something fierce.

Predatory.

Billie could not speak. She could only watch as he came ever closer, the air between them heating to a simmering pitch.

"You don't want to do this," she said.

"Oh, I do. I really do."

But he didn't. She knew that he didn't, and she could feel her heart breaking because she *did*. She wanted him to kiss her like she was the only woman he could ever dream of kissing, like he'd die if he didn't touch his lips to hers.

She wanted him to kiss her and *mean* it.

"You don't know what you're doing," she said, edging back a step.

"Is that what you think?" he murmured.

"You've been drinking."

"Just enough to make this perfect."

She blinked. She didn't have a clue what that meant.

"Come now, Billie," he mocked. "Why so hesitant? That's not like you."

"This isn't like *you*," she countered.

"You have no idea." He came even closer, his eyes glittering with something she was terrified to define. He reached out and touched her arm, just one finger to her flesh, but it was enough to make her tremble. "When have you ever backed down from a dare?"

Her stomach was flipping and her heart was pounding, but still her shoulders fell into a stiff, straight line. "Never," she declared, staring him straight in the eye.

He smiled, and his gaze grew hot. "That's my girl," he murmured.

"I'm not—"

"You will be," he growled, and before she could utter another word, his mouth captured hers in a searing kiss.

Chapter 17

He was kissing her.

It was the very definition of madness.

He was kissing *Billie Bridgerton*, the last woman in the world he should ever dream of wanting, but by God, when she'd glared up at him, and her chin had trembled and jutted out, all he could see were her lips and all he could smell was her scent.

And all he could feel was the heat of her skin beneath his fingers, and he wanted more. More of *that*.

More of her.

His other hand came around her with stunning speed, and he wasn't thinking, he *couldn't* be thinking. He just pulled her up against him, hard, and then he was kissing her.

He wanted to devour her.

He wanted to own her.

He wanted to fold her into his arms and hold her tight and kiss her until she finally saw sense, until she stopped doing crazy things and stopped taking crazy risks, and started behaving the way a woman ought while still being *her* and—

He couldn't think. His thoughts were jumbled, torn to bits by the sheer heat of the moment.

More . . . his mind was begging. *More* was the only thing that made any sense to him. More of this. More of Billie.

He captured her face in his hands, holding her still. But she wasn't still. Her lips were moving beneath his, kissing him back with the sort of fervor that was exactly Billie. She rode hard and she played hard and by God she kissed the same way, like he was her triumph and she was going to glory in it.

It was all so mad, so completely wrong and yet so deliciously perfect. It was every sensation in the world, wrapped into one woman, and he could not get enough. In that moment, in that room, he could never get enough.

His palm moved to her shoulder, then to her back, pulling her closer until his hips pressed hard against her belly. She was small, and she was strong, but she curved in all the best places.

George was no monk. He had kissed women before, women who knew how to kiss him back. But he had never wanted anyone as much as he wanted Billie. He had never wanted anything as much as this kiss.

This kiss . . . and all that could come after.

"Billie," he groaned. "Billie."

She made a sound. It might have been his name. And somehow that was what it took.

Good God. Reason came slamming back into him. His brain woke and his sanity returned, and he stumbled back, the electricity that had sparked so hot between them now jolting him away.

What the hell had just happened?

He breathed. No, he *tried* to breathe. It was an entirely different thing.

She had asked him what he wanted.

And he'd answered. He wanted *her*. He hadn't even had to think about it.

Clearly, he *hadn't* thought about it, because if he had, he wouldn't have done it.

He raked a hand through his hair. Then another. Then he just gave up and squeezed both, pulling on his scalp until he let out a growl of pain.

"You kissed me," she said, and he had just enough presence of mind not to say that she'd kissed him back. Because he'd started it. He had started it, and they both knew that she never would have done so.

He shook his head, tiny unthinking movements that did nothing to clear his mind. "I'm sorry," he said stiffly. "That wasn't—I mean—"

He swore. This was apparently the extent of his coherency.

"You kissed me," she said again, and this time she sounded suspicious. "Why did—"

"I don't know," he bit off. He swore again, raking his hand through his hair as he turned away from her. Bloody hell. Bloody, bloody—

He swallowed. "That was a mistake," he said.

"What?"

It was just one word. Not nearly enough for him to decipher her tone. Which was probably for the best. He turned around, forcing himself to look at her while at the same time not allowing himself to *see*.

He didn't want to see her reaction. He didn't want to know what she thought of him. "That was a mistake," he said, because it was what he had to say. "Do you understand me?"

Her eyes narrowed. Her face grew hard. "Perfectly."

"For God's sake, Billie, don't take bloody offense—"

"Don't take offense? Don't take offense? You—" She stopped herself, shot a furtive glance at the open door, and lowered her voice to a furious hiss. "I did not start this."

"I am well aware."

"What were you thinking?"

"Obviously, I wasn't," he practically spat.

Her eyes widened, flashing with pain, and then she turned, hugging her arms to her body.

And George finally knew the true meaning of remorse. He let out an unsteady breath, raking his hand through his hair. "I apologize," he said, for the second time in as many minutes. "I will marry you, of course."

"What?" She whirled around. "No."

George stiffened. It was like someone had taken an iron rod and shoved it right up his spine. "I beg your pardon?"

"Don't be daft, George. You don't want to marry me."

It was true, but he was not stupid enough to say so out loud.

"And you know I don't want to marry you."

"As you are making increasingly clear."

"You only kissed me because you're upset."

This was *not* true, but he kept his mouth shut on this point as well.

"So I accept your apology." Her chin rose. "And we will never speak of this again."

"Agreed."

They stood there for a moment, frozen in their painfully awkward tableau. He ought to be jumping for joy. Any other young lady would be screaming for the trees. Or for her father. And the vicar. And a special license woven into the shape of a noose.

But not Billie. No, Billie just looked at him with an almost preternatural haughtiness and said, "I hope *you* will accept *my* apology."

"Your—" *What?* His jaw dropped. What the devil did she have to apologize for? Or was she merely trying to get the upper hand? She'd always known how to unsettle him.

"It's not as if I can pretend that I didn't return the . . . ah . . ." She swallowed, and he took some pleasure in the fact that she blushed before she finished the statement. "The . . . ah . . ."

He took quite a bit of pleasure in the fact that she couldn't finish the statement at all.

"You liked it," he said with a slow smile. It was colossally unwise to goad her at such a moment, but he could not help himself.

She shifted her weight. "Everyone has to have a first kiss."

"Then I am honored," he said with a courtly bow.

Her lips parted in surprise, maybe even consternation. Good. He'd turned the tables.

"I was not expecting it to be you, of course," she said.

He stifled his irritation and instead murmured, "Perhaps you were hoping for someone else?"

She gave a jerky little shrug. "No one in particular."

He chose not to analyze the burst of pleasure that rushed through him at that statement.

"I suppose I always thought it would be one of your brothers," she continued. "Andrew, maybe—"

"*Not* Andrew," he bit off.

"No, probably not," she agreed, her head tilting to the side as she considered it. "But it used to seem plausible."

He stared at her with mounting irritation. While she was not wholly *un*affected by the situation, she was certainly not *as* affected as he thought she should have been.

"It wouldn't have been the same," he heard himself say.

She blinked. "I beg your pardon."

"If you had kissed someone else." He stepped toward her, unable to ignore the way his blood buzzed with anticipation. "It would not have been the same."

"Well . . ." She looked flustered, delightfully so. "I would expect not," she finally said. "I mean . . . different people . . ."

"Very different," he agreed.

Her mouth opened, and several seconds passed before words emerged. "I'm not sure to whom you're comparing yourself."

"Anyone." He moved even closer. "Everyone."

"George?" Her eyes were huge, but she wasn't saying no.

"Do you want me to kiss you again?" he asked.

"Of course not." But she said it too quickly.

"Are you sure of that?"

She swallowed. "It would be a very bad idea."

"Very much so," he said softly.

"So we . . . shouldn't?"

He touched her cheek, and this time he whispered it. "Do you want me to kiss you again?"

She moved . . . a little. He couldn't tell whether she was shaking her head *yes* or *no*. He had a feeling she didn't know, either.

"Billie?" he murmured, coming close enough so that his breath whispered across her skin.

Her breath hitched, and she said, "I said I wouldn't marry you."

"You did."

"Well, I said you didn't *have* to marry me."

He nodded.

"That would still be true."

"If I kissed you again?"

She nodded.

"So this means nothing?"

"No . . ."

Something warm and lovely unfurled in his chest. This could never mean nothing. And she knew it.

"It just means . . ." She swallowed, her lips trembling as they pressed together. ". . . that there are no consequences."

He brushed his lips against her cheek. "No consequences," he softly repeated.

"None."

"I could kiss you again . . ." His hand stole around to the small of her back, but he exerted only the barest of pressure. She could step away at any moment. She could remove herself from his embrace, cross the room, and leave. He needed her to know this. *He* needed to know that she knew this. There would be no recriminations, no telling herself that she had been swept away by his passion.

If she was swept away by passion, it would be her own.

His lips touched her ear. "I could kiss you again," he repeated.

She gave a little nod. A tiny nod. But he felt it. "Again," she whispered.

His teeth found her earlobe, gently nipping. "And again."

"I think—"

"What do you think?" He smiled against her skin. He couldn't quite believe how utterly delightful this was. He'd known kisses of passion, of raw, primal hunger and overwhelming lust. This was all that, but there was something more.

Something joyful.

"I think . . ." She swallowed. "I think you *should* kiss me again." She looked up, her eyes remarkably clear. "And I think you should shut the door."

George had never moved so fast in his life. He had half a mind to shove a chair under the door handle just to keep the damned thing closed.

"This still doesn't mean nothing," she said as his arms wrapped around her.

"Absolutely not."

"But no consequences."

"None."

"You don't have to marry me."

"I don't have to, no."

But he could. The thought flicked across his mind with warm surprise. He *could* marry her. There was no reason why not.

His sanity, perhaps. But he had a feeling he'd lost that the first moment his lips had touched hers.

She stood on her tiptoes, tilting her face to his. "If you're my first kiss," she said, her lips curving with subtle mischief, "then you might as well be my second."

"Maybe your third," he said, capturing her mouth with his.

"It's important to know," she said, getting just those four words out between kisses.

"To know?" His mouth moved to her neck, causing her to arch provocatively in his arms.

She nodded, gasping as one of his hands moved along her rib cage. "How to kiss," she clarified. "It's a skill."

He felt himself smile. "And you like to be skilled."

"I do."

He kissed her neck, then her collarbone, giving thanks to the current bodice styles, round and deep, baring creamy skin from her shoulders to the top swell of her breasts. "I predict great things for you."

Her only response was a gasp of surprise. About what, he wasn't quite sure—perhaps his tongue, flicking out along the sensitive skin peeking out from the lacy edge of her dress. Or maybe it was his teeth, nipping gently along the side of her neck.

He didn't dare tumble her onto the chaise; he did not trust himself that far. But he did nudge her until she was leaning against the sofa, lifting her the scant few inches required to set her atop the back.

And God love her, but Billie knew instinctively what to do. Her legs parted, and when he rucked up her skirts, she wrapped herself around him. Maybe it was just for balance, but as he pressed himself against her, he didn't care. Her skirt was still in the way, as were his breeches, but he *felt* her. He was hard, exquisitely so, and he pressed against her, his body knowing where it wanted to go. She was a country girl; she had to know what this meant, but she was lost in the same passion, and she pulled him closer, her legs tightening around his hips.

Dear God, at this rate he was going to spend himself like a green boy.

He took a breath. "It's too much," he gasped, forcing himself to pull away.

"No," was all she said, but her hands moved to his head, allowing him to kiss her even as he put a little distance between their bodies.

And so he kissed her. He kissed her endlessly. He kissed her carefully, skirting the edge of his own desire, all too aware how close he was to the brink of reason.

And he kissed her tenderly, because this was Billie, and somehow he knew that no one ever thought to be tender with her.

"George," she said.

He lifted his lips from hers, just a bit, just a breath. "Hmmm."

"We have to . . . we have to stop."

"Mmmm," he agreed. But he didn't stop. He could have done; he had a grip on his passion now. But he didn't want to.

"George," she said again. "I hear people."

He drew back. Listened.

Swore.

"Open the door," Billie hissed.

He did. With alacrity. Nothing sparked suspicion like a closed door. He looked at her. "You might . . ." He cleared his throat and made a motion near his head. "You might want to . . ."

He was no expert on ladies' coiffures, but he was fairly certain her hair did not look as it should.

Billie blanched and frantically smoothed her hair, her nimble fingers tugging on pins and then jamming them back into place. "Better?"

He grimaced. There was a spot behind her right ear where a chestnut lock looked as if it was sprouting from her head.

They heard a voice from the hall. *"George?"*

His mother. Good God.

"George!"

"In the drawing room, Mother," he called back, heading to the doorway. He could stall her in the hall for a few seconds at least. He turned back to Billie, sharing one last urgent glance. She took her hands from her hair and held them out, as if to say, *"Well?"*

It would have to do.

"Mother," he said, stepping into the hall. "You're up."

She offered her cheek, which he dutifully kissed. "I can't stay in my room forever."

"No, although surely you are allowed time to—"

"Grieve?" she interrupted. "I refuse to grieve. Not until we receive more definite news."

"I was going to say 'rest,' " he told her.

"I've done that."

Well done, Lady Manston, he thought. Funny how his mother still managed to surprise him with her resilience.

"I was thinking," his mother began, walking past him into the drawing room. "Oh, hello, Billie, I did not realize you were here."

"Lady Manston." Billie bobbed a curtsy. "I was hoping I might be of some assistance."

"That is very kind of you. I'm not sure what can be done, but your company is always appreciated." Lady Manston's head tilted to the side. "Is it very windy out?"

"What?" Billie's hand flew self-consciously to her hair. "Oh. Yes, a bit. I forgot my bonnet."

They all looked at the bonnet she'd left on a table.

"What I meant to say was that I forgot to put it on," Billie said with a nervous chuckle that George dearly hoped his mother did not detect. "Or rather, truthfully, I didn't forget. The air was so very fine."

"I won't tell your mother," Lady Manston said with an indulgent smile.

Billie nodded her thanks, and then an awkward silence fell over the room. Or maybe it wasn't awkward at all. Maybe George only thought it was awkward, because he knew what Billie was thinking, and he knew what *he* was thinking, and it seemed impossible somehow that his mother could be thinking of anything else.

But apparently she was, because she looked at him with a smile he knew was forced, and asked, "Have you given further thought to going to London?"

"Some," he replied. "I know a few people at the War Office."

"George was thinking of traveling to London to make inquiries," his mother said to Billie.

"Yes, he'd told me. It's an excellent idea."

Lady Manston gave a tiny nod and turned back to George. "Your father knows people as well, but . . ."

"I can go," George said swiftly, saving his mother the pain of having to describe her husband's current state of incapacitation.

"You probably know the same people," Billie said.

George glanced over. "Just so."

"I believe I will go with you," his mother said.

"Mother, no, you should stay home," George immediately said. "Father will need you, and it will be easier for me to do what needs to be done on my own."

"Don't be silly. Your father doesn't need anything but news of his son, and I can't do anything to further that cause from here."

"And you will in London?"

"Probably not," she admitted, "but at least there is a chance."

"I'm not going to be able to accomplish anything if I'm worried about you."

His mother raised one perfectly arched brow. "Then don't worry."

He gritted his teeth. There was no arguing with her when she was like this, and the truth was, he wasn't even sure *why* he didn't want his mother to come with him. Just this strange, niggling feeling that some things were best done alone.

"It will all work out," Billie said, trying to smooth over the tension between mother and son. George shot her a look of gratitude, but he didn't think she saw it. She was more like her own mother than anyone gave her credit for, he realized. She was a peacemaker, in her own inimitable way.

He watched as she took one of his mother's hands in hers. "I know that Edward will come home to us," she said with a light squeeze.

A warm, almost homey sense of pride swirled through him. And he could have sworn he could feel her, giving his hand a squeeze as well.

"You're such a dear, Billie," his mother said. "You and Edward were always so close."

"My best friend," Billie said. "Well, besides Mary, of course."

George crossed his arms. "Don't forget Andrew."

She glanced over at him with a frown.

Lady Manston leaned forward and kissed Billie on the cheek. "What I wouldn't give to see you and Edward together one more time."

"And you shall," Billie said firmly. "He will be home—if not soon, then at least eventually." She gave an excellent approximation of a reassuring smile. "We will be together again. I know it."

"We will *all* be together again," George said peevishly.

Billie gave him another frown, this one considerably more remonstrative.

"I keep seeing his face," his mother said. "Every time I close my eyes."

"I do, too," Billie admitted.

George saw red. He'd just bloody kissed her—and he was fairly certain her eyes had been closed.

"George?" his mother inquired.

"What?" he bit off.

"You made a noise."

"I cleared my throat," he lied. Had Billie been thinking of Edward when she kissed him? No, she wouldn't do that. Or would she? How would he know? And could he blame her? If she had been thinking of Edward, it wasn't anything she'd done on purpose.

Which somehow made it even worse.

He watched as Billie spoke quietly with his mother. Was she in love with Edward? No, she couldn't be. Because if she *was*, Edward would never have been so foolish as to not return the affection. And if that were the case, they'd be married by now.

Besides, Billie had said she had not been kissed. And Billie didn't lie.

Edward was a gentleman—maybe even more of one than George, after the events of today—but if he was in love with Billie, there was no way he'd have left for America without kissing her.

"George?"

He looked up. His mother was regarding him with some concern. "You don't look well," she said.

"I don't feel well," he said curtly.

His mother drew back ever so slightly, the only indication of her surprise. "I don't imagine any of us does," she said.

"I wish I could go to London," Billie said.

George snapped to attention. "Are you joking?" Good God, that would be a disaster. If he was worried about his *mother* being a distraction . . .

She drew back, visibly offended. "Why would I be joking?"

"You hate London."

"I've only been the once," she said stiffly.

"What?" Lady Manston exclaimed. "How is that possible? I know you didn't have a Season, but it's barely even a full day's ride."

Billie cleared her throat. "There was some hesitation on the part of my mother after what happened at my presentation at court."

Lady Manston cringed a little, then made a full recovery with a brightly declared: "Well, that settles it, then. We cannot live in the past."

George regarded his mother with a slow dose of dread. "Settles what, exactly?"

"Billie must go to London."

Chapter 18

And so it was that less than one week later Billie found herself stripped down to her unmentionables with two seamstresses jabbering on in French while they jabbed *her* with pins and needles.

"I could have used one of my gowns from home," she told Lady Manston for what was probably the fifth time.

Lady Manston did not even look up from the book of fashion plates she was perusing. "No, you couldn't."

Billie sighed as she stared out at the richly brocaded fabrics that draped the walls of the fancy dress shop that had become her second home here in London. It was very exclusive, she'd been told; the discreet sign hanging above the door said merely *Mme. Delacroix, tailoress*, but Lady Manston referred to the petite French dynamo as Crossy, and Billie had been told to do the same.

Normally, Lady Manston said, Crossy and her girls would come to *them*, but they hadn't much time to get Billie properly fitted and kitted, and in this instance it seemed more efficient to visit the shop.

Billie had tried to protest. She wasn't coming to London for a Season. It wasn't even the right time of year. Well, it would be soon, but it wasn't yet. And they absolutely had not traveled to London to attend parties and balls. Truth be told, Billie wasn't entirely certain why she was there. She had been utterly shocked when Lady Manston made her announcement, and it must have shown on her face.

"You just said you wished to go," Lady Manston had said, "and I will confess I am not being entirely unselfish. *I* wish to go, and I require a companion."

George had protested, which, under the circumstances, Billie had found sensible *and* insulting, but his mother was unstoppable.

"I can't bring Mary," she said firmly. "She's far too ill, and I doubt Felix would permit it in any case." At that she had looked over to Billie. "He's very protective."

"Quite so," Billie had mumbled . . . rather stupidly, in her opinion. But she couldn't think of anything else to say. Honestly, she never felt less sure of herself than in the face of an indomitable society matron, even one she'd known since birth. Most of the time Lady Manston was her beloved neighbor, but every now and then the Leader of Society shone through, issuing orders and directing people, and generally just being an expert on everything. Billie had no idea how to assert herself. It was the same way with her own mother.

But then George had jettisoned *sensible* and gone completely over to *insulting*.

"Forgive me, Billie," he'd said (while looking at his mother), "but she would be a distraction."

"A welcome one," Lady Manston said.

"Not to *me*."

"George Rokesby!" His mother was instantly incensed. "You apologize this minute."

"She knows what I meant," he said.

At that, Billie could not keep her mouth shut. "I do?"

George turned back to Billie with an expression of vague irritation. And clear condescension. "You don't really want to go to London."

"Edward was my friend, too," she said.

"There is no 'was' about it," George snapped.

She wanted to smack him. He was deliberately misunderstanding her. "Oh, for heaven's sake, George, you know what I meant."

"I do?" he mocked.

"What on earth is going on here?" Lady Manston had exploded. "I know the two of you have never been close, but there is no call for this sort of behavior. Good God, one would think the both of you were three years old."

And that was that. Both Billie and George were shamed into silence, and Lady Manston went off to pen a note to Lady Bridgerton, explaining that Billie had graciously agreed to accompany her to town.

Naturally, Lady Bridgerton had thought this a splendid idea.

Billie had thought she'd spend her days taking in the sights, perhaps attending the theater, but the day after their arrival, Lady Manston had received an invitation to a ball being given by a dear, dear friend, and much to Billie's surprise, she had decided to accept.

"Are you certain you're up to it?" Billie had asked. (At that point she had not thought that she was going to be roped in to attending as well, so it had to be said, her motives were purely altruistic.)

"My son is not dead," Lady Manston said, surprising Billie with her bluntness. "I am not going to act as if he is."

"Well, no, of course not, but—"

"Besides," Lady Manston said, giving no indication that she had heard Billie speak, "Ghislaine is a dear, dear friend, and it would be impolite to decline."

Billie had frowned, looking down at the sizable stack of invitations that had mysteriously appeared in the delicately scalloped porcelain dish resting atop Lady Manston's writing table. "How does she even know you're here in London?"

Lady Manston shrugged as she perused the rest of her invitations. "I expect she heard it from George."

Billie smiled tightly. George had reached London two days before the ladies. He'd ridden the whole way on horseback, lucky dog. Since her arrival, however, she'd seen him precisely three times. Once at supper, once at breakfast, and once in the drawing room when he came in for a brandy while she was reading a book.

He'd been perfectly polite, if a little distant. She supposed this could be forgiven; as far as she could tell he was busy trying to obtain news of Edward, and she certainly did not want to distract him from his objective. Still she had not thought that "no consequences" would mean "Oh, I'm sorry, is that you on the sofa?"

She didn't think that he had been unaffected by their kiss. She didn't have much—oh, very well, *any*—experience with men, but she knew George, and she knew that he had wanted her every bit as much as she wanted him.

And she had. Oh, how she had.

She still did.

Every time she closed her eyes she saw his face, and the crazy thing was, it wasn't the kiss she relived endlessly in her mind. It was the moment right before it, when her heart beat like a hummingbird and her breath ached to mingle with his. The kiss had been magical, but the moment before, the split second when she knew . . .

She'd been transformed.

He had awakened something inside of her she had not even known existed, something wild and selfish. And she wanted more.

Problem was, she had no idea how to get it. If ever there were a time to develop feminine wiles, this was probably it. But she was entirely out of her element here in London. She knew how to act back in Kent. Maybe she wasn't her mother's ideal version of womanhood, but when she was at home, at Aubrey or Crake, she knew who she was. If she said something strange or did something out of the ordinary it didn't matter, because she was Billie Bridgerton, and everyone knew what that meant.

She knew what it meant.

But here, in this formal town home, with its unfamiliar servants and pursed-lipped matrons coming to call, she was adrift. She second-guessed every word.

And now Lady Manston wanted to attend a ball?

"Ghislaine's daughter is eighteen, I believe," Lady Manston mused, flipping over the invitation and glancing at the back. "Maybe nineteen. Certainly of an age to marry."

Billie held her tongue.

"A lovely girl. So pretty and genteel." Lady Manston looked up with a wide, devious smile. "Shall I insist that George be my escort? It's high time he started looking for a wife."

"I'm sure he will be delighted," Billie said diplomatically. But in her head she was already painting Ghislaine's beautiful daughter with horns and a pitchfork.

"And you shall attend as well."

Billie looked up, alarmed. "Oh, I don't think—"

"We'll have to get you a dress."

"It's really not—"

"And shoes, I would imagine."

"But, Lady Manston, I—"

"I wonder if we can get away without a wig. They can be difficult to manage if you're not used to wearing them."

"I really don't like wearing wigs," Billie said.

"Then you won't have to," Lady Manston declared, and it was only then that Billie realized just how deftly she'd been manipulated.

That had been two days earlier. Two days and five fittings. Six, counting this one.

"Billie, hold your breath for a moment," Lady Manston called out.

Billie squinted over at her. "What?" It was bloody difficult to focus on anything other than the two seamstresses currently yanking her about. She'd heard that most dressmakers faked their French accents so as to seem more sophisticated, but these two seemed to be genuine. Billie couldn't understand a word they were saying.

"She doesn't speak French," Lady Manston said to Crossy. "I'm not sure what her mother was thinking." She glanced back up at Billie. "Your breath, darling. They need to tighten your corset."

Billie looked at Crossy's two assistants, waiting patiently behind her, corset laces in hand. "It requires two people?"

"It's a very good corset," Lady Manston said.

"Ze best," Crossy confirmed.

Billie sighed.

"No, *in*," Lady Manston directed. "Breathe *in*."

Billie obeyed, sucking in her stomach so that the two seamstresses could do some sort of choreographed crossways yank that resulted in Billie's spine curving in an entirely new manner. Her hips jutted forward, and her head seemed remarkably far back on her neck. She wasn't quite certain how she was meant to walk like this.

"This isn't terribly comfortable," she called out.

"No." Lady Manston sounded unconcerned. "It won't be."

One of the ladies said something in French and then pushed Billie's shoulders forward and her stomach back. "*Meilleur?*" she asked.

Billie cocked her head to the side, then twisted her spine a bit each way. It *was* better. Yet another aspect of genteel femininity she'd had no idea how to navigate: corset wearing. Or rather, "good" corset wearing. Apparently the ones she'd been wearing were far too permissive.

"Thank you," she said to the seamstress, then cleared her throat. "Er, *merci*."

"For you, ze corset should not be too uncomfortable," Crossy said, coming over to inspect her handiwork. "Your stomach is lovely and flat. The problem we have is your breasts."

Billie looked up in alarm. "My—"

"Very little meat to them," Crossy said, shaking her head sadly.

It was embarrassing enough to have one's breasts discussed like chicken wings, but then Crossy actually *grabbed* her. She looked over at Lady Manston. "We need to push them up more, don't you think?"

She then demonstrated. Billie wanted to die on the spot.

"Hmmm?" Lady Manston's face screwed up as she considered the placement of Billie's breasts. "Oh yes, I think you're right. They look much better up there."

"I'm sure it's not necessary . . ." Billie began, but then she gave up. She had no power here.

Crossy said something in rapid-fire French to her assistants, and before Billie knew what was happening, she'd been unlaced and relaced, and when she looked down, her bosom was most definitely not where it had been just a few moments earlier.

"Much better," Crossy declared.

"Goodness," Billie murmured. If she nodded she could actually touch her chin to her chest.

"He won't be able to resist you," Crossy said, leaning in with a confidential wink.

"Who?"

"There's always a who," Crossy said with a chuckle.

Billie tried not to think of George. But she wasn't successful. Like it or not, he was her *who*.

While Billie was trying not to think of George, he was trying not to think of fish. Kippers, to be precise.

He'd spent the better part of the week at the War Office, trying to gain information about Edward. This had involved several meals with Lord Arbuthnot, who, before he had developed gout, had been a decorated general in His Majesty's army. The gout was a bloody nuisance (was the first thing he'd said) but it did mean he was back on English soil, where a man could have a proper breakfast every day.

Lord Arbuthnot was apparently still making up for his years of improper breakfasts, because when George joined him for supper, the table had been laid with what was normally morning fare. Eggs three ways, bacon, toast. And kippers. Lots and lots of kippers.

All things considered, Lord Arbuthnot put away a lot of kippers.

George had met the old soldier only once before, but Arbuthnot had attended Eton with George's father, and George with Arbuthnot's son, and if there was a more effective connection to press in the pursuit of truth, George couldn't imagine what it was.

"Well, I've been asking," Arbuthnot said, slicing up a piece of ham with the vigor of a red-faced man who'd rather be outside, "and I can't get much about your brother."

"Surely someone must know where he is."

"Connecticut Colony. That's as precise as it gets."

George clenched his fingers into a fist beneath the table. "He's not supposed to *be* in Connecticut Colony."

Arbuthnot chewed his food, then looked at George with a shrewd expression. "You've never been a soldier, have you?"

"Much to my regret."

Arbuthnot nodded, George's reply clearly meeting with his approval. "Soldiers are rarely where they're supposed to be," he said. "At least not ones like your brother."

George pressed his lips together, working to maintain an even expression. "I'm afraid I don't catch your meaning."

Arbuthnot sat back, tapping his steepled fingers as he regarded George with a thoughtful, eye-narrowed gaze. "Your brother is hardly an enlisted man, Lord Kennard."

"Surely a captain must still follow orders."

"And go where he's told?" Arbuthnot said. "Of course. But that doesn't mean he ends up where he's 'supposed' to be."

George took a moment to absorb this, then said incredulously, "Are you trying to tell me that Edward is a spy?"

It was unfathomable. Espionage was a dirty business. Men like Edward wore their red coats with pride.

Arbuthnot shook his head. "No. At least I don't think so. Damned unsavory, spying is. Your brother wouldn't have to do it."

He wouldn't do it, George thought. Period.

"It'd make no sense, at any rate," Arbuthnot said briskly. "Do you really think your brother could pass himself off as anything but a proper English gentleman? I hardly think a rebel is going to believe that the son of an earl is going to sympathize with their cause."

Arbuthnot wiped his mouth with his napkin and reached for the kippers. "I think your brother is a scout."

"A scout," George repeated.

Arbuthnot nodded, then offered the dish. "More?"

George shook his head and tried not to grimace. "No, thank you."

Arbuthnot gave a little grunt and slid the rest of the fish onto his plate. "God, I love kippers," he sighed. "You can't get them in the Caribbean. Not like this."

"A scout," George said again, trying to get the conversation back on topic. "Why do you think this?"

"Well, no one has told me as much, and to be quite frank, I don't know that anyone here has the entire story, but putting together the bits and pieces . . . it seems to fit." Arbuthnot popped a kipper in his mouth and chewed. "I'm not a betting man, but if I were, I'd say that your brother had been sent afield to get the lay of the land. There hasn't been much action in Connecticut, not since that thing with Whatshisname Arnold in Ridgefield back in seventy-seven."

George was not familiar with Whatshisname Arnold, nor did he have a clue where Ridgefield was.

There are some damned good ports on that coast," Arbuthnot continued, getting back to the serious business of cutting his meat. "I wouldn't be surprised if the rebels were putting them to use. And I wouldn't be surprised if Captain Rokesby had been sent out to investigate." He looked up, his bushy brows dipping toward his eyes as his forehead wrinkled. "Does your brother have any map-making skills?"

"Not that I'm aware."

Arbuthnot shrugged. "Doesn't mean anything if he doesn't, I suppose. They might not be looking for anything so precise."

"But then what happened?" George pressed.

The old general shook his head. "I'm afraid I don't know, m'dear boy. And I'd be lying if I said I'd found anyone who did."

George hadn't expected answers, not really, but still, it was disappointing.

"It's a damned long way to the Colonies, son," Lord Arbuthnot said in a surprisingly gentle voice. "News is never as swift as we'd like."

George accepted this with a slow nod. He was going to have to pursue some other avenue of investigation, although for the life of him, he did not know what that might be.

"By the way," Arbuthnot added, almost too casually, "you wouldn't happen to be planning to attend Lady Wintour's ball tomorrow night, would you?"

"I am," George confirmed. He didn't want to, but his mother had spun some convoluted story that had ended in his absolutely *having* to attend. And frankly, he hadn't the heart to disappoint her. Not while she was so worried about Edward.

And then there was Billie. She'd been roped into attending as well. He'd seen the look of panic on her face when his mother had dragged her from her breakfast to visit the *modiste*. A London ball was quite possibly Billie Bridgerton's personal hell, and there was no way he could abandon her when she needed him most.

"Are you acquainted with Robert Tallywhite?" Lord Arbuthnot inquired.

"A bit." Tallywhite was a couple of years ahead of him at Eton. Quiet fellow, George recalled. Sandy hair and a high forehead. Bookish.

"He is Lady Wintour's nephew and will most certainly be in attendance. You would be doing a great service to this office if you would pass along a message."

George raised his eyebrows in question.

"Is that a yes?" Lord Arbuthnot said in a dry voice.

George tipped his head in affirmation.

"Tell him . . . pease porridge pudding."

"Pease porridge pudding," George repeated dubiously.

Arbuthnot broke off a piece of his toast and dipped it into his egg yolk. "He'll understand."

"What does it mean?"

"Do you need to know?" Arbuthnot countered.

George sat back, regarding Arbuthnot with a level stare. "I do, rather."

Lord Arbuthnot let out a bark of laughter. "And that, my dear boy, is why you would make a terrible soldier. You've got to follow orders without question."

"Not if one is in command."

"Too true," Arbuthnot said with a smile. But he still did not explain the message. Instead he regarded George with a level stare and asked, "Can we rely on you?"

It was the War Office, George thought. If he was passing along messages, at least he'd know he was doing it for the right people.

At least he'd know he was doing *some*thing.

He looked Arbuthnot in the eye and said, "You may."

Chapter 19

Manston House was quiet when George returned later that evening. The hall was lit with two candelabras, but the rest of the rooms seemed to have been shut down for the night. He frowned. It wasn't that late; surely someone ought to be about.

"Ah, Temperley," George said when the butler stepped forward to take his hat and coat, "has my mother gone out for the evening?"

"Lady Manston had her dinner sent up to her room on a tray, my lord," Temperley said.

"And Miss Bridgerton?"

"I believe she did the same."

"Oh." George shouldn't have been disappointed. After all, he'd spent the better part of the past few days avoiding both of the aforementioned ladies. Now they seemed to have done his work for him.

"Shall I have your dinner sent up as well, my lord?"

George thought for a moment, then said, "Why not?" It seemed he wasn't to have company that night regardless, and he hadn't eaten much of Lord Arbuthnot's repast.

It had to have been the kippers. Honestly, the smell had put him off the entire meal.

"Will you have a brandy in the drawing room first?" Temperley inquired.

"No, I'll go straight up, I think. It's been a long day."

Temperley nodded in that butlerish way of his. "For us all, my lord."

George regarded him with a wry expression. "Has my mother been working you to the bone, Temperley?"

"Not at all," the butler replied, the barest hint of a smile cracking through his somber mien. "I speak of the ladies. If I may be so bold as to offer my observation, they seemed rather tired when they returned this afternoon. Miss Bridgerton especially."

"I'm afraid my mother has been working *her* to the bone," George said with a half-smile.

"Just so, my lord. Lady Manston is never as happy as when she has a young lady to marry off."

George froze, then covered his lapse by devoting an inordinate amount of attention to the removal of his gloves. "That would seem somewhat ambitious, given that Miss Bridgerton does not plan to remain in town for the Season."

Temperley cleared his throat. "A great many parcels have arrived."

Which was his way of saying that every item required for a young lady to successfully navigate the London marriage mart had been purchased and delivered.

"I'm sure Miss Bridgerton will meet with every success," George said evenly.

"She is a very lively young lady," Temperley agreed.

George smiled tightly as he took his leave. It was difficult to imagine how Temperley had come to the conclusion that Billie was lively. The few times George had crossed her path at Manston House she had been uncharacteristically subdued.

He supposed he should have made more of an effort, taken her out for an ice or some such, but he'd been too busy hunting down information at the War Office. It felt so bloody good to *do* something for a change, even if the results were disappointing.

He took a step toward the stairs, then paused and turned back. Temperley had not moved.

"I always thought my mother hoped for a match between Miss Bridgerton and Edward," George said casually.

"She has not seen fit to confide in me," Temperley said.

"No, of course not," George said. He gave his head a little shake. How the mighty had fallen. He'd been reduced to dangling for gossip from the butler. "Good night, Temperley."

He made it to the stairs, his foot perched on the first step, when the butler called out, "They do speak of him."

George turned around.

Temperley cleared his throat. "I do not think it a breach of confidence to tell you that they speak of him at breakfast."

"No," George said. "Not at all."

There was a long beat of silence.

"We are keeping Master Edward in our prayers," Temperley finally said. "We all miss him."

It was true. Although what did it say about George that he missed Edward more now that he was missing than he ever had when he'd merely been an ocean away?

He walked slowly up the stairs. Manston House was much smaller than Crake, with all eight bedchambers clustered on one floor. Billie had been put in the second-best guest bedroom, which George thought was ludicrous, but his mother always insisted upon keeping the best guest bedroom free. *You never know who might unexpectedly visit*, she always said.

Has the King dropped by? he always parried. This generally earned him a scowl. And a smile. His mother was a good sport that way, even if the best room had gone empty these past twenty years.

He paused in the middle of the hall, not quite in front of Billie's door but closer to it than any other room. There was just enough of a crack under the door to show a faint flicker of candlelight. He wondered what she was doing in there. It really was much too early to go to sleep.

He missed her.

It came to him in a startling flash. He missed her. He was here, in the same house, sleeping just three doors down, and he missed her.

It was his own fault. He knew he'd been avoiding her. But what was he to do? He had kissed Billie, kissed her until he was nearly past the edge of reason, and now he was expected to make polite conversation with her at the breakfast table? In front of his *mother*?

George would never be as sophisticated as that.

He ought to marry her. He rather thought he'd like to, as mad as that might have seemed just a month earlier. He'd been quite warming to the idea back at Crake. Billie had said "You don't have to marry me," and all he could think was—

But I could.

He'd had just a moment with the idea. No time to think or analyze, only time to feel.

And it had felt lovely. Warm.

Like springtime.

But then his mother had arrived on the scene and started going on about how adorable Billie and Edward were together and what a perfect match they made and he couldn't remember what else but it was nauseatingly sweet and according to Temperley went very well over breakfast with toast and orange marmalade.

Toast and marmalade. He shook his head. He was an idiot.

And he had fallen in love with Billie Bridgerton.

There it was. Plain as day. He almost laughed. He *would* have laughed, if the joke weren't on him.

If he'd fallen in love with someone else—someone new, whose presence did not fill such a wealth of his memories—would it have been so clear? With Billie the emotion was such an about-face, such a complete departure from a lifetime of comparing her to a pebble in his shoe. He couldn't help but see it, shining in his mind like bright starry promise.

Was she in love with Edward? Maybe. His mother seemed to think so. She had not said as much, of course, but his mother had a remarkable talent for making sure her opinions were precisely known without ever actually stating them explicitly.

Still, it had been enough to render him insanely jealous.

In love with Billie. It was just the maddest thing.

He let out a long, pent-up breath and started walking again toward his room. He had to pass by her door, past that tantalizing flicker of light. He slowed, because he couldn't not.

And then the door opened.

"George?" Billie's face peered out. She was still in her day clothes but her hair was down, draped over her shoulder in a long, thick braid. "I thought I heard someone," she explained.

He managed a close-lipped smile as he bowed. "As you see."

"I was having supper," she said, motioning back into the room. "Your mother was tired." She gave a sheepish smile. "*I* was tired. I'm not very good at shopping. I had no idea it would involve quite so much standing still."

"Standing still is always more tiring than walking."

"Yes!" she said, quite animatedly. "I've always said that."

George started to speak, but then a memory sparked through his mind. It was when he'd been carrying her, after that debacle with the cat on the roof. He'd been trying to describe that odd feeling of when one's leg goes weak and bends for no reason.

Billie had understood perfectly.

The irony was that his leg hadn't gone weak. He'd been making it up to cover for something. He didn't even remember what.

But he remembered the moment. He remembered that she'd understood.

Mostly he'd remembered how she'd looked at him, with a little smile that said that she was happy to *be* understood.

He looked up. She was watching him with an expression of faint expectation. It was his turn to speak, he remembered. And since he couldn't very well say what he was thinking, he went for the obvious.

"You're still dressed," he said.

She glanced down briefly at her frock. It was the one she'd been wearing when he kissed her. Flowers. It suited her. She should always be in flowers.

"I thought I might go back down after I finish eating," she said. "Perhaps find something to read in the library."

He nodded.

"My mother always says that once you're in your dressing gown, you're in your room for the night."

He smiled. "Does she?"

"She says a great many things, actually. I'm sure I've forgotten whatever it is that I didn't ignore."

George stood like a statue, knowing he should bid her goodnight, but somehow unable to form the words. The moment was too intimate, too perfectly candlelit and lovely.

"Have you eaten?" she asked.

"Yes. Well, no." He thought of the kippers. "Not exactly."

Her brows rose. "*That* sounds intriguing."

"Hardly. I'm having a tray sent to my room, actually. I've always hated dining alone downstairs."

"I'm the same," she agreed. She stood for a moment, then said, "It's ham pie. Very good."

"Excellent." He cleared his throat. "Well, I . . . ought to go. Good night, Billie."

He turned. He didn't want to turn.

"George, wait!"

He hated that he was holding his breath.

"George, this is madness."

He turned back. She was still standing in the entrance to her room, one hand resting lightly on the edge of the door. Her face was so expressive. Had it always been so?

Yes, he thought. She'd never been one to hide her feelings beneath a mask of indifference. It was one of the things he'd found so annoying about her when they were growing up. She simply refused to be ignored.

But that was then. And this was . . .

Something else entirely.

"Madness?" he echoed. He wasn't sure what she meant. He didn't want to make assumptions.

Her lips trembled into a tentative smile. "Surely we can be friends."

Friends?

"I mean, I know . . ."

"That I kissed you?" he supplied.

She gasped, then practically hissed, "I wasn't going to say it quite so bluntly. For heaven's sake, George, your mother is still awake." And while she was frantically peering down the hall, George threw over a lifetime of gentlemanly behavior and stepped into her bedroom.

"George!"

"Apparently one *can* whisper and scream at the same time," he mused.

"You can't be in here," she said.

He grinned as she closed the door. "I didn't think you wished to conduct this sort of conversation in the hall."

The look she gave him was sarcasm in its purest form. "I believe there are two drawing rooms and a library downstairs."

"And look what happened last time we were in a drawing room together."

Her face flushed instantly. But Billie was a trouper, and after a moment of what appeared to be gnashing her teeth and telling herself to calm down, she asked, "Have you learned anything of Edward?"

Like that, his jaunty mood deflated. "Nothing of substance."

"But something?" she asked hopefully.

He didn't want to talk about Edward. For so many reasons. But Billie deserved a reply, so he said, "Just the suppositions of a retired general."

"I'm sorry. That must be terribly frustrating. I wish there was something I could do to help." She leaned on the edge of her bed and looked over at him with an earnest frown. "It's so *hard* to do nothing. I hate it."

He closed his eyes. Breathed out through his nose. Once again, they were in perfect agreement.

"Sometimes I think I should have been born a boy."

"No." His response was immediate and emphatic.

She let out a little laugh. "That's very kind of you. I suppose you have to say that after, well, you know . . ."

He knew. But not nearly enough.

"I would love to own Aubrey," she said wistfully. "I know every corner. I can name every crop in every field, and every name of every tenant, and half of their birthdays, too."

He looked at her in wonderment. She was so much more than he'd ever allowed himself to see.

"I would have been an excellent Viscount Bridgerton."

"Your brother will learn his way," George said gently. He sat down in the chair by the desk. She wasn't sitting down, but she wasn't exactly standing, either, and as he was alone with her behind a closed door, he rather thought *this* would not be the critical breach of propriety.

"Oh, I know he will," Billie said. "Edmund is very clever, actually, when he's not being annoying."

"He's fifteen. He can't help being annoying."

She gave him a look. "If I recall correctly, you were already a god among men by the time you were his age."

He lifted a lazy brow. There were so many droll rejoinders to such a statement, but he decided to let them all pass and simply enjoy the easy camaraderie of the moment.

"How do you bear it?" she asked.

"Bear what?"

"This." She raised her hands in a gesture of defeat. "The help-lessness."

He sat up a little straighter, blinking her into focus.

"You do feel it, don't you?"

"I'm not sure I catch your meaning," he murmured. But he had a feeling he did.

"I know you wish you could have taken a commission. I see it in your face every time your brothers talk about it."

Was he that obvious? He'd hoped not. But at the same time . . .

"George?"

He looked up.

"You'd gone very silent," she said.

"I was just thinking . . ."

She smiled indulgently, allowing him to think aloud.

"I *don't* wish I'd taken a commission."

She drew back, her surprise evident in the way her chin tucked into her neck.

"My place is here," he said.

Her eyes lit with something that might have been pride. "You sound as if you're only just realizing it."

"No," he mused. "I've always known that."

"You hadn't accepted it?" she prodded.

He chuckled wryly. "No, I had definitely accepted it. I just think I hadn't let myself . . ." He looked up, straight into her lovely brown eyes, and paused for a moment as he realized what he wanted to say. "I hadn't let myself *like* it."

"And now you do?"

His nod was quick and firm. "I do. If I don't—" He stopped, cor-rected himself. "If *we* don't care for the land and its people, what are Edward and Andrew even fighting for?"

"If they are going to risk their lives for King and Country," she said softly, "we should make it a *good* King and Country."

Their eyes met, and Billie smiled. Just a little. And they didn't speak. Because they didn't need to. Until finally she said, "They're going to be up with your food soon," she said.

He quirked a brow. "Are you trying to be rid of me?"

"I'm trying to protect my reputation," she retorted. "And yours."

"If you recall, I did ask you to marry me."

"No, you didn't," she scoffed. "You said, 'Of course I'll marry you,'"—this she said in a remarkable impression of a distempered crone—"which is not the same thing at all."

He eyed her thoughtfully. "I could get down on one knee."

"Stop teasing me, George. It's very unkind of you." Her voice wobbled, and he felt something tight, squeezing in his chest. His lips parted, but she pushed herself off the edge of her bed and walked over to her window, crossing her arms as she stared out into the night.

"It's not something you joke about," she said, but her words were oddly formed, round and wide, almost as if they were coming from somewhere deep in her throat.

He came quickly to his feet. "Billie, I'm sorry. You must know I would never—"

"You should go."

He paused.

"You should go," she said, more forcefully this time. "They'll be here with your dinner at any moment."

It was a dismissal, clear and sensible. It was a kindness, really. She was stopping him from making a fool of himself. If she wanted him to propose, wouldn't she have taken the bait he'd so casually dangled?

"As you wish," he said, executing a polite bow even though she was not facing him. He saw her nod, and then he left the room.

Oh, dear God, what had she done?

He could have proposed to her. Right then and there. *George.*

And she had *stopped* him. Stopped him because—bloody hell, she didn't know why. Hadn't she spent the entire day in a blue haze, wondering why he was avoiding her and how she might get him to kiss her again?

Wouldn't marriage ensure future kisses? Wasn't it *precisely* what she needed to achieve her (admittedly unladylike) goals?

But he'd been sitting there, sprawled out in the desk chair like he owned the place (which she supposed he did, or rather, would), and she couldn't tell if he meant it. Was he teasing her? Having a spot of fun? George had never been cruel; he wouldn't purposefully hurt her feelings, but if he thought *she* regarded the whole thing as a joke, then he might feel permitted to treat it as such . . .

It was what Andrew would have done. Not that Andrew would ever have kissed her, or that she'd have wanted him to, but if for some reason they'd been joking about marriage, absolutely he'd have said something ridiculous about getting down on one knee.

But with George . . . she just hadn't known if he'd *meant* it. And then what if she'd said yes? What if she'd said that she'd *love* for him to get down on one knee and pledge his eternal devotion . . .

And then found out he was joking?

Her face flamed just thinking of it.

She didn't think he would tease about such a thing. But then again, this was George. He was the eldest son of the Earl of Manston, the noble and honorable Lord Kennard. If he were going to propose to a lady, he would never do it slapdash. He'd have the ring, and he'd have the poetic words, and he certainly wouldn't leave it up to her to decide if he ought to do it on bended knee.

Which meant he couldn't have meant it, right? George would never be so unsure of himself.

She flopped on her bed, pressing both hands against her chest, trying to quell her racing heart. She used to hate that about George—his unshakable confidence. When they were children he always knew better than the rest of them. About everything. It had been the *most* annoying thing, even if now she realized that at five years their senior, he probably *had* known better about everything. There was no way the rest of them were going to catch up until they reached adulthood.

And now . . . now she loved his quiet confidence. He was never brash, never boastful. He was just . . . George.

And she loved him.

She loved him, and—*OH DEAR GOD, SHE HAD JUST STOPPED HIM FROM ASKING HER TO MARRY HIM.*

What had she done?

And more importantly, how could she undo it?

Chapter 20

George was always the first in his family to come down to breakfast, but when he stepped into the informal dining room the following morning, his mother was already at the table, sipping a cup
of tea.

There was no way this was a coincidence.

"George," she said immediately upon seeing him, "we must
speak."

"Mother," he murmured, stepping over to the sideboard to fix his
plate. Whatever it was she was het up over, he was not in the mood.
He was tired and he was cranky. He might have only *almost* proposed marriage the night before, but he had most definitely been
rejected.

It was not the stuff dreams were made of. Nor a good night's
sleep.

"As you know," she said, jumping right into it, "tonight is Lady
Wintour's ball."

He spooned some coddled eggs onto his plate. "I assure you it has not slipped my mind."

Her lips tightened, but she did not take him to task for his sarcasm. Instead she waited with heavy patience until he joined her at the table.

"It is about Billie," she said.

Of course it was.

"I am very concerned about her."

So was he, but he doubted it was for the same reasons. He pasted a bland smile on his face. "What is the problem?"

"She is going to need all the help she can get tonight."

"Don't be ridiculous," he scoffed, but he knew what she meant. Billie was not meant for London. She was a country girl, through and through.

"She lacks confidence, George. The vultures will see this instantly."

"Do you ever wonder why we choose to socialize with these vultures?" he mused.

"Because half of them are really doves."

"Doves?" He stared at her in disbelief.

She waved a hand. "Perhaps carrier pigeons. But that is not the point."

"I would never be so lucky."

She gave him just enough of a look to make it clear that while she had heard this, she was graciously choosing to ignore it. "Her success is in your hands."

He knew he would regret encouraging her to expand upon this point, but he could not stop himself from saying, "I beg your pardon?"

"You know as well as I do that the surest way to ensure a debutante's success is for an eligible gentleman—such as yourself—to pay her attention."

For some reason, this irritated him greatly. "Since when is Billie a debutante?"

His mother stared at him as if he were an idiot. "Why else do you think I brought her to London?"

"I believe you said you wished for her company?" he countered.

His mother waved that away as the nonsense she clearly saw it to be. "The girl needed some polish."

No, George thought, *she didn't*. He jabbed his fork into his sausage with far too much force. "She's perfectly fine the way she is."

"That is very gracious of you, George," she replied, inspecting her muffin before deciding to add an additional dab of butter, "but I assure you, no lady wishes to be 'perfectly fine.' "

He fixed a patient expression on his face. "Your point, Mother?"

"Merely that I need you to do your part this evening. You *must* dance with her."

She made it sound as if he thought it a chore. "Of course I'll dance with her." It would be awkward as hell, all things considered, but even so, he could not help but look forward to it. He'd been longing to dance with Billie since that morning back at Aubrey Hall when she'd looked up at him, planted her hands on her hips, and demanded, "Have you ever danced with me?"

At the time, he couldn't believe that he'd never done so. After all those years as neighbors, how could he not have danced with her?

But now he couldn't believe that he'd ever thought he *had*. If he had danced with Billie, music washing over them as he placed his hand on her hip . . . it was not something he could forget.

And he wanted it. He wanted to take her hand in his and dance her down the line, to step and dip, and feel her innate grace. But more than that, he wanted *her* to feel it. He wanted her to know that she was every bit as womanly and elegant as the rest, that she was perfect in his eyes, not just "perfectly fine," and if he could only—

"George!"

He looked up.

"Kindly pay attention," his mother said.

"My apologies," he murmured. He had no idea how long he'd been lost in his own thoughts, although generally speaking, with his mother even a second or two of woolgathering was not to be tolerated.

"I was saying," she said somewhat peevishly, "that you must dance with Billie twice."

"Consider it done."

Her eyes narrowed; she was clearly suspicious at the ease at which she was getting her way. "You must also be sure to allow at least ninety minutes to elapse between dances."

He rolled his eyes and did not bother to hide it. "As you wish."

Lady Manston stirred a bit of sugar into her tea. "You must appear attentive."

"But not too attentive?"

"Don't mock me," she warned.

He set down his fork. "Mother, I assure you that I am every bit as eager for Billie's happiness as you are."

This seemed to appease her somewhat. "Very well," she said, "I am pleased that we are in agreement. I wish to arrive at the ball at half past nine. This will give us the opportunity to make a proper entrance, but it will still be early enough that it won't be so difficult to make introductions. It gets so loud at these things."

George nodded his agreement.

"I think we should depart at nine—there will surely be a line of carriages outside of Wintour House and you know how long *that* takes—so if you could be ready by three-quarters past eight—"

"Oh, no, I'm sorry," George interrupted, thinking of the ridiculous message he was meant to pass along to Robert Tallywhite. "I cannot accompany you. I'll need to make my own way to the ball."

"Don't be absurd," she said dismissively. "We need you to escort us."

"I wish I could," he said quite honestly. He would have liked nothing better than for Billie to make her entrance on his arm, but he'd already given a great deal of thought to this evening's schedule, and he had determined that it was imperative that he arrive on his own. If he came with the ladies, he would have to practically abandon them at the door. And heaven knew *that* would never happen without a full interrogation from his mother.

No, better to get there earlier so that he could find Tallywhite and take care of the whole thing before they even arrived.

"What can possibly be more important than accompanying Billie and me?" his mother demanded.

"I have a previous engagement," he replied, lifting his own cup of tea to his lips. "It cannot be avoided."

His mother's lips pressed into a firm line. "I am most displeased."

"I am sorry to disappoint."

She began stirring her tea with increasing vigor. "I could be completely wrong about this, you know. She could be an instant success. We could be surrounded by gentlemen from the moment we arrive."

"Your tone seems to imply that you think that would be a bad thing," George said.

"Of course not. But you won't be there to see it."

In truth, it was the last thing George wanted to see. Billie, surrounded by a pack of gentlemen astute enough to realize what a treasure she was? It was the stuff of nightmares.

And a moot point, as it happened. "Actually," he told his mother, "I will likely arrive at Wintour House before you do."

"Well, then I see no reason you cannot circle back 'round from your errand and pick us up on the way."

He fought the urge to pinch the bridge of his nose. "Mother, it won't work. Please leave it at that and know that I will see you at the ball, where I shall dance such attendance upon Billie that the gentlemen of London will be waiting in line just to fall at her feet."

"Good morning."

They both turned to see Billie standing in the doorway. George stood to greet her. He wasn't sure how much she had heard, beyond his obvious sarcasm, and he very much feared she would take it the wrong way.

"It is very kind of you to agree to attend to me tonight," she said, her tone so sweet and pleasant that he could not quite gauge its sincerity. She walked over to the sideboard and picked up a plate. "I do hope it will not be too much of a chore."

Ah, and *there* she was.

"On the contrary," he replied. "I am very much looking forward to being your escort."

"But not so much that you will actually accompany us in the carriage," his mother muttered.

"Stop," he said.

Billie turned around, her eyes darting from Rokesby to Rokesby with unconcealed curiosity.

"I regret to inform you that I have an unbreakable commitment this evening," he told her, "which means I will not be able to drive to Wintour House with you. But I will see you there. And I hope you will save me two dances."

"Of course," she murmured. But then again, she could hardly say anything else.

"Since you cannot escort us this evening . . ." Lady Manston began.

George nearly threw down his napkin.

". . . perhaps you may assist us in some other way."

"Please," he said, "inform me how I may be of service."

Billie made a sound that might have been a snort. He wasn't sure. But it was certainly in her nature to find amusement in his rapidly dwindling patience with his mother.

"You know all of the young gentlemen better than I do," Lady Manston continued. "Are there any we should avoid?"

All of them, George wanted to say.

"And are there any we should particularly look out for? That Billie may plan to set her cap for?"

"That I may—*what*?"

Billie must truly have been startled, George thought. She dropped three slices of bacon on the floor.

"Set your cap, darling," Lady Manston said. "It's an expression. Surely you've heard it."

"Of course I've heard it," Billie said, hurrying over to take her place at the table. "I don't, however, see how it applies to me. I did not come to London to look for a husband."

"You must always be looking for a husband, Billie," Lady Manston said, then turned right back to George. "What about Ashbourne's son? Not the oldest, of course. He's already married, and as delightful as you are"—this, she said over her shoulder to the still-aghast Billie—"I don't think you could snag the heir to a dukedom."

"I'm fairly certain I don't want to," Billie said.

"Very practical of you, my dear. It's quite a lot of pomp."

"So says the wife of an earl," George remarked.

"It's not at all the same thing," his mother said. "And you didn't answer my question. What about Ashbourne's son?"

"No."

"No?" his mother echoed. "No, as in you don't have an opinion?"

"No, as in no. He is not for Billie."

Who, George could not help but note, was watching the mother-son exchange with an odd mix of curiosity and alarm.

"Any particular reason?" Lady Manston asked.

"He gambles," George lied. Well, maybe it wasn't a lie. All gentlemen gambled. He had no idea if the one in question did so to excess.

"What about the Billington heir? I think he—"

"Also no."

His mother regarded him with an impassive expression.

"He's too young," George said, hoping it was true.

"He is?" She frowned. "I suppose he might be. I can't remember precisely."

"I don't suppose *I* have any say in the matter," Billie put in.

"Of course you do," Lady Manston said, patting her hand. "Just not yet."

Billie's lips parted, but she appeared not to know what to say.

"How could you," Lady Manston continued, "when you don't know anyone but us?"

Billie put a piece of bacon in her mouth and began to chew with impressive force. George suspected this was to stop herself from saying something she'd regret.

"Don't worry, my dear," Lady Manston said.

George took a sip of his tea. "She doesn't look worried to me."

Billie shot him a grateful look.

His mother ignored him completely. "You will get to know everyone soon enough, Billie. And then you can decide with whom you wish to pursue an acquaintance."

"I don't know that I plan to be here long enough to form opinions one way or another," Billie said, her voice—in George's opinion—remarkably even and calm.

"Nonsense," Lady Manston said. "Just leave everything to me."

"You're not her mother," George said quietly.

To which his mother raised her brows and said, "I could be."

To which both George and Billie stared at her in openmouthed shock.

"Oh, come now, you two," Lady Manston said, "surely it can be no surprise that I have long hoped for an alliance between the Rokesbys and Bridgertons."

"Alliance?" Billie echoed, and all George could think was that it was a terrible, clinical word, one that could never encompass all that he had come to feel for her.

"Match, marriage, whatever you wish to call it," Lady Manston said. "We are the dearest of friends. Of course I should like to be family."

"If it makes any difference," Billie said quietly, "I already think of you as family."

"Oh, I know that, dear. I feel the same way. I've just always thought it would be wonderful to make it official. But no matter. There is always Georgiana."

Billie cleared her throat. "She's very young yet."

Lady Manston smiled devilishly. "So is Nicholas."

The look on Billie's face came so close to horror George almost laughed. He probably would have done if he hadn't been fairly certain his own face held the same expression.

"I see that I have shocked you," his mother said. "But any mother will tell you—it's never too early to plan for the future."

"I would not recommend mentioning this to Nicholas," George murmured.

"Or Georgiana, I'm sure," his mother said, pouring herself yet another cup of tea. "Would you like a cup, Billie?"

"Ehrm . . . yes, thank you."

"Oh, and that's another thing," Lady Manston said as she put a splash of milk in Billie's teacup. "We need to stop calling you Billie."

Billie blinked. "I beg your pardon?"

In went the tea, and then Lady Manston held the cup out and said, "Starting today we will use your given name. Sybilla."

Billie's mouth hung open for a brief—but noticeable—moment before she said, "That's what my mother calls me when she's cross."

"Then we shall begin a new, happier tradition."

"Is this really necessary?" George asked.

"I know it will be difficult to remember," Lady Manston said, finally setting the cup down near Billie's plate, "but I think it's for the best. As a name, Billie is so, well . . . I don't know that I would call it mannish, but I don't think it accurately represents how we wish to portray you."

"It accurately represents who she *is*," George practically growled.

"Goodness. I had no idea you would feel so strongly about this," his mother said, peering over at him with a flawlessly innocent expression. "But of course, it's not up to you."

"I would prefer to be called Billie," Billie said.

"I'm not sure it's up to you, either, dear."

George's fork came down heavily on his plate. "Who the devil is it up to, then?"

His mother regarded him as if he had asked *just* the stupidest question. "Me."

"You," he said.

"I know how these things work. I've done this before, you know."

"Didn't Mary find her husband in Kent?" George reminded her.

"Only after she gained her polish in London."

Good God. His mother had gone mad. It was the only explanation. She could be tenacious, and she could be exacting when it came to society and etiquette, but never had she managed to weave the two together with such complete irrationality.

"Surely it doesn't matter," Billie said. "Won't most everyone be calling me Miss Bridgerton, anyway?"

"Of course," Lady Manston conceded, "but they will hear us speaking with you. It's not as if they won't *know* your Christian name."

"This is the most asinine conversation," George grumbled.

His mother just flicked him A Look. "Sybilla," she said, turning to Billie, "I know you did not come to London with the intention of looking for a husband, but surely you see the convenience of it now that you're here. You'll never find so many eligible gentlemen in one place in Kent."

"I don't know," Billie murmured over her tea, "it's chock-full when all of the Rokesbys are home."

George looked up sharply just as his mother burst out in a trill of laughter. "Too true, Billie," she said with a warm smile (apparently forgetting that she meant to call her Sybilla), "but alas, I have only the one home right now."

"Two," George said incredulously. Apparently if one never went away, one wasn't counted as being home.

His mother's brows rose. "I was speaking of you, George."

Well, now he felt like a fool.

He stood. "I will call Billie what she wishes to be called. And I will see you at Wintour House as promised, when the ball is under-way. If you will excuse me, I have much to attend to."

He didn't actually, but he didn't think he could listen to another word of his mother's on the topic of Billie's debut.

The sooner they all got this wretched day over with the better.

Billie watched him walk away, and she wasn't going to say any-thing, honestly she wasn't, but even as she dipped her spoon into her porridge, she heard herself call out, "Wait!"

George paused at the door.

"Just a quick word," she said, hastily setting down her napkin. She had no idea what that quick word might be, but something was there inside of her, and it obviously needed to get out. She turned back to Lady Manston. "Pray excuse me. I'll be but a moment."

George stepped out of the small dining room and into the hall to afford them a spot of privacy.

Billie cleared her throat. "Sorry."

"For what?"

Good question. She wasn't sorry. "Actually," she said, "it's thank you."

"You're thanking me," he said softly.

"For standing up for me," she said. "Calling me Billie."

His mouth curved into a wry half-smile. "I don't think I could call you Sybilla if I tried."

She returned the expression in kind. "I'm not sure I would answer if it came from any voice other than my mother's."

He studied her face for a moment, then said, "Don't let my mother turn you into someone you're not."

"Oh, I don't think that's possible at this late stage. I'm far too set in my ways."

"At the grand age of three-and-twenty?"

"It's a very grand age when you're an unmarried female," she retorted. Maybe she shouldn't have said it; there were too many not-quite marriage proposals in their history. (*One*, Billie thought, was too many. Two practically marked her as a freak of nature.)

But she didn't regret saying it. She couldn't regret it. Not if she wanted to turn one of those almost-proposals into something real.

And she did. She'd been up half the night—well, twenty minutes at least—berating herself for her practically ensuring that he would not ask her to marry him. If she'd had a hair shirt (and any inclination for useless gestures), she'd have donned it.

George's brow furrowed, and of course her mind whipped into triple-speed. Was he wondering why she'd made a comment about her near-spinster status? Trying to decide how to respond? Debating her sanity?

"She did help me pick out a lovely gown for this evening," she blurted out.

"My mother?"

Billie nodded, then summoned a mischievous smile. "Although I did bring a pair of my breeches to town just in case I needed to shock her."

He let out a bark of laughter. "Did you really?"

"No," she admitted, her heart suddenly lighter now that he'd laughed, "but just the fact that I pondered it means something, don't you think?"

"Absolutely." He looked down at her, his eyes so blue in the morning light, and his humor was replaced by something more serious. "Please allow me to apologize for my mother. I don't know what's come over her."

"I think perhaps she feels"—Billie frowned for a moment, choosing the best word—"guilty."

"Guilty?" George's face betrayed his surprise. "Whatever for?"

"That neither of your brothers ever offered for me." Another thing she probably should not have said. But as it happened, Billie *did* think that Lady Manston felt this way.

And when George's expression slid from curiosity to something that might have been jealousy . . . well, Billie could not help but feel a little pleased.

"So I think she's trying to make it up to me," she said gamely. "It's not as if I was waiting for one of them to ask me, but I think she thinks I was, so now she wants to introduce me—"

"Enough," George practically barked.

"I beg your pardon?"

He cleared his throat. "Enough," he said in a much more evenly tempered voice. "It's ridiculous."

"That your mother feels this way?"

"That she thinks introducing you to a pack of useless fops is a sensible idea."

Billie took a moment to enjoy this statement, then said, "She means well."

George scoffed audibly at this.

"She does," Billie insisted, unable to suppress a smile. "She just wants what she thinks is best for me."

"What *she* thinks."

"Well, yes. There's no convincing her otherwise. It's a Rokesby trait, I'm afraid."

"You may have just insulted me."

"No," she said, maintaining an impressively straight face.

"I'll let it pass."

"Very kind of you, sir."

He rolled his eyes at her impertinence, and once again, Billie felt more at ease. Perhaps this wasn't how the more refined ladies flirted, but it was all she knew how to do.

And it seemed to be working. Of *that* she was certain.

Maybe she did have a touch of feminine intuition after all.

Chapter 21

*Later that night
At the Wintour Ball*

Ninety minutes in, and still he had not seen Tallywhite.

George tugged at his cravat, which he was certain his valet had tied far more tightly than usual. There was nothing out of the ordinary about Lady Wintour's Spring Soirée; in fact, he'd have gone so far as to say that it was so ordinary as to be dull, but he could not shake the odd, prickly sensation that kept crawling up his neck. Everywhere he turned, it felt like someone was looking at him strangely, watching him with far more curiosity than his appearance should warrant.

Clearly, it was all in his imagination, which led to a most salient point—that clearly, he was not cut out for this sort of thing.

He'd timed his arrival carefully. Too early, and he would draw unwanted attention. Like most single men of his age, he usually spent a few hours at his club before fulfilling his social obligations. If he showed up at the ball on the dot of eight, it would look strange. (And he would have to spend the next two hours making conversation with his nearly deaf great-aunt, who was as legendary for her punctuality as she was for her fragrant breath.)

But he didn't want to follow his usual schedule, either, which involved arriving well after the party was underway. It would be too difficult to spot Tallywhite in such a crush, or worse, he could miss him altogether.

So after careful consideration, he stepped into the Wintour ballroom approximately one hour after the designated starting time. It was still unfashionably early, but there were enough people milling about for George to remain unobtrusive.

Not for the first time, he wondered if perhaps he was overthinking this whole thing. It seemed an awful lot of mental preparation for the task of uttering a line from a nursery rhyme.

A quick check of the time told him that it was nearly ten, which meant that if Billie had not already arrived, she would do so soon. His mother had been aiming for nine-thirty, but he'd heard numerous grumblings about the lengthy line of carriages queued up outside Wintour House. Billie and his mother were almost certainly stuck in the Manston coach and four, waiting for their turn to alight.

He didn't have much time if he wanted to get this taken care of before they arrived.

His expression carefully bored, he continued to move about the room, murmuring the appropriate greetings as he brushed past acquaintances. A footman was circulating with glasses of punch, so he took one, barely moistening his lips as he peered out at the ballroom over the rim of the glass. He did not see Tallywhite, but he did see—damn it, was that Lord Arbuthnot?

Why the hell was he asking George to deliver a message when he could bloody well have done it himself?

But maybe there were reasons why Arbuthnot could not be seen with Tallywhite. Maybe there was someone *else* here, someone who could not be permitted to know that the two men were working together. Or maybe Tallywhite was the one in the dark. Maybe he didn't know that Arbuthnot was the one with the message.

Or . . .

Maybe Tallywhite *did* know that Arbuthnot was his contact, and the whole thing was a plan to test George so that they could use him for future endeavors. Maybe George had just accidentally embarked upon a career in espionage.

He looked down at the punch in his hand. Maybe he needed . . . No, he *definitely* needed something with a higher degree of alcohol.

"What is this rot?" he muttered, setting the glass back down.

And then he saw her.

He stopped breathing. "Billie?"

She was a vision. Her gown was of the deepest crimson, the color an unexpectedly vibrant choice for an unmarried miss, but on Billie it was perfection. Her skin was like milk, her eyes sparkled, and her lips . . . He knew she did not color them—Billie would never have patience for that sort of thing—but somehow they looked richer, as if they'd absorbed some of the ruby brilliance of her gown.

He had kissed those lips. He had tasted her and adored her, and he wanted to worship her in ways she'd likely never dreamed possible.

It was odd, though; he had not heard her being announced. He was too far from the entrance, or maybe he had simply been too enmeshed in his own thoughts. But there she was, standing next to his mother, so beautiful, so radiant that he could not see anyone else.

Suddenly the rest of the world seemed like such a chore. He didn't want to be here at this dance, with people he didn't want to talk to and messages he didn't particularly wish to deliver. He didn't want to dance with young ladies he didn't know, and he didn't want to make polite conversation with people he did. He just wanted Billie, and he wanted her all to himself.

He forgot about Tallywhite. He forgot about pease, porridge, *and* pudding, and he stalked across the room with such single-minded purpose that the crowds seemed to melt from his path.

And somehow, amazingly, the rest of the world had not yet noticed her. She was so beautiful, so uncommonly alive and *real* in this room full of waxen dolls. She would not go undiscovered for long.

But not yet. Soon he would have to fight the throngs of eager young gentlemen, but for now, she was still his alone.

She was nervous, though. It wasn't obvious; he was sure he was the only one who could tell. With Billie, you had to *know* her. She was standing proud, back straight and head high, but her eyes were flitting about, glancing through the crowd.

Looking for him?

He stepped forward.

"George!" she said delightedly. "Er, I mean, Lord Kennard. How lovely and"—she gave him a hidden smile—"unsurprising to see you."

"Miss Bridgerton," he murmured, bowing over her hand.

"George," his mother said, nodding her head in greeting.

He leaned down to kiss her cheek. "Mother."

"Doesn't Billie look beautiful?"

He nodded slowly, unable to take his eyes from her. "Yes," he said, "she looks . . . beautiful." But it wasn't the right word. It was far too prosaic. Beauty wasn't the fierce intelligence that gave her eyes depth, and it wasn't the wit behind her smile. She was beautiful, but she wasn't *only* beautiful, and that was why he loved her.

"I hope that you have saved your first dance for me," he said.

Billie looked over at his mother for confirmation.

"Yes, you may dance your first with George," she said with an indulgent smile.

"There are so many rules," Billie said sheepishly. "I couldn't remember if for some reason I was meant to save you for later."

"Have you been here long?" Lady Manston asked.

"An hour or so," George replied. "My errand took less time than I'd anticipated."

"It was an errand?" she said. "I thought it was a meeting."

If George hadn't been so entranced with Billie, he might have had the wherewithal to muster irritation at this. His mother was clearly fishing for information, or at the very least, attempting to scold him retroactively. But he just couldn't bring himself to care. Not when Billie was looking up at him with shining eyes.

"You really do look beautiful," he said.

"Thank you." She smiled awkwardly, and his gaze fell to her hands, which were nervously riffling against the folds of her skirt. "You look very handsome as well."

Beside them, Lady Manston was beaming.

"Would you care to dance?" he blurted.

"Now?" She smiled adorably. "Is there music?"

There wasn't. It was some testament to how foolish in love he'd become that he did not even feel embarrassed. "Perhaps a turn about the room," he suggested. "The musicians will begin again shortly."

Billie looked to Lady Manston, who gave her approval with a wave. "Go," she said, "but stay well within sight."

George was jolted out of his dreamy haze for long enough to shoot his mother an icy look. "I would not dream of doing anything to compromise her reputation."

"Of course not," she said airily. "I want to make sure she's *seen*. There are many eligible gentlemen here tonight. More than I expected."

George grabbed Billie's arm.

"I saw the Billington heir," Lady Manston continued, "and you know, I *don't* think he's too young."

George gave her a look of mild disdain. "I don't think she wants to be Billie Billington, Mother."

Billie choked down a laugh. "Oh, my, I hadn't even thought."

"Good."

"She's Sybilla now, anyway," his mother said, demonstrating her talent for hearing only what she wished to. "And Sybilla Billington has rather a nice ring to it."

George looked at Billie and said, "It doesn't."

She pressed her lips together, looking highly amused.

"His surname is Wycombe," Lady Manston said. "Just so you know."

George rolled his eyes. His mother was a menace. He held out his arm. "Shall we, Billie?"

Billie nodded and turned so they were facing in the same direction.

"If you see Ashbourne's son . . ."

But George had already led Billie away.

"I don't know what Ashbourne's son looks like," Billie said. "Do you?"

"Bit of a paunch," George lied.

"Oh." Billie frowned. "I can't imagine why she'd think of him for me, then. She knows I'm very active."

George made a murmuring noise that was meant to convey his agreement and continued his slow promenade along the perimeter of the ballroom, enjoying the proprietary sensation of her hand on his arm.

"There was quite a line of carriages to get in," Billie said. "*I* told your mother we should just get out and walk, since the weather is so fine, but she was having none of it."

George chuckled. Only Billie would make such a suggestion.

"Honestly," she grumbled, "you would have thought I'd asked if we could stop off and see the King for a cup of tea on the way."

"Well, seeing as the palace is quite across town . . ." George teased.

She elbowed him in the ribs. But lightly, so no one would see.

"I am glad you did not wear a wig," he said to her. Her hair had been styled elaborately, as was the fashion, but it was her own, and only lightly powdered. He liked that the rich chestnut color shone through; it was Billie without artifice, and if there was one thing that defined her, it was that she *had* no artifice.

He wanted her to enjoy her time in London, but he did not want her to be changed by it.

"Dreadfully unfashionable, I know," she said, touching the long lock of hair that had been left to drape over her shoulder, "but I managed to convince your mother that there was a good chance I would step too close to a sconce and set myself on fire."

George turned sharply.

"Given my history being presented at court," she said, "it was not as unreasonable as it sounds."

He tried not to laugh. He really did.

"Oh, please do," she said. "It has taken me this long to be able to make a joke of it. We might as well be amused."

"What did happen?" he asked. "Or don't I want to know?"

"Oh, you want to know," she said with an impertinent sideways look. "Trust me. You definitely want to know."

He waited.

"But you won't find out now," she declared. "A woman must have her secrets, or so your mother keeps telling me."

"Somehow I don't think setting fire to the Court of St. James was the sort of secret she had in mind."

"Considering how fervently she wishes me to be seen as a young lady of grace and refinement, I think it might be exactly what she had in mind." She glanced over at him with an arch expression. "Lady Alexandra Fortescue-Endicott would never accidentally set someone on fire."

"No, if she did it, I imagine it would be purposeful."

Billie snorted back a laugh. "George Rokesby, that's a terrible thing to say. And probably not true."

"You don't think so?"

"Much as it pains me to admit it, no. She's not that evil. Or clever."

He paused for a moment, then asked, "It *was* an accident, wasn't it?"

She gave him a look.

"Of course it was," he said, but he didn't sound nearly as certain as he ought.

"Kennard!"

At the sound of his name, George looked reluctantly away from Billie. Two university friends of his—Sir John Willingham and Freddie Coventry—were making their way through the crowd. They were both perfectly pleasant, utterly respectable, and exactly the sort of gentlemen his mother would wish him to introduce to Billie.

George found that *he* rather wished to hit one of them. It didn't matter which. Either would do, so long as he could aim for the face.

"Kennard," Sir John said, approaching with a grin. "It's been an age. I wouldn't have thought you'd be in town yet."

"Family business," George said noncommittally.

Sir John and Freddie both nodded and said something along the lines of *just so*, and then they both looked over at Billie with clear expectation.

George forced a smile and turned to Billie. "May I present Sir John Willingham and Mr. Frederick Coventry." There were murmurs all around, and then he said, "Gentlemen, this is Miss Sybilla Bridgerton of Aubrey Hall in Kent."

"Kent, you say," Freddie exclaimed. "Are you neighbors, then?"

"We are indeed," Billie said prettily. "I have known Lord Kennard all of my life."

George fought a scowl. He knew she could not use his Christian name in such a milieu, but it still grated to be referred to so formally.

"You are a lucky man indeed," Freddie said, "to have such loveliness so close to home."

George stole a glance at Billie to see if she was as appalled by the sugary compliment as he was, but she was still smiling placidly, looking for all the world like a sweet-tempered, gentle debutante.

He snorted. Sweet-tempered and gentle? Billie? If they only knew.

"Did you say something?" she asked.

He matched her smile with one of his own, equally bland. "Just that I am indeed lucky."

Her brows rose. "How odd that I might have missed a sentence of such length."

He gave her a sideways look.

Which she returned with a secret smile.

He felt something settle within himself. All was right with the world again. Or at least all was right with this moment. The world was a bloody mess, but right here, right now, Billie was smiling secretly . . .

And he was content.

"May I claim a dance, Miss Bridgerton?" Sir John asked Billie.

"And me as well," Freddie immediately put in.

"Of course," she said, again so prettily that George wanted to gag. She didn't sound like herself.

"She has already promised her first to me," he cut in. "And the supper set."

Billie regarded him with some surprise, since she had not promised him the supper set, but she did not contradict.

"Nevertheless," Freddie said with smooth amusement, "there are more than two dances at a ball."

"I should be delighted to dance with both of you," Billie said. She looked about the room as if in search of something. "I don't believe there are dance cards this evening . . ."

"We can survive well enough without them," Freddie said. "All we must remember is that when you are done with Kennard here, you will dance with me."

Billie gave a friendly smile and a regal nod.

"And then you're on to Sir John," Freddie noted. "But I'll warn you, he's an atrocious dancer. You'll want to watch your toes."

Billie laughed at that, full and throaty, and once again she became so incandescently beautiful that George was half-tempted to throw a blanket over her, just to stop anyone else from wanting her.

He should not begrudge her this moment in the sun. He knew that. She deserved to be adored and fêted, to have her much-deserved moment as the belle of the ball. But by God, when she smiled at Sir John or Freddie, it looked as if she actually meant it.

Who smiled like that without actually meaning it? Did she have any idea what a smile like that could lead to? The two gentlemen were going to think she was interested. George had a sudden vision of bouquets filling the front hall of Manston House, of young gentlemen queuing up for the privilege of kissing her hand.

"Is something wrong?" Billie asked quietly. Sir John and Freddie had been distracted by another acquaintance and had turned slightly away, so her words were for George alone.

"Of course not," he said, but his voice was somewhat more clipped than usual.

Her brow pleated with concern. "Are you certain? You—"

"I'm fine," he snapped.

Her brows rose. "Clearly."

He scowled.

"If you don't want to dance with me . . ." she began.

"*That's* what you think this is?"

"So there *is* something!" Her expression was so triumphant; she really ought to have had a Pall Mall mallet in her hand to complete the look.

"For the love of God, Billie," he muttered, "it's not a competition."

"I don't even know what *it* is."

"You shouldn't be smiling like that at other gentlemen," he said in a hushed voice.

"*What?*" She drew back, and he wasn't sure if it was out of disbelief or outrage.

"It will give them the wrong impression."

"I thought the whole purpose was for me to attract gentlemen," she practically hissed.

Outrage, then. And quite a lot of it.

George had just enough presence of mind not to blurt out the spectacularly inane, "Yes, but not *too* much attention." Instead he warned, "Do not be surprised if they come calling tomorrow."

"Again, isn't that the point?"

George had no answer, because there *was* no answer. He was being an idiot, that much was clear to both of them.

Good God, how had the conversation deteriorated to *this*?

"Billie, look," he said, "I simply—"

He frowned. Arbuthnot was making his way over.

"You simply . . ." Billie prompted.

He shook his head, and she was smart enough to know that the motion had nothing to do with her. She followed his gaze over toward Arbuthnot, but the older gentleman had stopped to talk with someone else.

"Who are you looking at?" she asked.

He turned back and fixed his full attention on her. "No one."

She rolled her eyes at the obvious lie.

"Kennard," Freddie Coventry said, returning to their sides as Sir John wandered off, "I do believe the orchestra is retaking their positions. You had best lead Miss Bridgerton to the dance floor or I shall have to accuse you of shady dealings." He leaned toward Billie and said with faux confidentiality, "It will not do for him to claim your first dance and then keep you here among the wallflowers."

She laughed, but only a little, and to George's ears it did not sound quite true. "He would never do that," she said, "if for no other reason than his mother would have his head."

"Oh-ho!" Freddie chortled. "So *that's* how it is."

George smiled tightly. He wanted to throttle Billie for emasculating him so efficiently in front of his friends, but he was still very much aware of Arbuthnot, just a few feet away, presumably angling for a moment alone.

Freddie's voice dropped to a murmuring tease. "I don't think he's going to dance with you."

Billie looked over at George, and when his eyes met hers, he felt like he'd found his entire world. He bowed and held out his arm, because bloody hell, he'd been waiting for this moment for what felt like years.

But of course that was when Arbuthnot finally arrived. "Kennard," he said, his genial greeting exactly what one might expect from a man to the son of a friend. "Good to see you here. What brings you to town?"

"A dance with Miss Bridgerton," Freddie drawled, "but he doesn't seem quite able to lead her to the floor."

Arbuthnot chuckled. "Oh, I'm sure he's not as incapable as that."

George couldn't decide which of them he wanted to kill first.

"Perhaps I should dance with *you*," Billie said to Freddie.

Forget the gentlemen. He'd kill Billie first. What the hell was she thinking? This was forward, even for her. Ladies did not ask gentlemen to dance, especially when their acquaintance was of five minutes' duration.

"A lady who speaks her mind," Freddie said. "How perfectly refreshing. I see why Lord Kennard speaks so highly of you."

"He speaks of me?"

"Not to him," George bit off.

"Well, he should," Freddie said with a flirtatious waggle of his brows. "You would certainly be a more interesting topic than our last conversation, which I believe was about oatmeal."

George was fairly certain this was not true, but there seemed no way to protest without seeming childish.

"Ah, but I find oats fascinating," Billie said, and George almost laughed, because he was the only one who knew that she wasn't joking. Her father's recent successes at harvest were a testament to that.

"A truly singular female," Freddie applauded.

The orchestra began to make the groaning noises that always preceded the actual music, and Billie glanced over at George, waiting for him to repeat his bow and lead her into the dance.

But before he could do so, he heard Lord Arbuthnot clear his throat. George knew what he had to do.

"I give her over to you, Coventry," he said with a bit of a bow. "Since you are so eager for her company."

He tried not to meet Billie's eyes, but he couldn't quite manage it, and when his gaze passed over her face, he saw that she was shocked. And angry.

And hurt.

"Her next shall be yours," Freddie said with good cheer, and George's heart twisted just a bit as he watched him lead her off to dance.

"I am sorry to deprive you of the company of the lovely Miss Bridgerton," Lord Arbuthnot said after a moment, "but I am sure there was more purpose to your time in town than a dance."

There was no one else in their small circle of conversation now that Billie had trotted off with Freddie Coventry, but Arbuthnot clearly wished for circumspection, so George said, "This and that. Family business."

"Isn't that always the case?" He tilted his head toward George. "It's damned exhausting, it is, being the head of the family."

George thought of his father. "I am most fortunate that this particular privilege is not yet mine."

"True, true." Arbuthnot took a large swallow of the drink he was holding, a drink that looked considerably more substantial than the ridiculous punch George had been served earlier that evening. "But you will be soon enough, and we can't pick our families, can we?"

George wondered if Arbuthnot was employing double-speak. If so, it was another indication that he was not cut out for a life of mysterious messages and secret meetings. He decided to take Arbuthnot's words at face value and said, "If we could, I daresay I would have picked my own."

"Well, *that's* a lucky man for you."

"I think so."

"And how fares your evening? Successful?"

"I suppose it depends on how one measures success."

"Is that so?" Arbuthnot said, sounding slightly irritated.

George felt no sympathy. *He* was the one who had started this layered conversation. He could damn well let George have a little fun with it, too. He looked Arbuthnot in the eye and said, "Alas, we come to these events in search of something, do we not?"

"You are rather philosophical for a Tuesday."

"Normally I save my great thinking for Monday nights and Thursday afternoons," George snapped.

Lord Arbuthnot looked at him with sharp surprise.

"I haven't found what I'm looking for," George said. Good God, the double-speak was giving him vertigo.

Arbuthnot's eyes narrowed. "Are you certain?"

"As I can be. It's rather a crush in here."

"That is most disappointing."

"Indeed."

"Perhaps you should dance with Lady Weatherby," Lord Arbuthnot said softly.

George turned sharply. "I beg your pardon?"

"Have you been introduced? I assure you she is a woman without equal."

"We have met," George confirmed. He'd known Sally Weatherby back when she was Sally Sandwick, the older sister of one of his friends. She had married and buried a husband in the intervening years and only recently had moved from full mourning to half. Luckily for her, she wore lavender quite well.

"Weatherby was a good man," Arbuthnot said.

"I did not know him," George said. He'd been quite a bit older, and Sally was his second wife.

"I worked with him from time to time," Arbuthnot said. "A good man. A very good man."

"It has been years since I spoke with Lady Weatherby," George said. "I don't know if I'll have anything to say to her."

"Oh, I imagine you'll think of something."

"I imagine I will."

"Ah, I see my wife over there," Lord Arbuthnot said. "She's doing that thing with her head that either means she needs my assistance or she's about to die."

"You must go to her, then," George said. "Clearly."

"I suppose she'll need my assistance either way," Arbuthnot said with a shrug. "Godspeed to you, son. I hope your evening proves fruitful."

George watched as Lord Arbuthnot made his way across the room, then turned to carry out his mission.

It seemed it was time to dance with Sally Weatherby.

Chapter 22

Mr. Coventry was an accomplished dancer, but Billie could give him no more than a fraction of her attention as he led her through the intricate steps of a cotillion. George had finished talking with the older gentleman, and now he was bowing before a lady of such staggering beauty it was a wonder all the people around her didn't need to shade their eyes from her miraculous glow.

Something seething and green churned within her, and the evening, once so magical, soured.

Billie knew that she shouldn't have asked Mr. Coventry to dance. Lady Manston would have had an apoplexy if she'd been there. She probably still would, once the gossip reached her. And it would. Billie might have avoided London for years, but she knew enough to realize that this would be all over the ballroom within minutes.

And all over town by the next morning.

She would be branded as overly forward. They would say she was chasing Mr. Coventry, that she was desperate for reasons no one quite knew, but she must have a wicked secret because why else would she throw over centuries of convention and ask a gentleman to dance?

And then someone would remember that unfortunate incident at court a few years earlier. Dreadful thing, really, they'd all cluck. Miss Philomena Wren's dress had caught on *fire* of all things, and by the time anyone knew what was happening, there was a pile of young ladies moored helplessly on the floor, unable to move against the awkward weight of their wide-hipped skirts. Wasn't Miss Bridgerton there? Hadn't she been on *top* of Miss Wren?

Billie had to clench her jaw just to keep from growling. If she had been on top of Philomena Wren, it had only been to put *out* the fire, but no one would ever mention that.

That Billie had also been the cause of the fire was still a closely held secret, thank heavens. But honestly, how could a lady be expected to *move* in full court dress? Court protocol demanded gowns with panniers far wider than anything women wore in day-to-day life. Billie normally had a wonderful sense of where her body stood in space—she was the least clumsy person she knew. But who wouldn't have had difficulty maneuvering in a contraption that had her hips jutting out nearly three feet in either direction? And more to the point, what idiot had thought it a good idea to leave a lit candle in a room populated with misshapen ladies?

The edge of her dress had been so far from her actual body that Billie hadn't even felt it when she'd knocked into the candle. Miss Wren hadn't felt it, either, when her dress began to smolder. And she never did, Billie thought with satisfaction, because *she'd* been sensible enough to leap atop the other girl, smothering the flame before it reached her skin.

And yet when all was said and done, no one seemed to recall that Billie had saved Miss Wren from death and disfigurement. No, her mother was so horrified by the entire situation that they'd abandoned their plans for Billie's London Season. Which, Billie had tried to remind herself, was what she'd wanted all along. She'd been fighting against a Season for years.

But she hadn't wanted to win her point because her parents were *ashamed* of her.

With a sigh, she forced her attention back to the cotillion she was apparently dancing with Mr. Coventry. She couldn't recall doing so, but she seemed to have taken the correct steps and not trod on any toes. Luckily she had not had to make too much conversation; it was the sort of dance that separated a lady from her partner as often as it brought them together.

"Lady Weatherby," Mr. Coventry said when he was near enough to speak.

Billie looked up with sharp surprise; she was quite certain Mr. Coventry knew her name. "I beg your pardon?"

They stepped apart, and then back together. "The woman Lord Kennard is dancing with," Mr. Coventry said. "Weatherby's widow."

"She's a widow?"

"Recently so," Mr. Coventry confirmed. "Just out of blacks."

Billie clenched her teeth, trying to keep her expression pleasant. The beautiful widow was very young, probably not more than five years Billie's senior. She was exquisitely dressed in what Billie now knew was the latest style, and her complexion was that perfect alabaster Billie could never achieve without arsenic cream.

If the sun had ever touched Lady Weatherby's perfect cheeks, Billie would eat her hat.

"She'll need to remarry," Mr. Coventry said. "Didn't give old Weatherby an heir, so she's living off the largesse of the new Lord Weatherby. Or more to the point . . ."

Again, the cotillion pulled them apart, and Billie nearly screamed with frustration. Why did people think it was a good idea to conduct important conversations while dancing? Did no one care about the timely impartation of information?

She stepped forward, back into Mr. Coventry's conversational sphere, and said, "More to the point . . . ?"

He smiled knowingly. "She must rely on the good graces of the new Lord Weatherby's wife."

"I am sure she will enjoy Lord Kennard's company," Billie said diplomatically. It wasn't going to fool Mr. Coventry; he knew perfectly well that Billie was jealous to the teeth. But she had to at least *try* to put on a show of indifference.

"I shouldn't worry," Mr. Coventry said.

"Worry?"

Once again, Billie had to wait for her answer. She stepped daintily around another lady, all the while cursing the cotillion. Wasn't there a new dance on the Continent that kept a lady and gentleman together for the entire song? It was being decried as scandalous, but honestly, could no one else see how very sensible it was?

"Kennard was not pleased to relinquish you to my care," Mr. Coventry said when he could. "If he has asked Lady Weatherby to dance, it is nothing more than tit for tat."

But that was not George's way. His humor might be sly, but his behavior never was. He would not ask one lady to dance for no purpose other than to make another jealous. He might have felt some pique, he might be furious with Billie for embarrassing him in front of his friends, but if he was dancing with Lady Weatherby, it was because he wanted to.

Billie felt suddenly sick. She shouldn't have tried to manipulate the situation earlier by saucily saying that she ought to dance with Mr. Coventry. But she had been so frustrated. The evening had all been going so well. When she had first seen George, resplendent in his evening clothes, she'd almost stopped breathing. She'd tried to tell herself that he was the same man she knew in Kent, wearing the same coat and shoes, but here in London, among the people who ran the country and quite possibly the world, he looked different.

He belonged.

There was an air of gravity around him, of quiet confidence and utter assurance of his place. He had this entire life that she knew nothing about, one with parties and balls and meetings at White's. Eventually he would take his seat in parliament, and she would still be the reckless Billie Bridgerton. Except that in a few years *reckless* would give way to *eccentric*. And after that it was all downhill to crazy.

No, she thought firmly. That was not what was going to happen. George liked her. He might even love her a little. She'd seen it in his eyes, and she'd felt it in his kiss. Lady Weatherby could never—

Billie's eyes widened. Where was Lady Weatherby?

And more to the point, where was George?

Five hours later George finally tiptoed through the front door of Manston House, tired, frustrated, and above all, ready to throttle Lord Arbuthnot.

When the general had asked him to deliver a message, George had thought—*How simple this will be.* He was already planning to attend the Wintour Ball, and Robert Tallywhite was precisely the sort of person with whom he might have an idle conversation. All in all, it would be ten minutes from his day, and he would be able to lay his head down that night knowing that he had done something for King and Country.

He had *not* anticipated that his evening would involve following Sally Weatherby to The Swan With No Neck, a somewhat unsavory pub halfway across town. It was there that he had finally found Robert Tallywhite, who appeared to be amusing himself by tossing darts at a tricorn hat pinned rather gruesomely to a wall.

Blindfolded.

George had delivered his message, the contents of which had not seemed to surprise Tallywhite in the least, but when he had attempted to take his leave, he had been compelled to stay for a pint of ale. And by compelled he actually meant *compelled*, as in shoved into a chair by two exceedingly large men, one of whom sported the most vivid black eye George had ever seen.

Such a bruise indicated a remarkable tolerance for pain, and George feared that this might correspond with a remarkable ability to *deliver* pain. So when old Violet Eye told him to sit down and drink up, George did as he was told.

He then spent the next two hours having a breathtakingly convoluted and inane conversation with Tallywhite and his henchmen. (Sally had disappeared immediately upon delivering him to the unfortunate neckless Swan.) They discussed the weather and the rules of cricket and relative merits of Trinity College versus Trinity Hall at Cambridge. They had then moved on to the health benefits of salt water, the difficulty of obtaining proper ice in summer, and whether the high cost of pineapples would affect the popularity of oranges and lemons.

By one in the morning, George suspected that Robert Tally-white was not entirely sane, and by two he was certain of it. At three, he finally managed to take his leave, but not before "accidentally" taking an elbow to the ribs from one of Tallywhite's large friends. There was also a scrape on his left cheekbone, the provenance of which George could not quite recall.

Worst of all, he thought as he trudged up the stairs at Manston House, he had abandoned Billie. He knew this night had been important to her. Hell, it had been important to *him*. God only knew what she thought of his behavior.

"George."

He stumbled in surprise as he entered his room. Billie was standing dead center in her dressing gown.

Her dressing gown.

It was only loosely belted, and he could see the fine peach silk of her nightdress peeking out from underneath. It looked very thin, almost sheer. A man could run his hands over such silk and feel the heat of skin burning through. A man might think he had the right to do so, with her standing a mere six feet from his bed.

"What are you doing here?" he demanded.

Her lips tightened at the corners. She was angry. In fact, he might go so far as to say she was breathtakingly furious. "I've been waiting for you," she said.

"That much I'd surmised," he said, tugging at his cravat. If it bothered her that he was disrobing in front of her, that was her own problem, he decided. She was the one who had taken up residence in his bedroom.

"What happened to you?" she demanded. "One moment you were foisting me off on poor Mr. Coventry—"

"I wouldn't pity him too much," George griped. "He did get my dance."

"You *gave* him your dance."

George kept working at his neckcloth, finally freeing it with one final yank. "I did not see that I had much choice," he said, tossing the now limp strip of linen on a chair.

"What do you mean by that?"

He paused, glad that he happened to be facing away from her. He had been thinking of Lord Arbuthnot, but of course Billie did not know—and could not know—of their dealings. "I could hardly do otherwise," he said, his eyes fixed on a random spot on the wall, "given that you'd asked him to dance."

"I did not precisely *ask* him."

He glanced over his shoulder. "Splitting hairs, Billie."

"Very well," she said, crossing her arms, "but I don't see that *I* had much choice, either. The music was starting and you were just *standing* there."

There was nothing to be gained by pointing out that he had been about to lead her to the dance floor when Lord Arbuthnot had arrived, so he held his tongue. They stared at each other for a long, heavy moment.

"You should not be here," George finally said. He sat down to pull off his boots.

"I didn't know where else to go."

He watched her intently, fiercely. What did she *mean* by that?

"I was worried about you," she said.

"I can take care of myself."

"So can I," she countered.

He nodded his *touché*, then turned his attention to his cuffs, pushing back the fine Belgian lace so that his fingers could work the buttons through their loops.

"What happened tonight?" he heard her say.

He closed his eyes, well aware that she could not see his expression. It was the only reason he allowed himself a weary sigh. "I wouldn't even know where to start."

"The beginning will do."

He looked over at her, unable to stop the wry smile that flitted across his lips. How very like her that statement was. But he just shook his head and said in a tired voice, "Not tonight."

She crossed her arms.

"For the love of God, Billie, I'm exhausted."

"I don't care."

That took him off guard, and for a moment he could only stare, blinking like some idiot owl.

"Where were you?" she demanded.

And because the truth was always best when possible, he told her, "At a pub."

Her head jerked back with surprise, but her voice was cool when she said, "You smell like it."

That earned her a grim chuckle. "I do, don't I?"

"Why were you at a pub? What could you possibly have been doing that was more important than—" She stopped herself with a horrified gasp, clasping her hand to her mouth.

He could not answer her, so he said nothing. There was nothing in the world that was more important than she was. But there *were* things more important than dancing with her, no matter how much he wished it were otherwise.

His brother was missing. Maybe tonight's absurd errand had nothing to do with Edward. Hell, George was certain it did not. How could it? Edward was lost in the wilds of Connecticut, and he was here in London, reciting nursery rhymes with a madman.

But he had been asked by his government to carry out this task, and more importantly, he had given his word that it would be done.

George would feel no compunction in refusing Lord Arbuthnot should he come with another fool's errand. He had not the temperament to follow orders blindly. But he had agreed this time, and he had followed through.

The silence in the room grew thick, and then Billie, who had turned away from him, hugging her arms to her body, said in a very small voice, "I should go to bed."

"Are you crying?" he asked, coming quickly to his feet.

"No," came her too-quick reply.

He could not bear it. He took a step forward without even realizing it. "Don't cry," he said.

"I'm not crying!" she choked out.

"No," he said gently. "Of course you're not."

She dragged the back of her hand inelegantly across her nose. "I don't cry," she protested, "and I certainly don't cry because of you."

"Billie," he said, and before he knew it, she was in his arms. He held her against his heart, and he stroked her back while her tears dropped one by one from her eyes.

She cried delicately, which seemed somehow unexpected. Billie had never done anything by half measure, and if she were going to cry, he would have thought she'd have done so with great big sobs.

And that was when he realized—she had been speaking true. She *didn't* cry. He had known her for twenty-three years, and he had never seen her shed a tear. Even when she'd hurt her ankle and had had to climb down that ladder on her own, she had not cried. For a moment she'd looked as if she might, but then she had steeled her shoulders, and swallowed her pain, and got on with it.

But she was crying now.

He had made her cry.

"I am so sorry," he murmured into her hair. He didn't know what he could have done differently, but that didn't seem to matter. She was crying, and every sniffle held the sound of his own heart breaking.

"Please don't cry," he said, because he didn't know what else to say. "It will be all right. I promise, everything will be all right."

He felt her nod against his chest, a tiny little movement, but one that somehow was enough to tell him that she had turned a corner. "You see," he said, touching her chin and smiling when she finally raised her eyes to his, "I told you, it's all right."

She took a shaky breath. "I was worried about you."

"You were worried?" He hadn't meant to sound pleased, but he couldn't help it.

"And angry," she continued.

"I know."

"You left," she said baldly.

"I know." He wasn't going to make excuses. She deserved better.

"Why?" she asked him. And when he did not reply she stepped out of his embrace and said it again. "Why did you leave?"

"I can't tell you," he said regretfully.

"Were you with *her*?"

He did not pretend to misunderstand. "Only briefly."

There was but one three-pronged candelabra in the room, but there was light enough for George to see the pain flash across Billie's face. She swallowed, the motion trembling through her throat.

But the way she was standing, with her arms wrapped protectively around her waist . . . she might as well have donned a suit of armor.

"I will not lie to you," he said quietly. "I may not be able to answer your questions, but I will tell you no falsehoods." He stepped forward, his eyes boring into hers as he made his vow. "Do you understand? I will *never* lie to you."

She nodded, and he saw something change in her face. Her eyes grew softer, more concerned. "You're hurt," she said.

"Not very much."

"But still . . ." She reached toward his face, her hand stopping an inch short of its destination. "Did someone hit you?"

He shook his head. He'd probably acquired the abrasion when he'd been persuaded to have a pint with Tallywhite. "I don't remember, honestly," he told her. "It was a very strange evening."

Her lips parted, and he could tell she wanted to question him further, but instead she said, very softly, "You never danced with me."

His eyes met hers. "I regret that."

"I'd wanted . . . I'd hoped . . ." Her lips pressed together as she swallowed, and he realized he was holding his breath, waiting for her to continue. "I don't think . . ."

Whatever it was, she could not bring herself to say it, and he realized that he needed to be as brave as she was.

"It was agony," he whispered.

She looked up, startled.

He took her hand and kissed her palm. "Do you have any idea how hard it was to tell Freddie Coventry to go ahead and dance with you? What it felt like to watch him take your hand and whisper in your ear like he had a right to be near you?"

"Yes," she said softly. "I know it exactly."

And then, in that moment, it all became clear. There was only one thing he could do.

He did the only thing he *could* do.

He kissed her.

Chapter 23

Billie wasn't stupid. She had known, when she decided to wait for George in his bedroom, that this might happen. But it wasn't *why* she had done it. It wasn't why she had crept so silently into his room, turning the door handle with practiced ease so it slipped through the locking mechanism without a click. It wasn't why she'd sat in his chair, listening for sounds of his return, and it wasn't why she had stared at his bed the whole time, achingly aware that this was where he slept, where his body lay at his most vulnerable, where, should he take a wife, they would make love.

No, she told herself, she had come to his room because she needed to know where he'd gone, why he'd left her at Wintour House. And she was worried. She knew she would not sleep until he was home.

But she'd known this might happen.

And now that it was happening . . .

She could finally admit that she'd wanted it all along.

He pulled her against him, and she made no show of surprise, no feigned outrage. They were too honest with each other; they always had been, and she threw her arms around him, kissing him back with every fevered breath.

It was like the first time he'd kissed her, but it was so much *more*. His hands were everywhere, and her dressing gown was thin, the material far more silky and fine than her day dress. When he cupped her bottom, she felt every finger, squeezing her with a desperation that made her heart sing.

He wasn't treating her like a china doll. He was treating her like a woman, and she loved it.

His body pressed against hers, length to length, she felt his arousal, hard and insistent. *She* had done this to him. Her. Billie Bridgerton. She was driving George Rokesby wild with desire, and it was thrilling. And it made her bold.

She wanted to nibble at his ear, lick the salt from his skin. She wanted to listen to the way his breath quickened when she arched her body against his, and wanted to know the exact shape of his mouth, not by sight but by feel.

She wanted all of him, and she wanted him in every possible way.

"George," she moaned, loving the sound of his name on her lips. She said it again, and then again, using it to punctuate every kiss. How had she ever thought that this man was stiff and unyielding? The way he was kissing her was heat personified. It was as if he wanted to devour her, consume her.

Possess her.

And Billie, who had never much liked letting anyone take charge, found she rather wanted him to succeed.

"You are so. Unbelievably. Beautiful," he said, not quite managing to say it like a proper sentence. His mouth was far too busy with other pursuits to string the words together smoothly. "Your dress tonight . . . I can't believe you wore red."

She looked up at him, unable to halt the playful smile that spread across her lips. "I don't think white suits me." *And after tonight*, she thought naughtily, *it never will*.

"You looked like a goddess," he rasped. And then he stilled, just a little, and pulled back. "But do you know," he said, his eyes burning with wicked intent. "I think I still like you best in breeches."

"George!" She couldn't help but laugh.

"Shhhh . . ." he warned, nipping at her earlobe.

"It's hard to be quiet."

He gazed down at her like a pirate. "I know how to silence you."

"Oh, yes, pl—" But she couldn't finish the sentence, not when he was kissing her again, even more fiercely than before. She felt his fingers at her waist, sliding under the silky sash that held her dressing gown against her body. It came undone and then slipped entirely to the floor, the silky material shivering across her skin as it fell.

Goose bumps rose on her arms as they were bared to the night air, but she felt no chill, only awareness as he reached out reverently to stroke her, slowly, from shoulder to wrist.

"You have a freckle," he murmured. "Right"—he leaned down and dropped a light kiss near the inside of her elbow—"here."

"You've seen it before," she said softly. It wasn't in an immodest spot; she had plenty of frocks with short sleeves.

He chuckled. "But I've never given it its proper due."

"Really."

"Mmm-hmm." He lifted her arm, twisting it just a bit so that he could pretend to be studying her freckle. "It is clearly the most delightful beauty mark in all of England."

A marvelous sense of warmth and contentment melted through her. Even as her body burned for his, she could not stop herself from encouraging his teasing conversation. "Only England?"

"Well, I haven't traveled very extensively abroad . . ."

"Oh, really?"

"And you know . . ." His voice dropped to a husky growl. "There may be other freckles right here in this room. You could have one here." He dipped a finger under the bodice of her nightgown, then moved his other hand to her hip. "Or here."

"I might," she agreed.

"The back of your knee," he said, the words hot against her ear. "You could have one there."

She nodded. She wasn't sure she was still capable of speech.

"One of your toes," he suggested. "Or your back."

"You should probably check," she managed to get out.

He took a deep, shuddering breath, and she suddenly realized just how much he was holding his passion in check. Where she was joyously setting herself free, he was waging a fierce battle against his own desire. And she knew—somehow she knew—that a lesser man would not have had the strength to treat her with such tenderness.

"Make me yours," she said. She had already given herself permission to let go. Now she was giving it to him, too.

She felt his muscles contract, and for a moment he looked as if he were in pain. "I shouldn't . . ."

"You should."

His fingers tightened against her skin. "I won't be able to stop."

"I don't want you to."

He drew back, his breath coming in shaky gasps as he put a few inches between their faces. His hands were at her cheeks, holding her absolutely still, and his eyes burned into hers.

"You *will* marry me," he commanded.

She nodded, her only thought to give her agreement as fast as she could.

"Say it," he said savagely. "Say the words."

"I will," she whispered. "I will marry you. I promise."

For about a second he stood frozen, and then before Billie could even think to whisper his name, he'd picked her up and practically thrown her onto the bed.

"You are mine," he growled.

She edged up onto her elbows and stared up at him as he stalked closer, his hands first tugging his shirt from his breeches and then moving to pull it over his head entirely. Her breath caught as his body was revealed. He was beautiful, as odd as that seemed to say about a man. Beautiful, and perfectly made. She knew he did not spend his days thatching roofs and plowing fields, but he must do some sort of regular physical activity because there was no softness to his form. He was lean and defined, and as the candlelight danced across his skin, she could see the muscles flex beneath.

She scooted up into a sitting position and reached out, her fingers itching to touch him, to see if his skin was as smooth and hot as it looked, but he was just beyond her grasp, watching her with hungry eyes.

"You are so beautiful," he whispered. He stepped closer, but before she could touch him he took her hand and brought it to his lips. "When I saw you tonight I think my heart stopped beating."

"And is it now?" she whispered.

He took her hand and laid it over his heart. She could feel it pounding beneath his skin, almost hear it reverberating through her own body. He was so strong, and so solid, and so wonderfully male.

"Do you know what I wanted to do?" he murmured.

She shook her head, too entranced by the low heat of his voice to make a noise of her own.

"I wanted to turn you around and push you right back through the door before anyone else saw you. I didn't want to share you." He traced her lips with his finger. "I still don't."

Heat flared within her, and she suddenly felt more daring, more womanly. "I don't want to share you, either."

He smiled slowly, and his fingers trailed down the length of her neck, across the delicate hollow of her collarbone, resting only when he reached the ribbon that tightened the neckline of her nightgown. Without ever taking his eyes from hers, he gave one of the strands a tug, sliding it slowly from the knot, its corresponding loop getting smaller and smaller until it finally popped through, and she was undone.

Billie watched his fingers, mesmerized, as they whispered across her skin, the edge of the now loosened bodice catching between his thumb and forefinger. The silk slipped from her shoulder, then slowly slid down her arm. She was so close to being revealed to him, but she could feel no modesty, summon no fear. All she had was passion, and the unrelenting need to follow it through.

She looked up, and so did he, almost as if they'd planned it. He caught her eyes with a questioning gaze, and she nodded, knowing exactly what he was asking. He drew a breath, its ragged sound speaking of desire, and then he nudged her nightdress over the rise of her breasts before allowing gravity to do the rest. The pale peach silk pooled luxuriously around her waist, but Billie didn't notice. George was staring at her with a reverence that took her breath away.

With a trembling hand, he reached out and cupped her breast, her nipple grazing lightly against his palm. Sensation shot through her, and she gasped, wondering how such a touch could make her abdomen clench. She felt hungry, but not for food, and the secret place between her legs tightened with what she could only assume was desire.

Was this how it was supposed to feel? As if she were incomplete without him?

She watched his hand as he caressed her. It was so big, so powerful, and so thrillingly male against her pale skin. He moved slowly, a stark contrast to the feverish kissing of just a few minutes earlier. He made her feel like a priceless work of art, and he was studying every curve.

She caught her bottom lip beneath her teeth, a little moan of pleasure slipping through her lips as his hand drew slowly away, teasing her skin until their only connection was his fingertips at her nipple.

"You like that," he said.

She nodded.

Their eyes met. "You'll like this even better," he growled, and then, as she gasped in surprise, he leaned down and took her into his mouth. His tongue rolled across her, and she felt herself tighten into a hard little bud—the sort she normally only felt in the chill of winter.

But she was the farthest thing from cold.

His touch was electric. Her entire body tightened, arching until she had to plant her hands on the bed behind her just to keep from falling over.

"George!" she practically squealed, and once again he shushed her.

"You never learn, do you?" he murmured against her skin.

"You're the one who's making me scream."

"That wasn't a scream," he said with a cocky smile.

She eyed him with alarm. "I didn't mean it as a dare."

He laughed aloud—although more quietly than she'd done—at that. "Merely planning for the future, when volume is not an issue."

"George, there are servants!"

"Who work for me."

"George!"

"When we are married," he said, lacing his fingers through hers, "we shall make as much or as little noise as we wish."

Billie felt her face go crimson.

He dropped a teasing kiss on her cheek. "Did I make you blush?"

"You know you did," she grumbled.

He looked down at her with a cocky smile. "I probably shouldn't take quite so much pride in that."

"But you do."

He brought her hand to his lips. "I do."

She lifted her gaze to his face, finding that despite the urgency in her body, she was content to take a moment just to look at him. She caressed his cheek, tickling her fingertips with the light growth of his beard. She traced his eyebrow, marveling at how such a straight, firm line could arch so imperiously when he wished. And she touched his lips, which were so improbably soft. How many times had she watched his mouth when he was speaking, never knowing that those lips could bring such pleasure?

"What are you doing?" he asked, his voice a husky smile.

Her lashes swept up as her eyes met his, and it was only when she spoke that she knew the answer. "Memorizing you."

George's breath caught, and then he was kissing her again, the levity of the moment giving way once again to desire. His mouth moved to her neck, teasing along the side, trailing fire in its wake. She felt herself descending, lying back against the bed, and then suddenly he was on top of her, skin to heated skin. Her nightgown slid past her legs, and then it was off completely. She was nude beneath him, without a stitch, and yet somehow it didn't feel awkward. This was George, and she trusted him.

This was George, and she loved him.

She felt his hands move to the fastening of his breeches, and then he swore under his breath as he was forced to roll off her in order to (in his words) "get the bloody things off." She couldn't help but chuckle at his profanity; he seemed to be having a much rougher time of it than she imagined was usual.

"You're laughing?" he asked, his brows rising into a daring arch.

"You should be glad I was already out of my gown," she told him. "Thirty-six cloth-covered buttons down the back."

He gave her a fearsome look. "It would not have survived."

As Billie laughed, one of George's buttons finally went flying, and his clothing fell to the floor.

Billie's jaw dropped.

George's smile was almost feral as he climbed back onto the bed, and she had a feeling he was taking her amazement as a compliment.

Which she supposed it was. With a healthy dose of alarm.

"George," she said cautiously, "I know that this *will* work, because, goodness, it *has* worked for centuries, but I have to say, this does not look comfortable." She swallowed. "For me."

He kissed the corner of her mouth. "Trust me."

"I do," she assured him. "I just don't trust *that*." She thought of what she had seen in the stables over the years. None of the mares ever seemed to be having a good time.

He laughed as his body slid over hers. "Trust me," he said again. "We just need to be sure you're ready."

Billie was not sure what *that* meant, but she was having a difficult time even thinking about it because he was doing very distracting things with his fingers. "You've done this before," she said.

"A few times," he murmured, "but this is different."

She looked at him, letting her eyes ask her question.

"It just is," he said. He kissed her again as his hand squeezed its way up the length of her thigh. "You're so strong," he said softly. "I love that about you."

Billie took a shaky breath. His hand was at the top of her leg now, spanning the whole width of it, and his thumb was very near to her center.

"Trust me," he whispered.

"You keep saying that."

His forehead rested against hers, and she had a feeling he was trying not to laugh. "I keep meaning it." He kissed his way back down her neck. "Relax."

Billie wasn't sure how *that* was possible, but then, just before he took her nipple in his mouth again, he said, "Stop thinking," and that was an order she had no trouble following.

It was the same as before. When he teased her this way she lost her mind. Her body took over, and she forgot whatever it was she'd thought she feared. Her legs parted, and he settled between them, and then *oh God*, he was touching her. He was touching her and it felt so wicked and so divine, and it just made her want more.

It made her hungry in a way she'd never been before. She wanted to draw him closer; she wanted to devour him. She grabbed his shoulders, pulling him down. "George," she gasped, "I want—"

"What do you want?" he murmured, sliding a finger within her.

She nearly bucked off the bed. "I want—I want—I just *want*."

"So do I," he growled, and then he was opening her with his fingers, spreading her lips, and she felt him pressing at her entrance.

"I'm told it will hurt," he said regretfully, "but not for long."

She nodded, and she must have tensed up, because he once again crooned, "Relax."

And somehow she did. Slowly he pushed inside. The pressure was stranger than it was great, and even when she felt a light stab of pain, that was overshadowed by her need to keep him close, then closer.

"Are you all right?" he asked.

She nodded.

"Are you sure?"

She nodded again.

"Thank God," he groaned, and he moved forward, entering her more deeply.

But she knew he was holding back.

He was gritting his teeth and holding hard, and she would swear he looked like he was in pain. But at the same time he was moaning her name as if she were a goddess, and the things he was doing to her—with his member and his fingers, with his lips and his words—were stoking a fire that consumed her.

"George," she gasped, when the tightness within seemed to grab her from the inside out. "*Please.*"

His movements grew more frenzied, and she pushed back, the need to move against him too overwhelming to ignore. "Billie," he groaned. "My God, what you do to me."

And then, just when she was certain she could take no more, the strangest thing happened. She grew stiff, and she shook, and then the moment she realized she could no longer so much as draw a breath, she shattered.

It was indescribable. It was perfect.

George's movements grew more frenzied, and then he buried his face in the crook of her neck, muffling his hoarse cry against her skin as he plunged forward one last time within her.

"I'm home," he said against her skin, and she realized it was the truth.

"I'm home, too."

Chapter 24

When George went down to breakfast the following morning, he was not surprised to learn that Billie was still abed.

She had not, he thought with some satisfaction, had a restful evening.

They had made love three times, and already he could not help but wonder if his seed was taking root within her. It was odd, but he'd never given much thought to having children before. He'd known he must, of course. He would one day inherit Manston and Crake, and he had a sacred duty to provide the earldom with an heir.

But even with all that, he had never *imagined* his children. He had never pictured himself holding a child in his arms, watching him learn to read and write, or teaching him to ride and hunt.

Or teaching *her* to ride and hunt. With Billie as their mother, his daughters would surely insist upon learning all the same skills as their brothers. And while he'd spent his childhood thoroughly annoyed by Billie's insistence upon keeping up with the boys, when it came to his daughters . . .

If they wanted to hunt and fish and shoot a pistol like a marksman . . .

They would hit the bull's-eye every time.

Although he might draw the line at jumping hedges at the age of six. Surely even Billie would now accept that that had been absurd.

Billie would be the *best* mother, he thought as he walked down the hall to the small dining room. Her children would not be trotted out once a day for her inspection. She would love them the way her own mother loved her, and she would laugh and tease and teach and scold, and they would be happy.

They would *all* be happy.

George grinned. He was already happy. And it was only going to get better.

His mother was already at the breakfast table when he entered the room, glancing at a recently ironed newspaper as she buttered her toast.

"Good morning, George."

He leaned down and kissed her proffered cheek. "Mother."

She looked at him over the rim of her teacup, one of her elegant brows set into a perfect arch. "You seem in an exceptional mood this morning."

He gave her a questioning glance.

"You were smiling when you entered the room," she explained.

"Oh." He shrugged, trying to quell the bubbles of joy that had had him nearly hopping down the stairs. "Can't explain, I'm afraid."

Which was the truth. He certainly couldn't explain it to *her*.

She regarded him for a moment. "I don't suppose it would have something to do with your untimely departure last evening."

George paused briefly in the act of spooning eggs onto his plate. He had forgotten that his mother would surely require an explanation for his disappearance. His presence at the Wintour Ball was the one thing she'd asked of him . . .

"Your presence at the Wintour Ball was the one thing I asked of you," she said, her voice sharpening with each word.

"I beg your forgiveness, Mother," he said. He was in far too good a mood to spoil it by quibbling. "It won't happen again."

"It is not *my* forgiveness you must obtain."

"Nevertheless," he said, "I would like to have it."

"Well," she said, momentarily flustered by his unexpected contrition, "it is up to Billie. I insist that you apologize to her."

"Already done," George said unthinkingly.

She looked up sharply. "*When?*"

Damn.

He took a breath, then returned to fixing his plate. "I saw her last night."

"Last night?"

He shrugged, feigning disinterest. "She was up when I came in."

"And when, pray tell, did you come in?"

"I'm not entirely certain," George said, subtracting a few hours. "Midnight?"

"*We* did not get home until one."

"Then it must have been later," he said equably. It was amazing what an excellent mood could do for one's patience. "I was not paying attention."

"Why was Billie up and about?"

He plopped four pieces of bacon onto his plate and sat down. "That I do not know."

Lady Manston's mouth clamped into a frown. "I do not like this, George. She must take more care for her reputation."

"I'm sure it's fine, Mother."

"At the very least," she continued, "*you* should know better."

Time to tread carefully. "I beg your pardon?"

"The instant you saw her, you should have gone to your room."

"I thought it behooved me to use the time to apologize."

"Hmmph." His mother did not have a ready response to that. "Still."

George smiled blandly and got down to the work of cutting his meat. A few moments later he heard footsteps coming toward them, but they sounded far too heavy to be Billie's.

Indeed, when a body filled the doorway a moment later, it belonged to the butler. "Lord Arbuthnot is here to see you, Lord Kennard."

"This time in the morning?" Lady Manston said with surprise.

George set his napkin down with a tight-jawed frown. He had anticipated that he would need to speak with Arbuthnot about the events of the previous night, but *now*?

George knew just enough about Lord Arbuthnot's dealings to know that they were inherently flavored with secrets and danger. It was unacceptable that he would bring his business to Manston House, and George would have no compunction telling him so.

"He is a friend of Father's," George said as he stood. "I will see what he needs."

"Shall I accompany you?"

"No, no. I'm sure that will be unnecessary."

George made his way to the drawing room, his mood growing blacker with every step. Arbuthnot's appearance this morning could mean only one of two things. First, that something had gone wrong after George had departed the Swan the night before and now he was in danger. Or worse, held responsible.

The more likely possibility, George thought grimly, was that Arbuthnot wanted something from him. Another message relayed, probably.

"Kennard!" Lord Arbuthnot said jovially. "Excellent work last night."

"Why are you here?" George demanded.

Arbuthnot blinked at his bluntness. "I needed to speak with you. Is that not why a gentleman usually calls upon another?"

"This is my home," George hissed.

"Are you saying I am not welcome?"

"Not if you wish to discuss the events of last night. This is not the time or the place."

"Ah. Well, I don't, actually. Nothing to discuss. It all came off brilliantly."

This was not how George would have described it. He crossed his arms, and stared Arbuthnot down, waiting for him to state his intentions.

The general cleared his throat. "I've come to thank you," he said. "And to request your help with another matter."

"No," George said. He did not need to hear anything more.

Arbuthnot chuckled. "You haven't even—"

"No," George said again, his fury cutting his words like glass. "Do you have any idea what I ended up doing last night?"

"I do, as it happens."

"You— What?" This was unexpected. When the hell had Arbuthnot learned of the farce at The Swan With No Neck?

"It was a test, m'boy." Arbuthnot slapped him on the shoulder. "You passed with flying colors."

"A test," George repeated, and if Arbuthnot knew him better, he'd have realized that the utter lack of inflection in George's voice was not a good sign.

But Arbuthnot didn't know him very well, and so he was chuckling as he said, "You don't think we'd trust just anyone with sensitive information."

"I think you'd trust me," George growled.

"No," Arbuthnot said with an odd, owlish solemnity. "Not even you. Besides," he added, his mien perking back up, " 'Pease, porridge, and pudding'? A bit of credit, if you will. We've more creativity than *that*."

George sucked in his lips as he pondered his next action. Tossing Arbuthnot out on his ear was tempting, but so was a well-thrown punch to the jaw.

"All in the past now," Arbuthnot said. "Now we need you to deliver a package."

"I think it's time you left," George said.

Arbuthnot drew back in surprise. "It's essential."

"So was pease, porridge, and pudding," George reminded him.

"Yes, yes," the general said condescendingly, "you have every right to feel abused, but now that we know we can trust you, we need your help."

George crossed his arms.

"Do it for your brother, Kennard."

"Don't you dare bring him into this," George hissed.

"It's a little late to be so high and mighty," Arbuthnot shot back, his friendly demeanor beginning to slip. "Do not forget that you were the one who came to me."

"And you could have declined my request for help."

"How do you think we go about defeating the enemy?" Arbuthnot demanded. "Do you think it's all shiny uniforms and marching in formation? The real war is won behind the scenes, and if you're too much of a coward—"

In an instant, George had him pinned against the wall. "Do not," he spat, "make the mistake of thinking you can shame me into becoming your errand boy." His hand tightened on the older man's shoulder, and then abruptly, he let go.

"I thought you wished to do your part for your country," Arbuthnot said, tugging on the hem of his jacket to smooth it out.

George nearly bit his tongue, stopping himself from making an untempered retort. He almost said something about how he had spent three years wishing he was with his brothers, serving with his rifle and sword, prepared to give his life for the good of England.

He almost said that it had made him feel useless, ashamed that he was somehow judged to be more valuable than his brothers by virtue of his birth.

But then he thought of Billie, and of Crake and Aubrey Hall, and all the people there who depended upon them. He thought of the harvest, and of the village, and of his sister, who would soon bring the first of a new generation into this world.

And he remembered what Billie had said, just two nights earlier.

He looked Lord Arbuthnot in the eye and said, "If my brothers are going to risk their lives for King and Country, then by God,

I am going to make sure it's a *good* King and Country. And that does not include carrying messages I do not know the meaning of to people I do not trust."

Arbuthnot regarded him soberly. "Do you not trust me?"

"I am furious that you came to my home."

"I am a friend of your father's, Lord Kennard. My presence here is hardly suspect. And that wasn't what I asked you. Do you not trust me?"

"Do you know, Lord Arbuthnot, I don't think it matters."

And it didn't. George had no doubt that Arbuthnot had fought—and continued to fight, in his own way—for his country. For all that George was furious that he'd been subjected to the War Office's version of an initiation rite, he knew that if Arbuthnot asked him to do something, it would be a legitimate request.

But he also knew—*now*, at last, he knew—that he was not the right man for the job. He would have made a fine soldier. But he was a better steward of the land. And with Billie by his side, he would be excellent.

He would be getting married soon. Very soon, if he had anything to do with it. He had no business running around like some sort of spy, risking his life without fully knowing why.

"I will serve in my own way," he said to Arbuthnot.

Arbuthnot sighed, his mouth twisting with resignation. "Very well. I thank you for your assistance last night. I do realize that it disrupted your evening."

George thought that he might have finally got through to him, but then Arbuthnot said, "I have just one more request, Lord Kennard."

"No," George tried to say.

"Hear me out," Arbuthnot interrupted. "I swear to you, I would not ask if the situation were not so critical. I have a packet that needs to go to a posting inn in Kent. On the coast. Not far from your home, I should think."

"Stop," George began.

"No, please, allow me to finish. If you do this, I promise I shall not bother you again. I will be honest, there is some danger involved. There are men who know it is coming, and they will wish to stop it. But these are documents of vital importance." And then Arbuthnot went in for the kill. "It could even save your brother."

Arbuthnot was good, George would give him that. He did not believe for a second that this Kent-bound packet had anything to do with Edward, and he still almost blurted his assent the moment the general had stopped talking.

"I'm not your man," he said quietly.

That should have been the end of it.

It *would* have been the end of it, but then the door slammed open and there, standing in the doorway, eyes shining with reckless purpose, was Billie.

Billie had not meant to eavesdrop. She had been on her way down to breakfast, her hair perhaps too hastily pinned due to her eagerness to see George again, when she'd heard his voice in the drawing room. She'd assumed he was with his mother—who else would be at Manston House this time in the morning?—but then she heard the voice of another gentleman, and he was saying something about the night before.

The night that George had said he could not tell her about.

She shouldn't have listened, but honestly, what woman could have pulled herself away? And then the man asked George to deliver a package, and he said it might help *Edward*?

She could not stop herself. All she could think was—*This is Edward*. Her dearest childhood friend. If she was prepared to fall out of a tree to save an ungrateful cat, she could certainly take a package to some inn on the coast. How difficult could it be? And if it was dangerous, if it was something that required discretion, surely she was an excellent decoy. No one would expect a woman to be making the delivery.

She didn't think. She didn't need to think. She just ran into the room and declared, "*I'll* do it!"

George didn't think. He didn't need to think. "The hell you will," he roared.

Billie froze for a moment, clearly not expecting this sort of reaction. Then she girded her shoulders and hurried in. "George," she said entreatingly, "we're talking about Edward. How can we not do everything—"

He grabbed her by the arm and yanked her aside. "You do not have all of the facts," he hissed.

"I don't need all the facts."

"You never do," he muttered.

Her eyes narrowed dangerously. "I can do this," she insisted.

Good God, she was going to be the death of him. "I'm sure you can, but you won't."

"But—"

"I forbid it."

Billie drew back. "You *forbid*—"

That was the moment Arbuthnot sidled over. "I don't think we were properly introduced last night," he said with an avuncular smile. "I am Lord Arbuthnot. I—"

"Get out of my house," George bit off.

"George!" Billie exclaimed, her face betraying her shock at his rudeness.

Arbuthnot turned to him with a thoughtful expression. "The lady appears to be quite resourceful. I think we could—"

"*Get out!*"

"George?" Now his *mother* appeared in the doorway. "What is all the yelling about? Oh, I'm sorry, Lord Arbuthnot. I did not see you there."

"Lady Manston." He bowed properly. "Forgive my early visit. I had business with your son."

"He was just leaving," George said, tightening his grip on Billie's arm when she started to squirm.

"Let me go," she ground out. "I might be able to help."

"Or you might not."

"Stop it," she hissed, now pulling furiously. "You cannot order me about."

"I assure you I can," he shot back, his eyes burning down into hers. He was going to be her husband, for God's sake. Did that not count for anything?

"But I want to help," she said, lowering her voice as she turned her back on the rest of the room.

"So do I, but this is not the way."

"It may be the *only* way."

For a moment he could do nothing but close his eyes. Was this a taste of the rest of his life as Billie Bridgerton's husband? Was he destined to live in terror, wondering what sort of danger she'd thrown herself into *that* day?

Was it worth it?

"George?" she whispered. She sounded uneasy. Had she seen something in his expression? A sign of doubt?

He touched her cheek, and he looked into her eyes.

He saw his whole world there.

"I love you," he said.

Someone gasped. It might have been his mother.

"I cannot live without you," he said, "and in fact, I refuse to do so. So no, you will not be going on some ill-advised mission to the coast to hand off a potentially dangerous package to people you don't know. Because if anything happened to you . . ." His voice broke, but he didn't care. "If anything happened to you, it would *kill* me. And I'd like to think you love me too much to let that happen."

Billie stared at him in wonder, her softly parted lips trembling as she blinked back tears. "You love me?" she whispered.

He nearly rolled his eyes. "Of course I do."

"You never said."

"I must have done."

"You didn't. I would have remembered."

"I would remember, too," he said softly, "if you'd ever said it to me."

"I love you," she said immediately. "I do. I love you so much. I—"

"Thank *God*," Lady Manston exclaimed.

George and Billie both turned. He didn't know about Billie, but he'd quite forgotten they had an audience.

"Do you know how *hard* I've been working toward this? My *word*, I thought I was going to have to beat you with a stick."

"You planned this?" George asked in disbelief.

She turned to Billie. "Sybilla? Really? When have I ever called you Sybilla?"

George looked over at Billie. She couldn't seem to stop blinking.

"I have waited a long time to call you daughter," Lady Manston said, tucking a lock of Billie's hair behind her ear.

Billie frowned, her head moving from side to side as she tried to puzzle it all out. "But I always thought . . . you wanted Edward. Or Andrew."

Lady Manston shook her head with a smile. "It was always George, my dear. In my mind, at least." She looked over at her son with a considerably more focused expression. "You *have* asked her to marry you, I hope."

"I might have demanded it," he admitted.

"Even better."

George suddenly straightened, glancing about the room. "What happened to Lord Arbuthnot?"

"He excused himself when the two of you started declaring your love," his mother said.

Well, George thought. Maybe the old man had more discretion than he'd thought.

"Why was he here, anyway?" Lady Manston asked.

"It doesn't matter," George said. Then he looked at his fiancée.

"It doesn't matter," she agreed.

"Well," Lady Manston declared with a beaming smile, "I can hardly wait to tell everyone. The Billingtons are hosting a ball next week and—"

"Can we just go home?" Billie interrupted.

"But you had such a wonderful time last night," Lady Manston replied. She looked over at George. "She danced every dance. Everyone loved her."

He smiled indulgently. "I am not surprised in the least."

She turned back to Billie. "We can make the announcement at the Billington ball. It will be a triumph."

Billie reached over and squeezed George's hand. "It already is."

"Are you sure?" he asked her. She had been so apprehensive about making her London debut. He would like nothing more than to go home to Kent, but Billie deserved to revel in her success.

"I am," she said. "It was a heady thing. And it's lovely to know that when I have to attend such functions that I can do it well and have a good time. But it's not what I love. I would rather be home."

"In breeches?" he teased.

"Only if I'm out in the fields." She looked over at Lady Manston. "A future countess must behave with some propriety."

Lady Manston chuckled at that. "You will be an excellent countess, although not too soon, I hope."

"Not for years and years," Billie said warmly.

"And you," Lady Manston said, looking at George with watery eyes, "my son. You look happier than I have seen you in a very long time."

"I am," he said. "I only wish . . ."

"You can say his name," his mother said softly.

"I know." He leaned down and kissed her cheek. "Edward is going to have to resign himself to missing the wedding, because I'm not waiting for him to get home."

"No, I expect you ought not," Lady Manston said, in just the right tone to make Billie blush ferociously.

"We will find him, though," George said. He was still holding Billie's hand, so he brought it to his lips and kissed his vow to her skin. "I promise."

"I suppose we're off to Kent, then," his mother said. "We could even leave today if that is your wish."

"Oh, that would be brilliant!" Billie exclaimed. "Do you think my mother will be surprised?"

"Not even a little bit."

"What?" Billie's mouth fell open. "But I hated him!"

"No, you didn't," George said.

She gave him a look. "You vexed me immensely."

"*You* were like a boulder in my shoe."

"Well, you—"

"Is this a competition?" Lady Manston asked in disbelief.

George looked at Billie, and when she smiled, it filled his soul. "No," he said softly, drawing her into his arms, "we're a team."

Billie looked up at him with such love it nearly stole his breath. "Mother," he said, never taking his eyes off his fiancée, "you might want to leave the room now."

"I beg your pardon?"

"I'm going to kiss her now."

His mother let out a little shriek. "You can't do that."

"I'm fairly certain I can."

"George, you're not married yet!"

He studied Billie's lips with the hot gaze of a connoisseur. "All the more reason to hurry things up," he murmured.

"Billie," his mother said firmly, transferring her attention to what she clearly considered to be the weaker link, "let's go."

But Billie just shook her head. "I'm sorry, but it's as he says. We're a team."

And then, because she was Billie Bridgerton and she'd never minded taking charge, she sank her fingers into his hair and pulled his mouth down to hers.

And because he was George Rokesby, and he was going to love her for the rest of his days, he kissed her right back.

Epilogue

Several months later
Crake House

"The results are final," Billie said, adding up the last column with a flourish. "I win."

George glanced up at her from his position on their bed—a large, lovely, four-posted piece that Billie had re-dressed in green a few weeks into their marriage. He was reading a book; Billie hadn't caught the title. He always read before they went to bed. She loved that about him. He was such a creature of habit. Another reason they were a perfect match.

"What is it this time?" he murmured.

She knew he was being indulgent, but she was so pleased by the numbers in front of her that she decided she didn't care. "The barley harvest," she said. "Aubrey Hall outdid Crake by a factor of . . . hold on one moment . . ." She chewed on her lower lip as she worked out another computation. "One point one!"

"Such a triumph."

She pursed her lips, trying for an unamused expression.

"Did you factor in Aubrey's greater barley acreage?"

"Of course!" She rolled her eyes. "Honestly, George."

His lips curved ever so slightly. "Might I remind you that you live at Crake?"

Billie felt herself smile in return.

"And that your name is Billie Rokesby now?"

"I'll always be a Bridgerton at heart. Well," she added, not liking George's frown, "a Bridgerton *and* a Rokesby."

He sighed. Just a little. "I don't suppose you've any plans to turn your formidable skills to the running of Crake."

Not for the first time Billie felt a rush of gratitude that George had not objected when she'd told him that she wanted to continue her work at Aubrey Hall. He was an uncommon man, her husband. He understood her. Sometimes she thought he might be the only person who did.

"My father still needs me," she said. "At least until Edmund is ready to take over."

George rose from the bed and walked over. "Your father's steward would be thrilled to finally earn his wages."

She glanced up. "I'm better than he is."

"Well, *that* goes without saying."

She batted him on the arm, then sighed when he leaned down and kissed her neck. "I should thank you," she said.

His lips stilled, and she felt him smile against her skin. "For what?"

"Everything, really. But mostly for being you."

"Then you're most welcome, Lady Kennard."

"I'll try to cut back a little," she said. George was right. She probably didn't need to do *quite* so much at Aubrey Hall. And the way they were going, she'd be pregnant sooner rather than later.

She was going to have to learn to let go of her life at Aubrey, or at least loosen her grip.

She pulled back so that she could look at his face. "You wouldn't mind if I took a more active role here at Crake? With the lands, not just the house?"

"Of course not! We'd be lucky to—" He stopped, his words interrupted by a knock at the door. "Enter!"

The door opened to reveal a visibly agitated footman. "A messenger, my lord," he said.

Billie blinked in surprise. "This time of night?"

The footman held out a folded missive. "It's addressed to Lord Manston, but he's—"

"In London," George finished for him. "I'll take it."

"He said it was urgent," the footman said. "Otherwise, I'd never give over your father's private correspondence."

"It's all right, Thomas," Billie said gently. "If it's urgent, it's more important that it is attended to quickly than it is to deliver it to Lord Manston."

George slid a finger under the wax but did not break the seal. "Does the messenger wait for a reply?"

"No, sir. But I directed him belowstairs for a hot meal."

"Very good, Thomas. That will be all."

The footman left, and Billie fought the urge to go to her husband's side to read over his shoulder. Whatever was in the missive, he'd tell her soon enough.

She watched as his eyes scanned left to right, quickly reading the words. About four lines down his lips parted and he looked up. Her heart stopped, and she knew what he was going to say even before the words left his lips.

"Edward's alive . . ."

About the Author

#1 *New York Times* bestselling author JULIA QUINN began writing one month after graduating from college and, aside from a brief stint in medical school, she has been tapping away at her keyboard ever since. Her novels have been translated into forty-three languages and are beloved the world over. A graduate of Harvard and Radcliffe Colleges, she lives with her family in the Pacific Northwest.

THE BRIDGERTON SERIES

THE DUKE AND I
Everyone likes Daphne Bridgerton, but no one truly desires her. Simon Basset, Duke of Hastings, intends to shun marriage and society. A sham attachment could benefit them both—unless love ignores every rule...

THE VISCOUNT WHO LOVED ME
Anthony Bridgerton has chosen a wife! The only obstacle is his intended's older sister, Kate Sheffield. Is the spirited schemer driving Anthony mad with her determination to stop the betrothal—or is it something else?

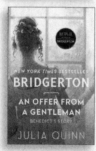

AN OFFER FROM A GENTLEMAN
Benedict Bridgerton has sworn to find and wed the mystery miss who fled the ball at the stroke of midnight. But will an oddly familiar maid entice Benedict to sacrifice his only chance for a fairy-tale love?

ROMANCING MISTER BRIDGERTON
Colin Bridgerton is the most charming man in London. Penelope Featherington has always loved him, but when she discovers his deepest secret, will she become his biggest threat—or his happy ending?

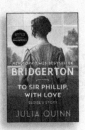

TO SIR PHILLIP, WITH LOVE

Eloise Bridgerton wrote a letter to Sir Phillip...and he stole her heart. But she could not accept the proposal of a man she'd never met. Or could this rough and rugged, imperfect brute of a man be her perfect match?

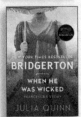

WHEN HE WAS WICKED

In every life there is a moment so tremendous and breathtaking that it changes one's life. For Michael Stirling, London's most infamous rake, that moment came the first time he laid eyes on Francesca Bridgerton...

IT'S IN HIS KISS

Hyacinth Bridgerton is smart, outspoken, and according to Gareth St. Clair, best in small doses—until he needs help to translate an old diary. But the answers they seek lie not in the diary, but in a single, perfect kiss.

ON THE WAY TO THE WEDDING

Gregory Bridgerton believes in true love, but love is never easy... And now, on the way to Lucy Abernathy's wedding, he must risk everything to ensure that when it comes time to kiss the bride, he is the man standing at the altar.

HAPPILY EVER AFTER

Ever wonder what happens after the Happily Ever After? This collection of "second epilogues"—stories that take place after the original books end—offers more from the Bridgerton characters.

THE BRIDGERTON PREQUELS

BECAUSE OF MISS BRIDGERTON
Everyone expects Billie Bridgerton to marry one of the Rokesby brothers. Yet, there is only one Rokesby Billie absolutely cannot tolerate, and that is George. But when Billie and George are quite literally thrown together, a whole new sort of sparks begins to fly. And when these lifelong adversaries finally kiss, they just might discover that the one person they can't abide is the one person they can't live without...

THE GIRL WITH THE MAKE-BELIEVE HUSBAND
With her brother, Thomas, injured on the battlefront in the Colonies, orphaned Cecilia Harcourt travels across the Atlantic, determined to nurse her brother back to health. But after a week of searching, she finds not her brother but his best friend, the handsome officer Edward Rokesby. Cecilia vows that she will save this soldier's life, even if staying by his side means telling one little lie...

THE OTHER MISS BRIDGERTON
Fiercely independent and adventurous, Poppy Bridgerton will only wed a suitor whose keen intellect and interests match her own. While visiting a friend on the Dorset coast, Poppy is pleasantly surprised to discover a smugglers' hideaway tucked inside a cave. But her delight turns to dismay when two pirates kidnap her and take her aboard a ship, leaving her bound and gagged on the captain's bed...

FIRST COMES SCANDAL
After Georgiana Bridgerton is abducted for her dowry, she is given two options: live out her life as a spinster or marry the rogue who has ruined her life. When Nicholas Rokesby discovers that Georgie Bridgerton—his literal girl-next-door—is facing ruin, he knows what he must do. Georgie doesn't want to be anyone's sacrifice, and besides, they could never think of each other as anything more than childhood friends...or could they?

MORE LADY WHISTLEDOWN!

Two sparkling anthologies written by Julia Quinn, Suzanne Enoch, Karen Hawkins, and Mia Ryan starring Lady Whistledown—the elusive Regency-era gossip columnist popularized in #1 *New York Times* bestselling author Julia Quinn's Bridgerton novels!

THE SMYTHE-SMITH SERIES

JUST LIKE HEAVEN

Honoria Smythe-Smith is to play the violin (badly) in the annual musicale performed by the Smythe-Smith quartet. But first she's determined to marry by the end of the season. When her advances are spurned, can Marcus Holroyd, her brother Daniel's best friend, swoop in and steal her heart in time for the musicale?

A NIGHT LIKE THIS

Anne Wynter might not be who she says she is. Daniel Smythe-Smith might be in mortal danger. But that's not going to stop either of them from falling in love.

THE SUM OF ALL KISSES

Sarah Pleinsworth can't forgive Hugh Prentice for the duel he fought three years ago that nearly destroyed her family and left Hugh himself with a badly injured leg. That's fine with Hugh, who can't tolerate Sarah's dramatic ways. But when the two are forced to spend a week together, they begin to change their minds...

THE SECRETS OF SIR RICHARD KENWORTHY

Sir Richard Kenworthy has less than a month to find a bride, and when he sees Iris Smythe-Smith hiding behind her cello at her family's infamous musicale, he thinks he might have struck gold. Iris is used to blending into the background, so when Richard courts her, she can't quite believe it's true.

AVONBOOKS
An Imprint of HarperCollins Publishers